MW01254256

DARK END OF THE STREET

ANDREW MADIGAN

"This book is dedicated to no one."

1

POUNDING THE PAVEMENT

HORVATH WAKES TO THE SOUND OF A HEAD SLAMMING AGAINST THE concrete outside his window. The noise is dull and hollow. There's no echo but you can feel it in your teeth and bones. There are sounds that can make a tough guy flinch. He put in a wake-up call last night, but this isn't exactly what he had in mind.

At first it's like a baseball hitting a brick wall at 90 mph. He thinks about this and sees the wind-up, the pitch and release. The impact. He imagines the ball, afterward, dropping to the ground as if exhausted from a long day's work.

Then he sees the man's dead eyes, the sweat, the pained rictus of his mouth. Arms and legs flopping like a ragdoll. And the other man, straddling a lifeless body. Clenched jaw, red eyes, bulging veins. Hands grabbing the man by the lapels, balled into fists as they pound him onto the unforgiving surface, again and again.

Horvath throws his legs over the side of the bed, scratches himself, yawns. Lights a cigarette.

He was dreaming of deep oceans and infinite deserts just a few minutes ago, and now this. Life's not a dinner menu, he thinks. You don't get to pick and choose, or place your order with a nice-looking waitress. No, they bring out any old thing and you have to eat it.

Two more head-slams, but the sound is different now. Softer and more precise. Like a musk melon whacked in half by a machete.

He can hear the man outside, breathing heavily. He can hear sweat drip down onto the pavement, blood pooling under the bodies. Or maybe it's just his imagination.

And then everything goes quiet.

The man's strength has suddenly drained, like motor oil into a drip pan. All you have to do is twist that nut and it all comes rushing out.

Horvath sees the limp arms and rubbery legs. Even his eyelids are exhausted. He knows how the guy feels. Like he hasn't slept in years. Empty, useless, going in circles. Running on cigarettes, bourbon, and cold soup he doesn't bother to reheat.

The man falls over, completely spent. He's now splayed out over his friend as if they're hugging. He makes some sort of noise, a soft moan.

The other man doesn't make a sound.

HORVATH GETS UP, stretches, makes a screechy noise as his fingertips reach for the ceiling.

One last puff before he crushes the cigarette into a square glass ashtray.

He looks over at the easy chair, where his wilting pants hang over the back. The belt is still attached, winding through the loops like an arm around someone's waist.

Time to get dressed. He sighs into the gray pants.

Shoes, shirt, jacket. No tie.

Wallet, keys, wristwatch, spare change.

Lighter, smokes.

Ready to go.

THE ELEVATOR IS MORE like a coffin. Small, dark and airless. Depressing.

Silent and unmoving, the passengers are more like corpses than living breathing humans. In fact, most of them have already died. They just don't know it yet.

Horvath presses the glowing *L*.

The doors shut, and the elevator moves.

The other passengers, a man and a woman, get off on the third floor.

There's a jagged crack in the mirror, like a lightning bolt, and the silver is wearing away, so it's more of a window than a looking glass. Anyway, he doesn't like what he sees. He used to look like that famous actor, or at least his less-attractive cousin, but now, when he looks at himself in a mirror, Horvath sees a child's drawing. The lurching caretaker of a haunted house, or a man released from the hospital a few days too early.

A tarnished brass plaque reads THE EXECUTIVE in a cursive script that's so ornate it's almost impossible to read. Horvath laughs soundlessly. No executives ever stayed in this dump, not in the last 20 years anyway.

This is the type of hotel where people don't stay the night. They stay for an hour, or they live here for weeks, months, maybe years. Some of them die here. Or they hide out until it's safe, then get dressed and walk down the street with a spring in their step, whistling on old tune until someone slips up behind them and sticks a knife in their back.

He lights up at the exact moment he sees the NO SMOKING sign. Actually, it says N_ SMOKING. The O has been melted off, incinerated. And the rest of the sign is scarred with cigarette burns, like an abused housewife who's going to do something about it one of these days.

DEAD MEN ARE HEAVIER THAN BROKEN HEARTS

It's still dark out.

The sky is gray, like a sidewalk after it rains.

Like those flannel pants my boss used to wear. He stops at the curb and takes a thoughtful drag, looking out across the sleeping city.

Mr. Lazlo. Regional Assistant Manager of Dominion Enterprises. Leslie Lazlo. Old Les.

Always wore a hat, carried an umbrella. And that stupid tie clip. What a prick.

That was my last real job. Good riddance, he says, not quite sure if he means it.

He looks at his watch. I'm never on the right schedule. Up before dawn, or *still* up when the sun comes out.

No one's around. The streets are empty. There's a telephone pole across the road, straight and tall like a finger raised to the lips telling you to be quiet. Even the rats and mice have scurried off somewhere. They don't want to be around when the cops got here. They've got better things to do than drink stale coffee and repeat the same story a hundred times until the detectives are satisfied.

Horvath walks around to the side of the building.

Nothing's moving around here, not yet, but somehow he can feel the newspaper trucks shuffling through the potholed streets, bakers rolling out dough, an aging streetwalker pouring herself a nightcap and telling herself a bedtime story. His eyesight's so good he can see things that aren't even there.

He walks a half-block down the west side of the hotel and turns right into an alley. Stained mattress, blue dumpster, couple trash bags next to it. The smell of rotten milk and even more rotten garlic. A screen door bangs shut.

The body sits there quiet and still, like he's having his portrait painted.

But there's no artist around here, not even a beret.

Horvath walks down the alleyway. In his mind the ground was made of concrete, but in reality it's asphalt. He finds this unsettling for reasons he doesn't understand.

The soles of his shoes stick to the gummy blacktop.

The stiff is at his feet now. He looks up to the third floor and sees the chalk mark on his windowpane. McGrath taught him that. So you always know where you are, even when you're on the outside looking in.

One last drag before flicking the butt against the brick wall. It lands next to a pair of rusty tin cans, standing around like a couple of old ladies arguing over a piece of fruit in the market.

He walks to the dumpster and opens the top.

Horvath pushes his jacket sleeves up a few inches, bends down, and grabs the guy by the wrists. He drags him back a few feet. Not too bad, he thinks. 180, 190. He remembers a rolled up rug in Cincinnati, couple years ago. His lower back remembers, too.

He drags the body over to the dumpster, puts his hands on his hips, and takes a few breaths. I'm getting too old for this. This guy's not a tackling dummy and I'm not on the JV football squad.

He gets down low, like a defensive linesman. It takes some doing, but he manages to hoist the body over his shoulder. Take it easy. Lift with your legs. There you go. He smiles and tosses the body into the mouth of the dumpster. I've got a few good years in me yet.

I could use a shot of whiskey, a good stiff belt.

This is the chorus to a song that's stuck in his head.

He grabs a few trash bags, a couple beer bottles, a hubcap, tosses it all into the dumpster. Newspapers, coffee cups, a broken umbrella that looks like a dead crow. Three stacks of old magazines tied up with frayed twine. A paper bag with hamburger wrappers inside, balled up and wrinkled like the stone of a plum.

He peeks inside the dumpster. There's a paint-splattered tarp at the guy's feet. He leans in, grabs it, spreads it out over the legs, which were still visible under the trash. There. You can't see him now. He's basically not even here. With any luck, the garbage men won't notice and he'll get to the city dump without anyone being the wiser.

Horvath looks down at his hands. They're covered in a sticky film of blood and something that makes him think of egg yolks. Pus? Internal organs? He doesn't know much about the inner workings of a human body but pictures it like a small suitcase, each item packed neat and tidy, everything in its proper place. Socks sleeping inside the shoes, clean shirts on top.

He smells his hands, but that doesn't tell him anything, so he wipes them on his pants.

The dry cleaning bill. He tries not to think about it.

Awake now, the sun is just starting to peak through the blinds, and Horvath has already put in a full day's work. Or at least it seems that way.

Hunger is a stranger's fist pounding insistently at the door.

He heads uptown and stops at a coffee shop on 5th and De Lucca for bacon, eggs, and two slices of crispy toast. He's earned it.

3

FALSE COLORED EYES

HE SCANS THE MENU, JUST TO MAKE SURE.

The waitress, green notepad in hand, skulks over.

"I'll have #37." He points to the item, even though she's not looking.

She nods, scribbles in her pad, steps over to the chrome counter.

The cook is bending over a skillet. He looks up at Horvath. It's still early, but his apron is as dirty as a butcher's at the end of a hard day's slaughter.

The waitress shouts, slapping the flimsy paper onto the silver carousel.

There's nothing to do while he waits for the coffee, not even an abandoned newspaper to read.

Horvath is looking for a distraction when she walks in. The first thing he's aware of is the stabbing of dagger heels on the tiled floor.

She sits at the counter, four stools down.

He moves his eyes without turning his head. Midnight blue skirt, just above the knee. It wraps tightly around her waist. Like coarse hands circling your throat, he thinks. Yellow blouse, primly buttoned to the neck. But there's nothing prim about her eyes, which tell you she knows all the four-letter words even if she's not going to say them out loud.

Pale green eyes with a band of gray around the outside. Red lips, like every other space on a roulette wheel. Dark brown hair tied up on top, with a few loose strands teasing the back of her neck. Fingernails painted that same casino red.

Seems familiar. Do I know her?

He flips through a Rolodex of women's faces, but comes up empty. The faces are all starting to look the same.

Not this one, though. I'd remember her. She stands out like a clown at a state funeral. A real heartbreaker. Knows I'm looking at her even though she can't see me. I can read it in her shoulders, her crossed legs, in the slim fingers touching that brooch pinned to her blouse.

The coffee arrives, eventually. Like the cavalry galloping in after all the foot soldiers have already been killed.

Horvath tries to remember if he's ever been heartbroken. Don't think so. My arms have been fractured. Couple ribs. Collarbone and nose, but no heart problems. I don't stick around long enough for that. He dreams a dream that he'd be too embarrassed to confess, even to himself.

When the food comes, he digs in as if he hasn't eaten for weeks.

Before she says anything, he feels her leaning over, senses the change in her breathing.

"Excuse me."

He turns.

"Can you pass the salt?"

"Sure. Here you go." He slides it down the slick counter.

He can feel the cook watching. His eyes are all over them, like the wet rag he uses to mop up spills.

She salts her eggs, then holds up the shaker with a wave. "Want it back?"

"Keep it. I'm good."

She gives him the once-over, twice. "Lana."

"Hi, Lana."

"No, *Lana*, like the actress."

"Oh right, her."

"You a movie buff?"

"Not really."

"What are you into, then?"

"Books."

"You like to read?"

"Yeah." He forks bacon into his mouth, on a mattress of runny eggs. Washes it down with black coffee. Bitter, but it gets the job done.

"What do you like to read, comic books?"

He laughs, turns his head.

Her smile is so thin it almost doesn't exist. Horvath thinks of teachers, politicians, and men of god. Always speaking, but when you try to grab hold of their words, there's nothing there. It all crumbles to dust in your hands.

"No, real books. *Literature.*"

"Oh, well. La-di-da. Didn't know I was dealing with such a scholar."

He laughs, for real this time. "I also like mystery, crime, westerns..."

"The whole kit and caboodle, huh? Well, I'll leave you to it." She pauses. "Sorry to bother you, professor."

"It's no bother."

"Well, I'm glad to hear that." Lana gives him a bigger smile, like you might hand a couple quarters to a bum. "What'd you say your name was?"

"I didn't."

"I know."

He moves one seat down, tells her his name.

"It suits you, I guess."

"I'll take that as a compliment."

Her eyebrows leap. "If you insist."

Lana was a real looker. No one could argue with that. But there's something in her eyes. Horvath can see it, clear as day, even though she tries to hide it. She might be talking to me, but she's thinking about something else. Or someone else.

"Never seen you in here before," she says.

"New in town."

She nods, sips her tea.

He mops up the remainders of breakfast with the last wedge of toast, which isn't so crispy anymore. The silver Greyhound bus pulls into his memory. He ate peanuts, read, and stared out the window through six identical states. Ripped seat cushions and squalid train station bathrooms. Payphones dressed in graffiti, with a Yellow Pages that pulled a runner and a silver cord with no receiver at the end. He can still hear the wiry man behind him, rocking in his seat and muttering to himself all the way from Bucks County, PA to Beckley, West Virginia.

"So, you a regular here?" Horvath swallows the dregs of his coffee.

"Yeah, more or less. I come in sometimes."

"Well—" He pays the bill, with 25¢ extra for the waitress. For all the hard work she didn't do and all the charm she didn't have. "— Maybe I'll pop back in one of these days."

"Lucky me."

Now it was his turn for a narrow smile, more of a rumor than a cold hard fact.

4
_____

YOU'VE GOT TO MOVE IN A STRAIGHT LINE

Horvath steps outside and looks both ways, but he has no idea where to go.

He's been doing a lot of walking for the past few months, ever since the repo men snatched his car, a '54 Chevy Bel Air. They came in the dead of night, when he was shooting pool over at Duff's. He loved that car, even if the transmission's shot.

He doesn't feel like himself, a stranger in a new town. The people walk a little different, talk a little different. Their clothes are a bit off, and even the way they drink coffee isn't quite right. The buildings look down at him, sneering as if they know something he doesn't.

He tries to blend in, but it's not easy. Walking around town, he can feel their eyes burn into his back. They know he's not from around here.

His back aches and his feet are covered in blisters. He hasn't worn holes through the bottom of his shoes, not yet anyway, but he does feel about half an inch shorter.

Man alive, the blisters. Horvath considers himself a fairly tough customer, but he's got the skin of a baby calf. Rowing a boat, raking leaves, walking around in new shoes—his hands and feet get sore and rip open at the slightest aggravation.

5

MAN WALKS INTO A BAR

HORVATH HAS TIME TO KILL SO HE STARTS WALKING UPTOWN, BLISTERS be damned.

It's early spring. The sun is shining, birds are singing, flowers are in bloom, all that pretty stuff.

Full belly, fresh pack of smokes, sun on his face. What more could a guy want?

He stops in a record store and starts flipping through through the albums lined up in wooden bins. He's been meaning to buy the new one from that young guy. Beard, steely gaze. Washington Somethingorother. Or maybe Somethingorother Washington.

A clerk is walking by. He's got one of those faces that Horvath just can't stand. Prim little mouth, upturned chin, untrustworthy eyes. Hair that spends too much time in front of the mirror, admiring itself. He's got black-framed glasses, a little mustache, and a hat perched on the side of his head like a guy who's about to jump off a building.

He stops the clerk, against his better judgment. "Excuse me."

"What is it?"

The way he says this, it sounds more like *Why the hell are you bothering me? I got things to do, places to be.*

"I'm looking for a record."

The clerk gives him a *no-shit* glare.

"Washington...something. Young jazz player. Alto sax, maybe."

The clerk is silent, inspecting his nails. Guy works in a record store, but he thinks he's the King of Siam.

"I heard good things."

"I have no idea." The clerk sighs. "I mean, Washington's a really common name, you know? Especially for jazz musicians."

He's lucky I haven't been drinking, Horvath thinks. And that I'm not in the mood for any rough stuff.

"It's the name of a city, too." The clerk walks off toward the back room. He's got teeth to polish, lines to memorize.

He thinks of all the Washingtons he's passed through. Charmless, forgettable little nothing towns. Dirty, foul, rat-infested sewers. Feral beasts covered in grime and corruption instead of fur. Of course, there's also Washington, DC, the filthiest town of all.

They've got a whole section of Lester Young. That's a good sign.

He grabs the record Young made with Roy Eldridge and Harry Edison and heads for the listening booth. A peroxide blonde smiles at him from the blues aisle, but he's not in the mood for small talk. And from the looks of her, the talk would be pretty damn small.

The first side starts to spin. When the needle hits the groove, Horvath thinks of a trolley car rolling across town on steel tracks.

Lester Young could blow sax like other men breathe. He didn't follow a path. When he played, it was like a Chrysler racing down the side of a mountain. You always felt it would spin out of control, though it rarely did.

He didn't bother with Side 2. There's no way it could live up to the first half.

On the way out he sees the blonde, who's sizing up a tall thin man looking at R&B singles.

The clerk looks over at Horvath and scrunches his eyebrows like a couple of hedgehogs wrestling. Cheap bastard, he thinks. Didn't even buy a newspaper.

It's time for a drink so Horvath turns left and heads downtown. The streets are dirtier but the whiskey's cheaper. That's a pretty good trade-off, as far as he's concerned.

Smith's Tavern. The locals probably call it Smittie's.

He pushes through the front door and takes a seat at the bar.

The place is dark, nearly empty. It's quiet and there aren't a lot of pictures on the walls. Just the way he likes it.

Two young men huddle at a table by the window, heads together, wearing faces they borrowed from a gangster movie. They think they're a couple of tough guys. He sees a bulge under the arm, where a holster should be.

An older woman sits alone at the end of the bar. She stares at the empty glass in front of her the way you'd look at a man's suit hanging in the closet after he died. She's falling fast and one of these days she's going to hit rock bottom.

The bartender's standing there, looking down at Horvath.

"Whiskey, neat."

The bartender makes the smallest movement that would count as a nod. He follows this by reaching down to the rail for a bottle of rye without taking his eyes off the customer.

"You got a jukebox?" he asks.

"No."

"Good."

It takes a couple seconds, but the bartender smiles.

He has a few drinks, but not a few too many. He needs to keep his wits about him.

He thinks about that Lester Young record. Would've been nice, but he's running low on cash. And he likes to travel light. Only a sucker walks around all day with a shopping bag. Never know when you might need your hands.

After the first drink, Horvath starts thinking about the stiff he dumped in the trash bin.

They told me there'd be bodies. This is a bad town, and everybody knows it.

Wasn't my guy. That much I know. But who was he? Didn't have an ID or billfold.

What does it have to do with me? Nothing, maybe. Could be a coincidence.

But no, Horvath doesn't believe in those.

Happened right outside my window. Did they see the chalk mark? Were they trying to tell me something? Maybe it was a message, a little postcard sealed in blood.

I better check in. He raises his chin at the bartender, who sees him but doesn't move an inch. He's got a newspaper in his mitts, pretending to read it.

After a few long seconds, the bartender puts down the paper and walks over real slow like he's got anvils where his feet should be. He yawns, leans against the bar, looks down at Horvath with eyes like crosshairs.

He says nothing the way other men say *Yeah, this better be good.*

What is it with bartenders?

"Whaddya need, pal?"

"You got a payphone?"

"Yeah, in back." He jerks his head over his shoulder.

Horvath sees a dark hallway behind the bar.

"Change for a dollar?"

The bartender makes change, begrudgingly, and slaps it on the bar. "Want me to take the air out of your glass?"

"Sure, make it a double this time."

The bartender pours the drink, pushes it forward.

"Say, you Smith?"

He looks at Horvath with dead eyes.

"You know, *Smith's Tavern.* You the owner?"

The bartender shakes his head. "There ain't no Smith, far as I know."

"It's just a name, huh? Doesn't mean anything?"

"Something like that. Guy named Childers runs the place." The bartender aims the double barrel of his eyes at Horvath. "Why you wanna know?"

"Just curious."

The men are quiet now, but the bartender doesn't back away.

"Thanks for the drink."

The bartender nods, shuffles back to his paper.

He downs the whiskey, hops off the barstool, and walks around the bar. One of the young men by the window looks over for a second, but then goes back to his conversation. The old woman doesn't even notice he's there. Just keeps staring at that empty glass.

Dartboard, cigarette machine, ashtray that needs to be dumped.

Big empty room off to the left. He remembers the old days, when women weren't allowed in the bar. Had to sit in a side room if they wanted a drink.

He walks down the hallway, decorated in early Mildew with accents of Water Damage and Wood Rot. I guess you'd call the style Eclectic. They keep the lights dim so you can't see just how decrepit the place really is.

At the end of the hallway, there's a sliver of light coming from a small room. He puts his ear to the door. Two men are talking, arguing. Maybe there's three of them. Silence walks in when they stop to drink.

Phone's on the wall, to his right. He puts in a couple dimes and calls Ungerleider, his contact at the firm.

It's a short call. Ungerleider doesn't have much to say because he never does. To him, a couple grunts is like a Shakespeare play. Horvath keeps it short, too. He's just checking in. Telling them what he knows, which isn't much, and seeing if they have any new information. They don't.

He hangs up and checks the slot for change. Empty.

The boys in the back room are still quiet. It must be time to shut up, sit back and drink. He smiles. After a few more rounds they'll be arguing again, and then the fists will come out to play.

He lights up and leans back against the wall. There's one thing he didn't tell Ungerleider. He found something in the alley, near the body. A clue.

That's another thing McGrath taught him—always hold something back, just in case.

Plus, he isn't sure it's a clue, not yet. He needs to poke his nose around first. Life is filled with leads that turn into nothing but dead-ends.

6

PASTIES & RED VELVET

HORVATH GOES BACK TO THE EXECUTIVE, TAKES OFF HIS SUIT, AND LAYS down on the bed. The mattress is old and thin, and it doesn't smell very good, but that doesn't keep him from falling asleep.

When he wakes up the sun is taking its own nap.

Horvath skipped lunch and slept through dinner.

He walks over to the sink, splashes cool water on his face, dries himself with a coarse white towel.

Time to have another look at that clue, if that's what it is.

In his pants pocket, a small sheet of paper. Pale blue with lines. Ripped across the top and folded in quarters.

It says *R. Johnson*, with a local phone number. Shaky handwriting. A man's, he guesses.

There's a phone book on the bedside table. He flips through it. 14 Johnsons, but none of them R's.

He tries the last number. *Johnson*, no first name.

The number's been disconnected. A dead-end. He's not surprised, but it usually takes longer before he runs out of options.

Time for dinner. He could use a thick steak and a baked potato. Maybe a bowl of stew. Couple whiskeys, too. All that food could use a bath.

He gets dressed, combs his hair, and whistles a Pharaoh Sanders tune as he walks out the door.

In the elevator he sees a business card jammed into the corner of the mirror frame. An outline of a nude woman sitting in a giant martini glass. He thinks about the leggy brunette from the coffee shop.

He punches the *L* and waits.

The elevator stops at the second floor, but no one's there.

Something clicks in Horvath's mind. He looks back at the card.

Ron Johnson's Paradise City.

R. Johnson. He pulls the paper out of his pocket and checks the number. It's the same.

Not such a dead-end after all.

He grabs the business card and stuffs it into the breast pocket of his suitcoat. Looks like he'll have to pay them a visit.

But first he needs a little fuel.

DINNER'S PERFECT. Strong whiskey and a steak so rare it's practically wearing a bell around its neck.

His meal came with with greens on the side, which made Horvath feel like a regular health nut. Pretty soon, he thinks, I'll be eating dandelions and sitting cross-legged on a pillow.

Outside, he walks to the corner and sticks out his arm.

Cab pulls over a few seconds later.

He gets in back, leans forward, holds up the business card. "You know where this is?"

The driver squints, moves the toothpick to the other side of his mouth. "Yeah. Uptown."

"How long will it take to get there?"

"20 minutes. More with traffic."

Horvath pulls out a couple bills, hands them to the driver. "Make it 15."

"You got it, buddy."

The cabbie doesn't seem like he's in a hurry. Sticks to the speed limit, stays in one lane, doesn't run any yellows. But 12 minutes later there's a big flashy sign and that woman swimming like an olive in a martini glass.

Guy knew it wouldn't take 20 minutes, or 30. Horvath shakes his head. Everybody's working the angles.

Nightclubs everywhere you look. The whole strip is covered in neon and blinking lights.

Horvath gets out of the cab and walks toward the glowing entrance. There's so much wattage here the rest of the town must have a lightbulb shortage.

He hands the doorman a buck and goes inside.

There's a small bar to his left, sort of a tiki lounge. Women in grass skirts and flowers in their hair serve overpriced cocktails to fat salesmen from Toledo and Jeff City. He's been here a million times before, in other towns.

He goes straight, down a long narrow hallway.

At the end is a lobby, with a cloakroom off to the right. A girl in a low-cut top stands behind a wooden counter, smiling for tips. A single lightbulb hangs from the ceiling, buzzing.

There are framed photos on the wall, but he doesn't recognize any of the faces.

To the left, a small café or restaurant with a half-dozen round tables. A handful of gray suits are sitting alone. Eating, drinking, smoking. Nobody talks. A heavy chandelier hangs from the ceiling like a bad memory.

He nods to the coat-check girl and keeps moving. Another hallway, not quite as dark.

Bathroom. Stairs to the second floor. Supply closet. Phone booth.

He keeps walking.

Elbow-high table, with a banker's lamp. To the side, a doorway and red velvet curtain.

A big man in a dark suit and bulging forehead stands there gawking at Horvath like the caveman days are still in full swing.

"Are you...here for...the enter-tain-ment, sir?"

This *is* the show, he thinks. Gorilla in a suit who can sound out words.

"Sure. What kind of show is it, exactly?"

"A bur-le, bur-le. It's an...all-nude revue, sir."

"Sounds good. How much?"

"Two dollars."

Horvath slips him a few extra. "Mr. Johnson in tonight?"

The amazing talking gorilla looks up and to the right, but just for a second. "No, sir."

"Oh, that's too bad. Say, you got anything else going on tonight? You know, aside from the revue?"

The man stares at him like he's speaking Ancient Greek, or English.

"Anything...a little more special?"

The man stares at him long and hard. "Nothing like that, sir. Enjoy the show."

He parts the velvet curtain and Horvath walks inside.

The tables are even smaller here, with a little lamp in the middle of each one. The lampshades are red velvet, just like the curtains, but with gold tassels.

It's a big room, size of a football field.

A cigarette girl walks by smiling like she's got three rows of teeth, maybe four.

The hostess greets him, walks him to a table. The hem of her fake silk dress is so short he can see all the way up to Altoona, where she grew up.

He picks up the cocktail menu. Fake leather, gold tassel. This place has so much class they've got to cram some of it in storage, or at least that's what they want you to think.

When Horvath opens the menu and looks at the prices, he gets whiplash. Who pays that much for a drink? Christ, hope they reimburse me for this. He reaches into his coat pocket and pulls out a jar of aspirin. He twists it open, shakes a handful into his palm, throws them down.

"Want a chaser with that, sir?"

He looks up at the waitress, who's wearing the same get-up as the hostess, only shorter. "Good one. Are you the next act?"

"I could be."

She smiles at him, but it's the kind of smile that makes you want to take a shower afterward.

"What can I get you?"

"Singapore Sling."

"Anything else, sir?" Her drinks tray is painted with wet circles.

"No, that'll do it. If I need something else, I'll talk to my bank manager and see about a loan."

This time the smile is clean, and real. He can almost see the girl she used to be, before she wandered into this place.

The music starts and, a few moments later, the stage curtains open.

The men clap politely until the dancer struts out in a gold lamé dress. Busty redhead with good legs and a cruel mouth. A dim spotlight follows her around.

Without warning, the music gets louder and the stage lights explode. Now you can see a three-piece set up in a corner of the stage. The drummer looks like he's sleeping. A cigarette, dangling from the corner of his mouth, wears pajamas and a nightcap.

The gold dress doesn't stay on for long.

Clapping gets louder. A few hoots and hollers.

Silver bikini comes and goes.

Now she's standing there in pasties, swinging those tassels like her life depends on it. And maybe it does.

The tassels are gold, just like on the menu. Real class.

"Here you go, sir."

The waitress lingers, for a tip.

Horvath slides a bill into her palm.

"Johnson still run this place?"

"I wouldn't know about that, sir."

"Let me guess. You just keep your mouth shut and serve drinks?"

"Well, I do a lot more than that."

"I'll bet."

The waitress raises an eyebrow, empty drink tray at her hip. She's looking for another tip, or maybe a side job.

"So who is your boss? He around?"

"Sorry, sir. I've got other tables."

The waitress walks away and the exotic dancer takes off what's left of her outfit.

The audience claps and whistles. The men slap each other on the back. They're really living the high life.

ONE HIGHBALL and two dancers later, Horvath sees his waitress across the room whispering to a stocky guy in a cheap suit. Muscle, by the looks of him.

She points in his direction and the guy looks over.

Time to leave.

A dancer floats across the stage on a cloud of cigarette smoke, or maybe hidden wires.

He moves quickly, but not so you could tell. Head down, hands stuffed in his pockets.

Passing the cloakroom, he speeds up and thinks of McGrath. Don't check your coat. That was another one of his favorites. You never know when you'll have to make a fast exit, so travel light and keep your coat handy.

Not that he needs one tonight. Outside, the heat's gone down but somebody turned the humidity all the way up. This town is no picnic, that's for sure.

There aren't any taxies at the curb so he turns right and starts walking.

At the main road he takes a left and blends in with the crowd. The sidewalks are full of smiling people going nowhere.

After three blocks he stops and looks in a storefront window. Squadrini's Hardware. Hammers and chisels are on sale.

Couple goons are on his tail. Not the doorman gorilla, but two of his cousins. Chimps, maybe.

Whoever they are, they're not pros. Following too close. Staring right at me. Flashy ties, like they're in Miami or someplace. Suits are too tight. You can see their pieces bulging out like goiters. He shakes his head. That's how you draw heat from the boys in blue. Stupid.

Or maybe they own the police. Got 'em under their thumb. No need to hide anything.

He walks another few blocks, crosses against the light, turns a corner.

The goons are struggling to keep up. They're running across the intersection, or trying to. Their species can only stand upright for so long.

He double-times it down a side street. Newsstand, pawn shop, tobacconist.

It's a short block. Wino stands on the corner like a wobbly street sign.

After the first cross street, he looks back. The muscle has just rounded the corner. It's dark and the streets are thick with cars. They might not see him yet.

He makes a quick left into an alley.

There's a streetlamp, but it's burned out.

Brick walls on either side. Fire escapes. The alley backs up to a row of small shops. Butcher, jeweler, dive bars and foreign restaurants. He can practically see the red-and-white tablecloths, candles melting into old bottles of chianti. Whole chickens hanging in windows. Old man bent over a workbench, loupe jammed in his eye.

An open door, restaurant maybe.

He bolts inside, slowly closes the door. Locks it and throws the deadbolt. Tries to keep himself from breathing too loud.

After a few seconds he takes his bearings. It's not a kitchen. No heat from the ovens, no garlic or onion, no one barking out orders. No spatulas scraping against skillets or knives banging against chopping blocks.

It's dark but his eyes are adjusting. He can see outlines and vague shapes. Wooden crates, carboard boxes.

He flicks his lighter, looks around.

It's a storeroom, for a shop or restaurant. Must be closed for the night. Maybe it's their day off.

Small room. Metal shelves. Jars and cans lined up in nice tidy rows, like soldiers on parade. Couple wooden barrels. Boxes stacked on the floor.

Cobwebs, large bottle of cleanser, roll of paper towels, bucket, a neat pile of old rags, broom and dustpan. Two 55-gallon vats, shoulder to shoulder like a pair of bouncers outside a nightclub.

There's something else, in the corner. A black shadow. Horvath aims the lighter.

He's not alone.

When she smiles, her white teeth are a flashlight in the darkness.

He expects a scream. Or a smack to the back of his head with a tire iron. But all he gets is that smile.

The Chinese woman steps forward and stops about eight inches away from him. She crosses her arms and looks him up and down, a boxer sizing up the competition.

He puts her at 85 pounds, soaking wet. She wouldn't even qualify as flyweight.

The woman's no more than five feet tall. 70 years old, maybe more. She's got on one of those black pajama outfits they like to wear.

He leans forward, whispering. "Sorry, ma'am. Just hiding for a few minutes. I don't mean any harm."

She keeps staring, wordlessly.

"I won't hurt you."

She laughs now. Those shiny teeth are turned all the way up to floodlight.

"Quiet." He points outside, raises a finger to his lips. "Bad men. Out to get me."

She nods, puts a hand on his shoulder.

Now it's his turn to size her up. Old and wrinkled, all bones with a little skin painted on. But with tight compact muscles and veins popping out all over like a roadmap. She looks tough and strong. If Charles Atlas was an old Chinese lady, this is what he'd look like.

They huddle in the darkness and listen to the footsteps outside.

The goons run up and down the alley, stop a few feet from the door. Voices, heavy breathing. They're quiet for a few seconds, probably looking around and plotting their next move. One of them tries the door.

Horvath hears them walk away, slowly. They're in no hurry to get back to the club. Their boss won't be happy when he hears the bad news. He knows the feeling. Nobody likes to go home empty-handed and get chewed out by the boss.

The woman starts to speak, but he holds up a hand to stop her.

A minute later he reaches into his coat pocket, takes out a cigarette, lights up, blows smoke at the ceiling. "Thanks, ma'am."

"I know how to keep my mouth shut."

"That's a good quality in a woman."

"In a man, too."

"You got that right." He reaches into his pocket for a few dollars. "You never saw me, alright?"

She waves her hands, purses her mouth. "Not necessary."

"Suit yourself."

"I'll take one of those cigarettes, though."

"Sure." He takes a handful out of the pack. "Here's some for later, too."

"Thank you."

He lights her up and they puff in silence for a few minutes. The unventilated storage room is getting thick with smoke, but they don't mind.

7
—————

THE ANT HILL

"YOU HUNGRY?" SHE ASKS.

"Always."

"Come."

He follows her through a steel door on the other side of the room.

They're in a hallway. The floor tiles are old and cracked, the walls could use some paint, and the ceiling needs a little plaster, but the place is clean.

He follows her down the hall, past a row of doors. A mop leans against the wall like an old man taking a cigarette break.

She stops, takes a metal ring out of her pocket, finds the right key without looking, and unlocks a door. "Come. Upstairs."

The stairs are rickety and the light's not really pulling his weight, but he walks up.

The door at the top of the stairs is also locked, but she lets them in.

While his hand reaches for the doorknob, Horvath hears a low vibrating sound, like the hum of electrical wires or a transformer box.

He walks into a small vestibule. Just ahead is a doorway leading to a large room with a high ceiling. He steps inside.

There are no overhead lights, but smaller lamps are watching him from various points in the room. There's natural light, too. Candles and glowing cigarettes.

"I live up here. We all do."

Horvath looks around. It's an old warehouse or sweatshop that's been divided into hundreds of little rooms, maybe more. None of them bigger than the storeroom downstairs, and most of them a lot smaller. *Home* is definitely the wrong word. *Apartment* would be an overstatement. *Living space*, maybe. If you can call it living. *Hovel* is the word that comes to mind. Some of the more modest compartments don't even have solid walls. They're more like glorified chicken coops.

"I'm not sure this place is up to code."

She laughs. "No, I don't think so."

The woman shuffles toward the city of makeshift rooms and walks through a slim entrance. He has to turn sideways, suck in his belly, and squeeze through. The woman looks back and watches, but doesn't laugh. She's alright in his book.

The chatter is deafening. Hundreds of people sitting still, trying not to make too much noise. There's no room to breathe.

She turns right, left, left. Scrambles up a wooden ladder, which is also the wall of someone's room. Horvath looks at the man inside, eating noodles out of a black lacquered bowl. He sits cross-legged on the floor and wears a white sleeveless t-shirt. His space is tidy and clean, almost fussy.

The second floor is more cramped and the ceiling is so low he has to bend over. Now he feels like the ape. But no one looks up or takes notice as they scuttle through the labyrinth, even though he's the only white face around.

Another ladder. Up to the third floor.

She stops in front of an unpainted plywood door and unlocks it. Horvath thanks god or whoever's in charge around here that there's no more climbing.

They walk inside.

Horvath feels like a giant. The walls are closing in and he's starting to sweat uncontrollably. He's out of breath from scaling the human anthill.

She laughs, moving books and pillows out of the way to make space. "Let me get you some water."

"Thanks."

He wonders how high you've got to climb to get to the communal bathroom, if there is one. The woman lives in a single room. No closets or cabinets. No icebox. No fan, unless you count the folding one she's got in her hand. He can touch almost every wall from where he's sitting, and the ceiling isn't too far out of reach. He remembers a third-floor walk up in Astoria, which doesn't seem so bad anymore. A toilet and sink, no ladders to climb.

"What do you want to eat?"

"Anything's fine. Whatever's easiest for you."

"You like leftovers?"

"It's the only thing I know how to cook."

She slaps him on the back and smiles, popping one of his cigarettes into her mouth.

He lights it, and one for himself.

She blows a perfect smoke ring and holds up the cigarette. "Good flavor. Thanks."

"Any time."

"Back in a minute."

She shuffles outside and jogs down the hallway until Horvath can no longer hear the soft footsteps. I should be so nimble at her age, he thinks.

Hell, at my age.

A few minutes later the woman comes back with a metal bin in her hands. She turns on a hotplate, grabs a wok that's hanging from the wall, throws in a little cooking oil, and empties the tin into the wok.

"We have kitchen downstairs, but hotplate is good for reheating."

He nods.

Soon, the food is sizzling.

"Smells good. What is it?"

"Egg foo young."

"What's that?"

"Eggs, onion, carrot, peas…famous Chinese dish."

She stirs the food a few times, waits, then dumps it on two plates.

"More water?"

He shakes his head *no*.

She hands him a fork but grabs chopsticks for herself.

They eat in silence. No music, no small talk. He feels right at home.

She wolfs down the food with a serious expression, like a scholar pouring over old books. They're both finished in under two minutes.

"Thank you. That was good."

She bows.

"What's your name, anyway?"

"Fang. That's Chinese for *pleasant*. Or a plant that smells good."

"Means something else in English."

"I know." She laughs.

He tells the old woman his name.

"What does it mean?"

"I don't know. Nothing, probably."

Horvath lights a cigarette, hands one to Fang.

She lights it from a short red candle squatting next to a copper Buddha. "Drink?"

"Why not."

She reaches into a wooden box at the base of her bed, which is a thin mattress wedged into the corner. Fang holds up a bottle of clear liquor and pours it into small ceramic cups.

"What is it?"

"Chinese drink. *Baijiu*. Don't know the word for it in English."

"There probably isn't one," he says. "Bottom's up."

They clink glasses and drink. It's strong. Not good, but strong.

"You like it?"

"It does the trick."

"One more, for luck."

"Is that what they say in China?"

"I don't know, but I say it."

Her smile is a spotlight. Horvath feel's like one of the dancers at the revue.

"You have any family here?" he asks.

"No."

"What do you do for work?"

"I clean this place. And downstairs."

"Bathrooms must be a mess, with all these people…"

She throws up both hands. "Don't remind me."

"Well, I better get going. Thanks for the food, and everything."

She shrugs.

"Here, keep the rest." He tosses the pack of cigarettes on the table. "And if you ever need anything, I'm at the Executive."

She nods while he stands up.

Horvath slips from the room and she reaches for the bottle.

8

NIGHT TRAIN

HE MAKES IT BACK TO THE STOREROOM WITHOUT TOO MANY WRONG turns. Before he opens the door to the alley, he stops and listens. No one's there. It's safe.

Back at the main road, he turns left and heads away from Paradise City. The muscle should be long gone by now, but there's no use taking chances.

The sidewalks and streets are still crowded. Nobody sleeps in this town, he thinks.

Crossing a busy intersection, he trips on what he thinks is a granite paving stone. But no, it's a steel track. He looks up. Catenary wire runs overhead, like dialogue in the funny pages. He looks around but there's no trolley stop. Maybe they don't run anymore.

He keeps moving. There are no more bars or shops. Just a few lonely houses, with dead grass and mailboxes leaning over like street-corner drunks. A rusty bicycle pump stands by the curb, like it's waiting for a ride. The edge of town is drawing near.

Up ahead, there's an elevated platform. Of course, the subway killed off the tramcars.

He bounces up the metal staircase. The platform is empty, and there's no sign of a train.

Horvath walks closer to the tracks and looks out over the city. Skyline, rooftops, pigeon coops, water towers. He remembers sleeping on a tar-covered roof when he was a boy. On hot summer nights his bedroom was an oven.

The crows are smudges against the blue-black sky. A child's drawing.

He thinks about what brought him here, to this dying town.

Train should be here by now. He checks his watch. Is the station closed for repairs? There aren't any signs posted.

Too bad I'm not packing a flask.

He can see her plain as day, as if she was standing right there on the platform. The woman from the coffee shop. Lana. Her legs were long and lean, but powerful. They could make a man lose his mind, or at least forget what he was doing for a few minutes.

It's been almost half an hour. Something's wrong.

He's about to turn around and leave when he sees them. The goons are walking side by side, creeping along in the shadows by the staircase.

Did they set this up? Hell, they don't control the train schedule, do they?

Is there another way out? No, just one set of stairs.

Horvath looks up and down the tracks, at the covered roof of the station. The platform's not wide enough to run past them.

The gorillas are getting closer. He can hear their knuckles dragging. There's only one way out.

He jumps off the platform and sprints across the tracks. Climbs up the other side, races across the platform, and takes the stairs.

The goons are right behind him. Their shoes slap hard against the concrete like it's a substitute for his face.

At the street, he turns right and heads back into town.

He makes a few quick turns, slows down.

Apartment buildings, locksmith, electrician, Elk's lodge, coffee shop.

There's a bar on the corner. Dom's. The lights are on but he can't hear anything. The streets are empty now.

Can't hear the goons anymore so he stops running, pops into an alley.

He pats his pockets but can't find the smokes. That's right. Gave them to Fang.

The alley is dark and narrow. Red brick walls rise up on either side of him, which makes him think of the two men on his tail. It makes him think of other things, too. Life is closing in.

There's a No Parking sign on the wall. A streetlight looks down at him.

Horvath crosses the alley, hides behind a dumpster. He crouches down to stay out of view.

He didn't choose this life, not really. It just fell in his lap. He didn't have a choice in the matter, or at least that's what he tells himself. Sometimes he feels like a tough guy. Fistfights, black eyes, stab wounds, stakeouts. Hunting men down. Collecting information for the firm. But he doesn't feel tough right now, cowering next to a trashcan in a filthy alley.

After 20 minutes he decides it's safe, and his knees can't take it anymore. He stands up and walks carefully up the alley. If there's one thing he's learned over the years, it's how to move without making a lot of noise.

The streets are even more quiet now, like a graveyard.

A cat dashes underneath a Ford, staring at him with wary yellow eyes.

Man stumbles out of the bar across the street, hails a cab that isn't there.

The wind whistles and a tin can rolls down the blacktop like a clanking tumbleweed.

He keeps walking toward the center of town. The Executive is a good 20 minutes away, on foot. The cabbies are probably in bed by now, dreaming of beautiful women and magic carpets.

It's almost peaceful, a quiet walk with no one around. No cars honking, no screeching women, no dumb lunks trying to act hard. He sometimes wishes the daytime could be just like the night.

A shadow moves in the doorway of a grocery store, and there they are.

They block the sidewalk, hands on hips.

"Oh, hey. It's the knuckle-draggers. How you fellas doing?"

They don't answer. One of them cracks his knuckles.

"Thought you'd be back at the treehouse by now. Swinging on vines, eating bananas. Maybe picking fleas off each other."

The goons bare their teeth and flex their neck muscles at the same time, like it's a dance routine.

"You guys must be happy. Zookeeper letting you out of the cage for so long."

Horvath laughs, but it's all a bluff. He's just playing for time.

This would be good time to carry a gun, he thinks. But McGrath was clear about that. No sidearms. They cause more problems than they solve.

"How'd you boys get into this racket, anyway?" He stuffs his hands in his pockets, like they're just shooting the shit. "You already had the flashy ties and pin-striped suits, so the boss just hired you on the spot? Saved him a few bucks in wardrobe?"

He laughs. The thugs don't.

"Or I know...you and the boss are from the same species, right? You went to Chimp College together. Met in some, uh, advanced chest-beating seminar?"

The goons have square heads and hair short as tennis ball fuzz. They're built like mailboxes—barrel chests and short legs.

Goon 1 makes a fist and steps forward.

Goon 2 reaches into his jacket.

They may not be smart, he thinks. Or quick on their feet. And they don't keep up with the latest developments in quantum physics. But they've got fists and guns and they probably know how to use them.

"Come on fellas, why don't we sit down, have a drink, talk things over."

The one in front laughs, or maybe grunts, then turns his head a few inches to say something to his pal.

Horvath doesn't need an invitation.

He takes a step forward, brings the heel of right foot down on the guy's knee as hard as he can. It makes an ungodly sound, like a dump truck driving over a row of skulls. The guy doesn't scream or even call out, but he drops to his knees. Horvath lands two quick jabs square on the nose, which makes him fall to the cement.

Goon 2 draws his gun.

Horvath holds up his hands. "Alright. I give up. You got me."

The goon keeps his gun on Horvath, lightly kicks his pal on the shoulder.

The guy doesn't move. His pal kicks him again, a little harder this time.

He moans.

"You okay?"

He moans again, but in a slightly lower pitch.

Goon 2 nods. He seems to understand his pal's grunts and groans. Must be their native language.

The thug gets to his hands and knees, looks up at Horvath. He's in pretty bad shape. His bones creak like the back door of an abandoned house.

Horvath knows his way around a boxing ring, but he didn't hit the guy all that hard. The sidewalk did more damage than his fists. When you're a big man, that's usually the case.

"C'mon," his pal says. "Get up already."

He sees a car slow down and circle around.

The goon is having a hard time standing up. His head hit the ground pretty hard and his eyes aren't focusing. Goon 2 reaches down and grabs him by the shoulder.

He looks over at the curb, 30 feet up the road. The car is waiting. It's a cab.

The driver nods.

The goon starts getting to his feet and his pal helps him up. He moans louder this time and, for a moment, his pal lowers the gun and looks away from Horvath.

That's all the time he needs.

He kicks the gun out of the goon's hand, drives a left into the side of his head, and lands a solid uppercut to the jaw.

The goon reels and his pal drops back to the ground.

Horvath sprints for the taxi. The driver is revving up.

He jumps into the back seat and the driver steps on the gas. Horvath turns around and watches the muscle through the rear window. Looks like Goon 2 has a broken nose. They're both standing now, waving their arms and arguing about whose fault it is.

He turns around, takes a deep breath, and settles into his seat. The driver scrolls through the static looking for a good song on the radio, which isn't easy, and at the same time he speeds up to make the yellow light.

9

BUILDS YOU UP, JUST TO PUT YOU DOWN

HORVATH SLEEPS THROUGH THE NIGHT LIKE A BIG BABY WITH A FIVE o'clock shadow.

He checks the clock. It's nearly 11:00 am.

Haven't slept this well since the last time someone slipped me a mickey.

He reaches for a pack of cigarettes that isn't there, groans, thinks of the two apes who followed him all over town.

What are the hiding at that nightclub? What does it have to do with my man?

How many more thugs are they going to send looking for me?

His bladder's about to burst. He gets up, walks to the bathroom, takes a slash, washes his hands and face.

No time for a shave. No good blades, anyway.

Grabs a shirt. Clean, but not as white as it used to be. He puts on a fresh suit, this one a slightly darker shade of gray.

Wallet, keys, watch, change, lighter.

He grabs his dirty clothes and heads out the door.

. . .

THE YOUNG MAN at the front desk gives him a prissy look and points to the laundry. "Would you like to leave that with us?"

"What, you kidding? You guys charge an arm and a leg."

"Well, if you can't afford it..."

"For what you're asking to iron a couple shirts, I could hire a girl to come over here and stitch me a new suit from scratch. And then fry up some steaks afterward."

The desk clerk inspects his fingernails, nose in the air. It looks like he gets his eyebrows waxed, and he's got enough oil in his hair for a dozen lube jobs.

Why do these guys always have to be such arrogant pricks? he asks himself. Even at a dump like this. "Look, much as I'd like to sit around and jaw all day, I've got things to do. You know where there's a gym around here?"

The clerk looks him up and down.

"Somewhere I can go a few rounds."

"Three blocks north on Russell, left on Quaker Lane. You can't miss it. Big ugly green building."

"Uglier the better."

The desk clerk touches a moleskin notepad with gold lettering embossed on the cover. He speaks without making eye contact. "Say, I know a little secret you'd probably like to hear."

"Oh yeah?"

"Yeah."

Horvath lays out two bills.

The clerk looks down at the money like it's a pile of dog shit. "Well, I guess it's not that important after all."

He lays down another bill.

The clerk scoops up the money, folds it, sticks it in the breast pocket of his Italian suit.

"Last night, a lady was waiting around the lobby, looking for you. She seemed rather impatient, and *agitated*."

"You talk to her?"

"No."

"Who did?"

"Rafael."

"He here now?"

"No, it's his day off." The fussy little man adjusts his orange pocket square.

"Alright, keep going."

"She was a blonde, with legs." He raises a dark, sculpted eyebrow.

"With legs, huh?"

"Yes, sir. You know who the lady is?"

"I've got a pretty good idea." He stares at the ledger, the service bell, the warren of pigeonholes behind the clerk. "What else did this Rafael say?"

"Hm...you know what? I'm getting a little foggy."

He lays down another bill.

When the clerk reaches out his hand, Horvath clamps it down, hard. "Your memory needs to improve, quick."

"Yes, sir." He's wincing, ready to cry. The sarcasm and self-importance have drained from his voice.

He lets go of the young man's hand.

The clerk straightens his tie, adjusts his immoveable hair.

"Your hands are soft," Horvath says.

"Moisturizer." He releases a thin smile.

"So the lady. What'd she say?"

"Not much. But she wanted to speak with you. Urgently, I'd say. She was waiting in the lobby for almost two hours."

Two chairs and a table. That's a lobby? "You see her?"

"I caught a glimpse."

Horvath nods.

"But I didn't talk to her."

"So you said."

The clerk straightens a few papers on the counter, his eyes darting around like pachinko balls. His Windsor knot is as wide as a fist.

"She leave me a message or anything?"

"No, but Rafael said he's seen her around."

"Oh, yeah? Where?"

"Frank's."

"What's that, a bar?"

The clerk nods. "22nd and Delaney. The place ain't fancy."

"Didn't think it was."

Ain't? Horvath thinks, as he pushes through the revolving door. I guess Mr. Fancy Desk Clerk isn't all that fancy, when it comes down to it. We're all pretending to be someone we're not.

He heads uptown, toward 22nd. Bound to pass a dry cleaner along the way.

3rd avenue is wide and almost impressive. A few trees, a small plaza with a statue of somebody who used to be important. But the streets are just as dirty here, and so is the air.

Office buildings, swank apartments, nice restaurants. A fat doorman standing under a canopy, hands clasped behind his back, dressed in a long frock coat and a swanky cap like he's the grand marshal of a parade.

He turns right, walks two blocks, makes a left up a side street.

Shoe repair, bakery, hardware store, bodega, café. This is more like it.

Chinese take-away, butcher, toy shop, bar. Apartments stacked like wooden crates in a warehouse.

He likes walking, even with the blisters and sweat. You feel alive when you're moving through the city on your own two feet.

Dry Cleaner. Bingo.

The sign says One Hour Martinizing. Everything spick-and-span in 60 minutes, without dangerous chemicals. What'll they think of next.

He drops off his clothes and takes the ticket.

Drugstore at the end of the block. He stops in for a few things.

Cigarettes, aspirin, razor blades, styptic pencil, socks. Pen, steno pad. Two paperbacks—science fiction and a western. There's a luncheonette in back. After he pays for his things, Horvath walks over and takes a stool at the counter.

A big lady waddles over. She's got a rat's nest of bottled red hair and little glasses perched on the end of her nose, but she knows the job. Pours him a steaming cup of joe without asking, or making small talk.

He leans down, takes a sip. Doesn't matter how bad your night was. That first sip washes it all away.

The smokes are staring him down. Horvath caresses the pack, takes off her crinkly cellophane dress. He can't do anything about the stupid smile on his face, but hopefully he's not salivating.

A few quick puffs and a smoke ring. Long slow sip of coffee.

He feels almost human again. Reanimated, like Frankenstein's monster.

It's not so far-fetched, he thinks. Could even work on a pile of old tires and busted plywood. If you fill anything with strong coffee, cigarettes and whiskey, it's bound to stand up straight and walk around for a while.

He remembers when cigarettes were wrapped in tin foil. Those were the days...

Man alive, I'm getting old.

Horvath chews on this for a while. *Getting*? Hell, I'm already older than my old man when he died. He's never thought about this before.

A waitress catches him staring absentmindedly into the distance, or maybe at the one-armed busboy, Rick. She snaps in his face. "Hey, mister. You wanna order, or what?"

He's already forgotten what he was daydreaming about. "Sure. Scrambled eggs and bacon, side of crispy toast."

"Got it."

He looks up at her. She's a lot younger than the one who poured his coffee. Too young. This town's going to eat her alive. And she's skinny, too skinny. Narrow drooping shoulders. Pale splotchy skin. Sickly looking, like a dope fiend. But she doesn't seem the type. There's still some life in those hazel eyes. Lank dirty-blonde hair, piled up high with a couple pencils stuck inside. If someone smacked her around they'd fall out like candy from one of those Mexican piñatas.

He eyes the notepad in her left hand. "You plan on writing down my order?"

"Naw, I'll remember." She taps the side of her head to show how smart she is, which you only do if you're not very smart.

She walks back to the kitchen.

He hunches over the coffee, tapping his butts into the saucer.

A few minutes later the young waitress swoops in with the coffee pot. "Nother round?"

"Always."

She doesn't leave. Instead, she sets down the pot, leans on the counter, pulls a folded up section of newspaper out of her apron pocket. With a wrinkled forehead she studies the paper like she's considering a longshot in the sixth race.

She's working a crossword, but the grid is almost completely blank.

"Say, mister. What's a nine-letter word for *long, arduous campaign*?"

"Breakfast."

She squints at the crossword. He can see her lips move as she counts the squares. Don't blow a fuse in your head, young lady. You might need it someday.

"It fits. Thanks." She starts writing, but stops short. "Hey, you having me on?"

"No, I wouldn't do that, kid. Need any more help with that thing?"

"You bet." She smiles and twirls a loose strand of hair, flirting like she's read about it but hasn't actually tried it out yet. "You know, you're alright."

"My mother used to think so."

The cook smacks the silver buzzer.

He looks over. His meal is steaming on the chrome countertop.

"How 'bout a two-word phrase for *behind schedule*? Four letters each."

"Cold food?"

"No, doesn't fit."

The older waitress carries over his meal. "Why don't you leave the customers alone, Maggie."

"He likes it, right?"

"Sure."

The older waitress shakes her head, though you almost can't see it, before shuffling off to clear some dishes and wipe up a mess two stools down.

"How's your food?" the waitress asks.

"Fine."

"Sunny-side up, just like you ordered."

"Yeah, just about."

She watches him eat for a few moments, then goes back to her puzzle.

A bald man with little round glasses takes a seat at the counter. The waitress keeps plugging away at the crossword, oblivious.

Eventually, the other waitress frowns her way over to pour the schmuck some coffee.

Horvath comes up for air a minute later, breakfast half-gone. "You're really something, kid."

"I know." She scribbles a few letters, then erases them. "You need anything else?"

He spears a runny glob of egg and soggy toast, shovels it into his mouth, chases the whole mess with a landslide of black coffee.

"Just the check."

OUTSIDE, he looks around. The street sign says 19th and Michigan. Frank's is on 22nd and Delaney.

Will she be at the bar this early? He lights up and checks his watch. Sure, why not.

Slender fingers of sunlight reach out between two buildings and swipe at his face.

He squints, covers his eyes with his hand, and keeps walking.

After a few blocks he sees Delaney, cuts right.

There it is. Fran_'s.

The k skipped town. Gambling debts, maybe.

A stray dog is curled up at the entrance, eyes closed, soaking up the sunlight.

Before he can step over the threshold, an old drunk waddles up from the side of the building. Ripped trousers, gray suspenders, filthy white undershirt. He's holding onto the scarred bricks so he won't fall down. The brim of his tattered fedora is hanging so low it's covering his eyes.

He reaches out to Horvath, who takes his arm.

"You okay, old-timer?"

"Will be, if you can give me a quarter."

He fishes a few coins out of his pocket, hands them over. "What are you going to do with the money, go to night school?"

The man laughs through a nearly empty mouth. His teeth are a white picket fence with most of the slats missing. "Ha, good one. No siree, I'm going to get me a nice cold beer."

"Enjoy it." He tips the man's brim up out of his eyes, and spins him around so he's pointed at the door. "There you go."

"Thanks, Joe." The man gives him a wave and stumbles into the bar.

He waits a few beats, then follows him inside.

It's dark. Making his way to the bar, he feels as blind as the old drunk.

Vic Damone is singing on the jukebox. The Velvet Fog. Not bad for a crooner.

The stool is wobbly. He looks around. The people in here are a little wobbly, too.

No sign of a bartender. The drunk's grinning to himself at a booth near the window, mumbling something. Who says you need two people for a conversation.

There's red paint on the floor near his feet. Or maybe it's blood. He puts his feet up on the brass rail.

Place hasn't seen a broom or dustpan in a while. A few dirty glasses are loitering along the bar. Back near the bottles, there's a white plate splattered with ketchup. Hunks of gristle and toast crumbs are scattered across the plate. Fork and knife sit there quietly, eyewitnesses to a crime.

Man walks toward him from the bathroom, wiping his hands on

his pants. Hasn't shaved in a few days. Hair looks like it's trying to make a run for it.

It's the bartender. He flips up the hinged plank of unpainted wood at the end of the bar, slips through, grabs a bottle of gin, and pours himself three fingers. Down the hatch.

He doesn't pay attention to his customers. Doesn't even seem to know they exist.

The dog from outside wanders in, walks alongside the tables by the wall, throws up on the leg of a chair. Grass, mostly. Probably better than eating here.

The bartender doesn't blink.

I've been in worse dives, he thinks. But only in Ohio.

This place should be condemned, but it's not quite good enough for that. Boys at the Health Department wouldn't bother. It'll fall apart on its own soon enough. Death by natural causes.

What is it with this town? Everything's ramshackle, broken-down, missing something. Can't they fix anything around here? It's one big dump.

The bartender takes another drink, shakes his head, scratches himself. He looks over at Horvath with dead eyes and a mouth that hangs open like a broken drawer.

"Whiskey."

"Rocks?"

"Neat."

The bartender pours the drink, walks it over, and sets it down, sloshing a quarter-ounce on the bar.

Horvath nods, takes a sip.

The man plants his hands on the bar and watches him, mouth gaping. The way you'd look at a space alien or talking goat who sat down and asked for a cocktail.

"Food?"

"No. This'll do it for me."

The bartender doesn't move.

"You know a brunette?" Horvath asks. "Tall, good legs, calls herself Lana."

The bartender does his best imitation of a statue.

Horvath wants to say something about her eyes, how they're filled with tenderness and cruelty, but that would be too much poetry for a corner bar on a weekday afternoon.

"So you ever seen her? She comes in here sometimes, from what I hear."

The bartender points backwards with his thumb, like he's throwing salt over his shoulder for good luck.

When he turns, Lana's right there, her dress brushing against the side of the bar. She smiles at Horvath like he's a big juicy steak and it's time for the first bite.

He nods.

She grabs a heavy glass ashtray and slides it down the bar. "You'll need this."

He looks at his cigarette. The tower of ash is about to collapse. "Thanks."

"Don't mention it."

Black heels, red dress, black hat with a little veil.

She walks over with long precise steps as if auditioning for a role, and maybe she is.

10

THE WOMAN IN RED

They stare at one another in silence, two prizefighters about to step into the ring.

The bartender walks off. Busy day, he's got places to scratch.

"What's in your little bag?" she asks.

"I had to pick up a few things at the drugstore."

"Nothing serious, I hope."

He grins. "Just needed cigarettes and razors."

"You going to slit your throat or just burn a few holes in your arm?"

"Enough with the banter." He finishes the whiskey. "I heard you were snooping around my hotel."

"You call that a hotel?"

"Good point, but were you?"

"Maybe."

"Why don't you tell me what you *maybe* wanted."

Lana nods to the bartender and, quick as a flinch, a gin and tonic appears. Horvath didn't think the guy could move so fast. She must have some pull around here.

He pushes his empty glass across the bar and the man walks off for the whiskey bottle, a little slower this time.

"Here's looking up your old address." She raises the highball to her lips, pinkie out like a lady, and takes a cautious sip.

When his drink arrives he stamps out his cigarette before having a slug.

She takes another drink, more thirsty this time, puts the glass down. "My friend is missing."

"What kind of friend?"

"The kind that sleeps over occasionally."

"But not always?"

"A girl needs time to herself."

He lets this sink in. "So why do you think I can help?"

"You seem like the kind of fella who knows how to handle himself."

"I do, most of the time."

"What about the rest of the time?" she asks.

"That's when I can't."

Lana opens her purse, takes out a cigarette case.

Horvath flicks his lighter.

She bends down, eyes locked on Horvath. "Thanks."

"Don't mention it." He pauses. "Thing is, you don't even know me. Why not ask one of your pals?"

"Who, like Sammy over there?" Lana points to the old drunk, muttering to himself by the window.

"Not him, but somebody you know and trust."

"I don't trust anybody."

"What about me?"

"I'm still trying to work that one out." She finishes her drink, eyes never letting go of Horvath.

He downs the rest of his whiskey.

The bartender comes over with a fresh cocktail and a bottle of bourbon. He's about to pour the whiskey, but Horvath puts his hand on the bottle. "Leave it."

The bartender skulks off.

He tries to read her face but it's a mystery with a dozen pages missing, and her thin eyebrows are accents marks in a foreign language.

Lana takes a healthy swig of gin, but it doesn't seem to affect her. She can hold her liquor. He likes that, but it could mean trouble.

"So, let's get down to brass tacks," he says.

"Fine by me."

"How'd you know where I was staying? Who told you?"

"Nobody told me anything. I tailed you."

"Huh..."

"Yeah, *huh*."

He takes a closer look at the woman. Her eyes don't give anything away, and neither does her mouth. But the body's a different story. It gives everything away, for free. She isn't wearing that red dress. It's painted on. Closer to the skin than most tattoos. Lana looks great and she knows it. Horvath might be getting played for a fool, and he knows it too. A woman like her could break a dozen hearts before breakfast, and the suckers wouldn't even be angry. They'd thank her for it.

She blows smoke from the corner of her mouth.

He just sits there, thinking.

"*Huh*," Lana repeats. "That all you got to say?"

"It's enough."

"Anyone ever tell you you were a great conversationalist."

"Not yet."

"Didn't think so."

"So you shadowed me? That's the truth?"

"Honest to god. Thought you were too slick for that, didn't you?"

I should've known, should've *felt* it. The booze is tapping him on the shoulder.

Lana smiles. "The best marks are the ones who don't think they're marks."

"I've heard that one before."

"Then you should know better." She blows a smoke ring, watches it float toward the ceiling and disappear. "You underestimated me."

"Guess so."

"My first husband did the same thing."

"How'd that work out?"

"Bout like you'd expect," she says. "So will you do it? Look around for my friend?"

"I'm already looking for someone myself."

"Great, then it's a double feature."

Horvath leans closer to Lana. "Maybe you can help me find the guy I'm looking for."

"What's his name?"

He tells her.

"Never heard of him."

He has his doubts. She plays her cards close to the chest.

"What do you say?" she asks.

"I'm not supposed to take any side jobs. The people I work for wouldn't like it."

"I won't tell anyone."

"No, don't suppose you would."

"So?" She wipes her mouth with a tissue.

"What's his name, this friend of yours?"

"Al Kovacs. But sometimes he goes by Kupchak. Or Bill Covington."

"Fake names, huh? Sounds like a real boy scout."

"Yeah, he's got the neckerchief and everything."

"What's he look like?"

"Shorter than you. Medium build, maybe 185 pounds. Dark hair, dark eyes. Likes shoes with a small heel, and bright red ties. Wears a cream-colored suit."

"A regular man about town."

"He may not be much, but he's all I got."

"I've heard that one before, too."

She shrugs. "I watch too many movies."

He nods, trying to take it all in. "What else can you tell me?"

"That's it. I don't know anything else."

"Somehow, I don't believe you."

"Try me."

"Maybe I will."

She smiles, like a lion after a kill. "Look at Mr. Smooth-talker over here."

"Do you think your friend might have skipped town?"

"No way. He left everything behind. Spare suit, pair of shoes, hair oil. Even his best fedora. He'd never leave without that."

His eyebrows jump. "Best fedora, huh? No comment."

"Like I said, he's all I got."

"Does he owe anyone money?"

"No."

"What'd he do, anyway?"

"Nothing."

"So they grabbed him, worked him over, maybe killed him. All for no reason."

She shrugs. "It happens."

Does it? He pours himself another three fingers, and a thumb for good measure. "So he didn't run. It was foul play?"

"That's my take."

"How long's he been gone?"

"Two days, maybe three." She crosses her legs slowly, leans against the bar.

Horvath sits back and enjoys the show.

Lana grabs the olive from her empty glass, pops it in her mouth.

The bartender takes a half-step forward, but she cuts him off with a hand raised a few inches off the bar.

She looks great, he thinks, even in this crummy light. But she's dead tired. That's one thing she can't hide from me. Hasn't been sleeping much. She's got enough bags under her eyes for a weekend trip to Paris.

"So, will you do it?" she asks.

"Sure, why not." I could use the money for a new set of wheels, he thinks. And a new suit, too.

"How much?"

He names a price.

"I can handle that."

"Plus expenses."

"Expenses, huh? Just don't pad the bill. I'll be keeping an eye on you."

"I'm sure you will."

She picks a flake of tobacco off her tongue. "It's a deal, then."

They shake hands.

"One more thing?"

"What is it?" Lana asks.

"What do you know about this clip joint, Paradise City? Couple thugs chased me all around town last night, pulled a gun on me. Was lucky to make it out in one piece."

"What'd you do to deserve all that?"

"I asked a few innocent questions."

"I'll bet. Sticking your nose where it isn't wanted, that'll get you killed in this town."

"So who runs the place?"

"Well, it's not Ron Johnson, that's for sure."

"No?"

"They found him in the river a few months ago."

"Cement shoes?"

"I don't know about his footwear, but he wasn't dressed for a swim."

"What happened?"

"He was into the syndicate for 20 large. Least that's what I heard."

"From who?"

"From everyone. It all over town."

"What else do you know?"

"That's about it. Syndicate runs the place now. They got some stooge to act like he's the new owner, but he's just a stuffed shirt. Doesn't fool anybody."

"Not even the police?"

She laughs. "Good one."

"So the cops don't make a move without asking the syndicate for permission?"

"Bingo."

"Who's this stooge?"

"No idea. You'd need to ask around."

"I'll do that."

"Look, I have to go." Lana hands him a discreet roll of bills. "That's to get you started. Let me know if you find anything."

"How do I get in touch with you?"

She laughs like you do when something's not funny. "Easy. Just stop by my office."

"What, you run this place?"

"You catch on quick."

Horvath turns and walks away before he says anything he'll regret.

11

PULP

THE REST OF THE DAY IS A BLUR.

He walks across town, looks in a few shops, eats dinner, crushes out cigarette butts under his heel. A normal day, but he's not getting any closer to the truth. He doesn't know where his guy is, and he doesn't have any good leads.

His eyes are open and his mouth is shut. When all else fails, keep a low profile. That's another one of McGrath's proverbs. He should write them all down and have them framed. Hang them on the wall next to his marriage license, college degree, and old shopping lists. All those useless scraps of paper.

He calls Ungerleider, his contact at the firm, and gets an address. North side of town. Rowhouse. He's told to check it out, as soon as possible. That's all the information he has. He asks about Lana's friend Kovacs, but Ungerleider's never heard of the guy.

WHEN HE GETS to the house at dusk, the place is empty.

Really empty. Broken windows, splintered door, stained mattress in the corner. Icebox doesn't have so much as a jar of horseradish or an old can of sardines. Doesn't hum, either. Electricity's been shut off. Water, too. Even the tumbleweeds have scrammed.

He climbs to the second floor and opens a closet. The clothes are gone and, when he touches the flimsy metal hangers, they rattle like skeleton bones.

Place looks like the cops busted in. Or maybe a gang of crooks. Somebody. Whoever it was, they were looking for something.

He doesn't see any blood. Maybe he got wised up at the last minute and beat it.

Horvath shakes his head. Ungerleider has been useless, for months now. All his leads are dead-ends. His words are as empty as this goddamn rowhouse.

On the way out he stops for a second on the front porch. The floorboards creak and the wind whistles through the windowless house.

He hears something.

Next door, a little girl is holding onto the unpainted wooden railing. She must be about six or seven. Horvath can't tell. Pigtails, braids, pink ribbons. Plaid dress with a white collar. Little white socks, patent leather shoes. The whole bit.

"Hi, mister."

He nods.

She keeps staring.

"Didn't anyone ever tell you it's not polite to stare?"

"Yeah."

She doesn't take the hint.

"You live here?" He points to the attached home next door.

"Yes."

"Hear anything from this place lately? Fighting, yelling, loud voices?"

"No."

"Do you know who lives here?"

"No."

"Ever see anybody go in or out."

She looks down at her fingers, still gripping the rail, looks back up at the strange man. "No."

Course not. "Look, sorry to ask, but...are you telling me the truth? Cause it's important."

"Yes, mister. It's the truth. I don't know anything."

"Alright."

"You got any candy?"

He laughs. "No, sorry. I'm fresh out."

She frowns, hangs her head.

"Take it easy, kid."

Horvath walks for another hour or two, without direction. Doesn't eat or drink or ask any more questions. His mind is shut off and he barely registers the people and objects passing by. He's just one more shmuck in a gray suit.

Back at the Executive, he sits on the edge of his bed and takes off his shoes. The heels are wearing thin, but so is his wallet.

He takes off his suit, splashes water on his face, drinks some water.

Climbs into bed, gets under the covers.

His books are stacked in an orderly pile on the end table. He grabs the western and opens to the bookmark on page 38. The hero's riding from Cheyenne to Sioux Falls. That's over 500 miles with a lot of rough terrain in the middle. Hostile Indians, too. He's only got 10 days to make it. A couple frontier soldiers are also looking for him, but that's the least of his worries. What he needs right now is a nice soft bed and someone to warm it up for him.

Horvath adjusts the pillow behind his back and starts reading.

It's a good book, even though he can see exactly where the story's going.

Eventually, he falls asleep with the book flopped across his chest like a sleeping baby.

IN THE MORNING he reaches for a smoke, lights up, and enjoys the first one staring at the ceiling. The book fell off his chest at some point during the night, and tumbled over next to the chair. The spine isn't broken, though. He takes this as a good sign.

He reads for a good hour. The Indians are closing in, and so is the Army. He's not sure if the hero will make it out alive, but at the same time he does.

THE ELEVATOR'S no bigger than a garbage chute, and it smells just as rotten. His lungs felt more clean upstairs, smoking.

The front desk clerk pretends not to see him, but he's trying too hard. Bad acting.

He's never seen a chambermaid in the Executive. Guess cleaning's not on top of their list.

Horvath walks a few blocks to the coffee shop where he met Lana. For the thick bacon and strong coffee, not the memories. At least that's what he tells himself.

His brain switches on somewhere during that first cup.

Should I find a nice sweet girl, settle down? Rustle up a few brats and a nice fat mortgage. Dinner at 5:30 on the dot. Meat, veg and potato. New car and a white picket fence.

The word *fence* makes him think of stolen goods. Which reminds him who he is. No, a nice girl's not in the cards for a guy like me. Even if I found her, she wouldn't give me the time of day. And why would she?

Scrambled eggs on a raft of crispy toast, floating down a river of black coffee. Heaven couldn't be any better than this. You don't have to be a theologian to know that.

Hell is when you start thinking.

The case is going nowhere and it's getting there pretty damn fast. So far I've found a dead body, but not much else. 200 miles on a bus and my hands are empty.

There's Lana, too. But he isn't sure if he has her, or if she has him. If life is an accounting ledger, he doesn't know which column to put her in.

Thinking's no good. Like McGrath always said, the best way to work out a problem is to not work on it at all. Erase it from your mind. Have a nice steak, wash it back with a couple drinks, and when you wake up the next day your answer will be sitting there, like a stack of fresh towels from the maid.

Boxing's the best way to clear his mind so he throws his gear into a gym bag and heads out.

20 yards away from the building, and he starts to hear it. Foot-work in the ring. The heavy bag. Grunts, groans, heavy breathing. A haymaker connecting. Medicine ball smacking someone's chest. Guy on the floor doing pushups. Big man skipping rope. Trainers shout-ing. A body going down, head bouncing on the mat.

On the way in, he passes a palooka in a gray sweat suit coming out. Blood's splashed all over his neck and collarbone, dripping down the side of his face. He's covered in sweat and his knuckles are raw. There's more blood circling his wrist like a bracelet. His nose is way out of joint, like something painted by one of those modern artists.

Horvath smiles. My kind of place.

Two middleweights are in the ring, sparring. One is quick on his feet, light, plenty of energy. He lands an uppercut, makes a few combinations, dances around. The other guy is tired, punchy, slow on his feet. Trainer stands outside the ropes, shouting. The first guy smiles, lands two quick jabs to the gut, then tries an overhand punch to the face. A near-miss. He fakes with the left, the right, the left again. Pause. Head-bob. Jab to the face. His partner's playing peek-a-boo, but the shot still does a little damage. The guy reels, almost trips on his feet. It's clear who's the contender and who's the journeyman.

"Alright, enough." The trainer climbs into the ring. "Hit the bags, go for a run, then come find me after you wash up."

The boxer nods, heads over to the speedbag.

His sparring partner can barely see through all the blood. There's a cut next to his right eye, which is practically swollen shut. He's been beaten to a bloody pulp to help someone else's career, and it won't be the last time. His union card reads: human punching bag.

Horvath looks around. Hoodlums, wise guys, ne'er-do-wells, petty thugs, a few brawlers. Men who like to beat the crap out of each other. A typical gym.

In back, near the locker room, there's a small office with a big square window. Lights on. Man in a desk chair, leaning over some papers. An older man stands on the other side of the desk, talking. Rolled up towel wrapped around his neck and tucked inside his shirt. He grips it with both hands,

He walks over to the room.

The door's shut, but not all the way. He can hear voices, low and muffled. Insistent.

He waits a few seconds before knocking.

Pause.

"Come in."

It's not what you'd describe as a welcoming voice.

It occurs to him, in the moment before he speaks, that no one else in the gym is wearing a suit. Stupid mistake. Never stand out; always blend in.

"Sorry to bother you fellas, but I'm passing through town and wanted to train. Alright if I pay for the day and go a few rounds?"

Trainer looks down at the boss, who looks right back. Their eyes are silent but somehow a message gets passed back and forth.

"Sure." The manager flinches.

There's a short row of lockers behind the boss. He leans back, chewing on the end of a ballpoint pen. The back of his chair dings the metal lockers.

"Where you from?" the boss asks.

"All over. East coast, mostly."

"Oh, yeah. Me, too. Where exactly?"

"Pittsburgh."

It's as good an answer as any, and more or less true.

The boss nods. He's trying to size up the stranger.

Horvath wonders if he's the owner, or just the manager. Either way, he's really going to town on that pen, like a lion brunching on gazelle. Pretty soon he'll hit a vein and black-ink blood will splatter all over the office.

"You can do all the PT you want, but I don't know about getting in the ring. Not sure who's available."

"Simpkins maybe." The trainer pops a stick of gum in his mouth.

"Yeah, maybe him. Tony? Big Keith?"

The trainer looks at Horvath. "He's a little small for Keith."

"Yeah, but Keith's slow. You got quick hands?"

"No one's ever said they were slow."

The boss smiles. "I like your style. We'll fix you up with a partner, if we can. Have to wait and see."

"Thanks. I just need a good sweat. Whether or not I get in the ring."

"Yeah, I get it."

"Should I pay now?" He reaches for his wallet.

"No, settle up later."

He nods, gives them a one-finger salute, backs out of the room.

The men watch him leave and then stare at him through the window as he walks toward the locker room.

He switches on the light, puts his bag on the slender wooden bench, and starts changing.

It's warm, humid, damp. A dim yellow lightbulb hangs from the ceiling. Mold and mildew reach out from every corner. The smell of jockstraps and dirty sweat socks crowds the room like a packed subway car at rush hour.

He ties his shoes and heads for the door.

Back in the gym, he finds a quiet corner. Toe touches, jumping jacks, running in place. He doesn't like to be too limber. Muscles need to be a little tense. If not, they can't spring into action when you need them. It's like trying to stab someone with a wet noodle.

25 push-ups. 25 sit-ups. 20 chin-ups.

25 dips on the parallel bars. Shadow-boxing.

He's getting tired, already.

I'm out of shape, he thinks, or maybe just getting old. Every year it takes a little longer to get back in trim.

The place is nearly empty. Trainer's in the ring now, holding a fighter's wrists. Showing him how to jab, pushing his elbows down.

Horvath grabs a pair of dumbbells. He always starts with the shoulders.

Near the end of his second set, a man walks over. Boxing shorts, stained undershirt. Hair shaved close to the scalp. Head square as a cinderblock. Big arms, thick neck. Skinny legs, though. Most people would confuse him for a tough guy, but not Horvath. The eyes give him away. Uncertain, always moving. Scared. He's got the gloves and the outfit, but he's no boxer. Why'd they set me up with this guy? Do they want me to knock a little sense into him? Or maybe they underestimate me. He thinks of Lana.

"You the new guy?"

"Yeah. Just here for a few days."

"Simpkins."

"Horvath."

"Working up a sweat, huh?"

"You got it."

He does another set of shoulder presses.

The man nods, looks at Horvath, looks down at the floor. "So you fight?"

"Yeah."

"Any good?"

"I can hold my own."

"I played football." The man crosses his arm, puffs out his chest. "Chicago Cardinals, running back."

He nods, still breathing hard.

"How about you? Ever play ball?"

"Rugby."

"That's some kind of Limey sport, right?"

He was getting tired of this clown. "Rugby's sort of like football, but for men."

"Hey, pal, watch it."

He laughs. "Don't take it personally. I'm just having you on."

"You're not so tough."

"How do you figure?"

"I'm twice your size."

He laughs. "You don't know much about being a tough guy, do you?"

The man shrugs. "I know enough."

"It's got nothing to do with how big you are or how much weight you can lift."

"So what's so great about rugby, huh?" His hands are on his hips now, and he takes a step closer to Horvath. "I never seen a game. What's it like?"

He thinks back to his days on the rugby pitch. Seems like another lifetime, another man. "No pads, for one thing. And no helmet."

"That's nuts."

"Play doesn't stop every couple seconds. You keep going, for 90 minutes. Run, pass, tackle, get up, keep playing."

The man doesn't have anything to say about that.

"And there's no such thing as offense and defense. Every man plays every minute of the game. So it's nothing like football. You don't get to hide behind a helmet and pads, you don't get a little break every five seconds, and you don't sit out half the game."

"You calling me a wimp?"

"No, just telling you how it is."

The man takes another step toward Horvath, sticks his chest out a little more. "Cause if you want a mouthful of bloody Chiclets, I can arrange that."

"Settle down, boys." The trainer walks over. "Save it for the ring, alright?"

Horvath starts a set of 20 squat thrusts.

"You two want to go a few rounds?" The trainer cracks his knuckles.

"No, I got better things to do." Simpkins grabs a jump rope from a hook on the wall, walks over to the other side of the gym.

The trainer follows him with his eyes. "You scared him off."

Horvath shrugs. "He wasn't much."

"You can tell?"

"I've got eyes, don't I?"

The trainer laughs. "You're a fighter, a real one."

"I've got a few moves."

"I'll bet you do." He looks the stranger up and down, jams another stick of gum in his mouth. "Well, he may be your only chance for a fight today."

"That's alright. Just need to get the blood pumping."

The trainer nods, walks back to the office.

Horvath drops to the floor for another set of push-ups. After that, it's arm curls and maybe the heavy bag.

HE SHOWERS, dries off, sits on the wooden bench. Elbows on his knees, head down. It's been a while. Even though he didn't step into the ring, it feels like he took a beating.

He doesn't move, or make a sound.

Sweat drips from his body onto the floor. A few towels lie under the bench, like dope fiends nodding off.

Two men are whispering, in the first row of lockers by the shower stalls.

Did they just walk in? he wonders. Or have they been here the whole time? Man alive, I'm really out of it.

He's sitting in a dark corner, back of the room. A towel cart is parked in the aisle, partially blocking off his row.

They're talking about someone called Gilroy who's got a few girls lined up. They laugh.

Big night out, Horvath thinks. Couple drinks, couple of girls. Brag about busting some guy's teeth in at the gym. Enough to make them feel like real men. Enough to get them through the night with a little left over for the next day.

Belt buckles, zippers, socks slipping quietly onto feet. He pictures them yawning into undershirts.

Sounds are muffled, words garbled. Locker doors slam shut on nouns and verbs.

Tonight. Jaworski. 9:15, 9:30.

Few drinks, meet up with—

They're whispering. He can't hear anything.

Laughter. Locker door opening.

Bunch of new girls. Younger. 8, 9, 10 years old.

Need to move them, quick.

He can't hear everything, but he hears more than enough.

Boys, too. Young. Whatever you want.

Anything goes.

Their voices echo off the tiles and tinny metal lockers.

They can't see me. They don't know I'm here. Don't make a sound.

Horvath hears a few names and numbers. Prices, maybe. He keeps still. Very still.

The men are quiet. Shoes on, bags packed. They're leaving.

He scoots over slowly, squints around the edge of the lockers.

A tall thin man with broad shoulders, long neck and crooked back. Blue pants, gray knit shirt.

His pal is medium height, average build. Bald as a cue ball.

McGrath was right. Once you stop looking for something, you find it.

Horvath gets dressed, grabs his bag, walks out the door.

There's a water cooler 10 yards away, next to a supply closet. He gets a drink.

The two men from the locker room are standing in front of the office. Tall guy's talking, moving his arms. Other guy's hanging back, arms crossed, staring at the ground. Trainer leans in the doorway, listening. He laughs. Tall guy smiles, turns to his friend, bumps him with his shoulder.

The trainer says something. The men nod. They shake hands, and the men turn to leave. The tall guy shoots Horvath a look across the ring.

He walks over to the office to settle up.

The trainer is inside now, but the owner's gone.

He knocks on the open door. "How much I owe you?"

The trainer tells him.

He reaches for his wallet, eyes locked on the trainer. He's older. 55, 60. Face like a sack of potatoes. Nose splintered with red lines, arrows pointing towards the nearest bar. But his eyes don't shift and the mouth never laughs at something it's not telling you. A face you can trust.

He lays a few bills on the desk. "Who were those fellas you were just talking to?"

"Local boys." He pauses, snaps the gum in his mouth. The towel stuffed into his shirt looks like a neck brace. "They've been coming around here for years."

"Boxers?"

"Not really."

"I see. So what do you know about these guys?"

The trainer shrugs.

He lays a few more bills on the desk. "You know what, I'll pay for the whole year."

"Thought you were just passing through?"

"Maybe I'll stick around for a while."

The trainer collects the money, stuffs it into his pants pocket.

"I heard something in the locker room. Something sick."

The trainer nods, sits down behind the desk, looks up at Horvath. "What are you doing here, anyway? Who sent you?"

"No one. I'm just a guy who collects information." He lights a cigarette, blows smoke toward the ceiling.

"Better watch it. Those things'll kill you."

"Not if something else gets me first." He pauses. "So what do you know?"

"Not much."

"You know Gilroy?"

The trainer laughs, but the sound is hollow. "Everybody knows Gilroy. The name, anyway. Never met the man himself."

"How can a guy like me get in touch with him?"

"He can't."

"Right." Horvath pauses. "He's a big man in the syndicate?"

"He *is* the syndicate."

"What's his game?"

"I really shouldn't be telling tales out of school."

"Stays between us. Come on, spill it."

The trainer taps his foot on the ground, looks out the window. "Shut the door."

He quietly closes the door, locks it.

The trainer sinks back in his chair. He looks smaller and older now, Horvath thinks. Seems like a good man. Doesn't want to fink on his pals, but he has to.

"So, tell me about his operation."

"The usual rackets. Numbers, drugs, girls, extortion. Blackmail, protection. Counterfeit goods, armed robbery..."

"Right. The whole package, plus a little tax evasion for dear old Uncle Sam."

Trainer takes a cigar out of the desk drawer, smells it, and lights up.

"I take it Gilroy has all the matches fixed?"

The trainer nods. "Most of them, anyway."

"They tell you who's going to win, who's taking a fall, how many rounds they'll go."

"You got it."

"And here I was hoping to stop by on Friday night and see a fair fight."

"Fat chance."

"Your pals from before, what's their story?"

"They're nothing. Just deliver messages. Go-betweens. Gophers, really."

"They may be small time, but they've got big mouths."

The trainer scratches the side of his face, crosses his arms.

"I heard another name—Jaworski."

"One of Gilroy's lieutenants."

"He the one who runs the show? With the kids, I mean."

"Don't know if he's in charge, but he's a big part of it."

"I see."

These two little words are almost always a lie. Horvath doesn't see much of anything, not yet, but he's getting there.

"And this Gilroy character. Does he have a front, construction or something?"

"Trucking."

"Figures."

"Owns a couple dry cleaners, too. That's where he got his start."

"What about the police?" Horvath asks.

"What about them?"

"They in Gilroy's pocket?"

"Yeah. Not that it makes a difference. Even before Gilroy came to town, the cops weren't too keen on catching bad guys. Those clowns couldn't catch a cold."

"So Gilroy runs the whole city?"

"Pretty much. Police, mayor, city council. Hell, he's probably got his claws in the League of Women Voters."

Horvath pauses, tries to take it all in. "So, tell me more about the child prostitutes."

The trainer raises both hands, like it's a stick-up. "I don't know anything, I swear."

"I believe you." He looks down at the trainer. "You told anyone else about this?

"No."

"Then why are you being so helpful all the sudden?"

"I don't know. Because you're the first one to ask, I guess. Look, this is some awful stuff. I don't want any part of it, but what can I do? I was a prizefighter once, long time ago. Stuck around the gym afterward, to help out the younger guys. It's all I knew, and I liked the work. But then Gilroy moves in, and his men start leaning on us. Old owner gets pushed out. New guy shows up the next day."

"The guy who was in here before?"

"You got it."

"When was this?"

"Five, six years. Something like that. Wasn't a bad little town in the old days."

"Apple pie, school dances, white picket fences, the whole bit?"

Trainer shrugs. "You're not far off. Gilroy ruined this place."

You're wrong about that, he thinks. One man can't make a good town bad. The corruption was already here, just waiting for someone to take control of it.

"Anyway, it started with the fix, but pretty soon things got worse, a lot worse. Pushing dope in the locker room. At the fights, girls were walking around making dates. They use the office to make deals, and they store a few things in back..."

"Like what?"

"Guns, stolen goods, whatever. I was told two things: keep your mouth shut and do what you're told. Or else."

"That's three things."

"I was never any good at math."

Horvath smiles.

"Then I heard whispers about other things, like kids, but I knew the score. They were going to do whatever they wanted. Thought about going to the cops, but..."

"Are these kids for sale, or are they just rented out by the hour?"

"No idea."

He nods. "How long's it been going on?"

"Few months, maybe a year."

"Anything else you can tell me?"

"Look, I don't know where it happens or who's involved, but it's a big operation. That's my take. Lately, they've sent more guys around, new guys. In here, talking to the boss."

"You there for any of these meetings?"

"No, they always tell me to take a hike. But something's up. The whispers have become shouts."

Outside the window, a boxer is heading for the door. Shiny gloves tied together and flopped over his shoulder.

"That it?"

"There's a warehouse on the east side. I don't know what happens there, but it's worth a look." He writes an address on a scrap of paper. "Here."

"Thanks."

Horvath opens the door and walks out. The trainer unwraps the towel from around his neck and mops the sweat off his forehead.

12

IN A QUIET PLACE

HE'S STARVING, AS USUAL.

Horvath stands on the corner a few blocks from the gym, looking around. Red awning across the street, and down the block. *Rossino's* is painted in white on the square window. Plate of spaghetti sounds good right about now.

Early dinner. He's got a headache, so he pops a few aspirin. Call it an appetizer.

The doorway is narrow, two steps down from the street.

He bows his way into the restaurant and looks around. The place is dark with low ceilings. Copper pipes wriggle like snakes overhead. Walls are dark wood, covered in old paintings and family photographs. Old lady eats by herself in the corner. Empty martini glass. She's wearing a big white hat with an even bigger feather.

There's no waiter but the cooks are shouting in back.

He sits in a wooden booth, and waits.

Waiter marches through the swinging doors from the kitchen. He's got small eyes and a crooked gash of a mouth. He was probably out back by the trash cans, having a smoke. Or maybe it was something else. Horvath can't help but assume the guy was up to no good.

If Gilroy has his fingers in every pie, then maybe even the waiters are on the take.

He eyes Horvath, but walks the other way to see if the old lady wants another drink. He leaves her empty plate where it is.

The waiter saunters—that's definitely the right word for it—over to the bar and mixes another martini. White shirt, black vest. Wine glasses hang like unfinished thoughts above his head. He takes his sweet time, brings her the drink, then yawns his way over to Horvath.

"Yeah?" He acts like he's doing him a favor. Must be the owner's nephew, or his no-good son.

"Spaghetti."

"You want garlic bread with that?"

"Sure."

"Anything else?"

"Whiskey, neat."

"Double?"

"Can't see why not."

The waiter goes back to the kitchen.

Horvath looks around. Wooden floors are starting to splinter. Water damage on the wall, near the ceiling. Bucket in the corner, collecting the drips. Rossino's is unnervingly quiet. The cooks aren't banging ladles anymore, or shouting orders. The waiter is off on one of his little breaks. Even the cockroaches and rats are silent. Must be wearing slippers.

I've got a million leads but they're all heading in different directions. Which is the same as having no leads at all. There's no structure here, no design or logic. Just chaos and corruption. Horvath went to college. He knows how important it is to find a pattern, to reach into the muck and mayhem to find some order. Or if you can't find it, make it yourself.

McGrath knows it too, but he never went to college. Didn't need to.

He can hear his mentor now. The words are as crisp and clear as if he was standing right in front of him. *Sure, I went to college. School of*

Hard Knocks. Our colors were black and blue. An old joke, and a bad one. Repeats it every chance he gets, but Horvath doesn't mind.

Waiter brings the old lady a new drink. A green olive floats at the bottom of the empty glass like a stiff dumped in the East River.

He drifts over to Horvath with the whiskey, plops it on the table.

"Already?" He pretends to look at his watch. "It's only been 20 minutes. You sure work fast around here."

The young man punches Horvath with flexed eyebrows and a clenched jaw. Even his ears look angry.

The waiter skulks off.

Horvath takes a sip. A smile sneaks up and spreads across his face. The whiskey's a lot better than he would've thought. This is enough to convince him that it's going to be a good day.

So, what do I have so far? No sign of my man. No sign at all. A dead body. Paradise City, a crooked nightclub. Two musclebound thugs looking to rearrange my face. Smith's Tavern seems pretty shady, too.

Lana.

Her missing friend.

Boxing club, as bent as everything else around here. The cops and mayor are on the take. Gilroy. Jaworski. The syndicate. Couple knuck-leheads getting chatty about a child prostitution ring. This is one sick town.

What I got is a lot of numbers, but none of them add up. Feels like a wild goose chase. How's it all connected? Where's my guy hiding out? Or is he dead? And what about Lana's missing pal? Is any of it connected?

He has another sip and tries to figure out where to go from here.

Few minutes later a middle-aged guy with a white apron and thick hairy forearms comes out with a steaming plate of spaghetti. Swarthy, balding, bad teeth. His apron's covered in grime, and his hands don't look much better. He drops the plate in front of Horvath. There's a small hunk of buttered toast at the very edge of the sauce, like a young lady sitting by the side of a swimming pool working up the nerve to jump in.

He looks up. "Thanks."

The dishwasher turns and walks off without a word.

Waiter must be busy. Standing around looking surly's a full-time job. Who says service isn't what it used to be?

He digs in.

The plate looks like a serving platter, and the meatball's big enough to hit with a Louisville Slugger. There's a lot of food here, he thinks, and it's good. Man alive, though. These Italians don't go light on the pepper and garlic.

Headache's gone. He's not sure if it's the aspirin, the drink, or getting his stomach filled. Or maybe it's sitting alone in a cool, dark place.

His gym bag sits in the booth next to him, like they're having dinner together.

He looks over at the old lady. So quiet, so still. On her table, empty martini glasses stand around in a circle, guests at a funeral reception. She stares at the wall, and occasionally remembers to have a sip. Tough old broad. She can sure handle her liquor, I'll give her that.

Horvath mops up every last bite. *Clean plate club.* The words run through his head like they always do after a meal. He thinks of his mother, god rest her soul. Some women always pick the wrong men.

The waiter swoops in, eyeballs the empty glass. "Take the air out of that?"

"No, I'm okay. What's the damage?"

He slaps a bill on the table, then slinks back through the swinging doors to the kitchen.

Horvath takes out his wallet, leaves a few bills under the salt shaker, then he adds a little extra, to pay for charm school.

HE TAKES the long way home, to clear his head.

It's getting dark early. The streetlights are slowly waking up, like they're fighting off a nasty hangover.

There are few things better than a nice long walk. It helps clear the mind, helps him relax. But at the same time he always keeps his eyes open and his mind alert. You never know what's waiting around the next corner. Death could step out from the shadows and then your number's up. You just never know.

The streets are clear and quiet. He thinks of the empty martini glasses on the old lady's table. Her only company.

A teenager rides by on a bicycle, baseball cards rattling in the spokes.

He can smell a bakery nearby.

There's a bridge in the distance, carrying people to the next state over.

He picks up his dry cleaning and heads back to the hotel. The western is sitting there on the corner of his bed, asking to be read.

He gets undressed, washes up, drinks water from the sink. Grabs the book, crawls under the covers. He'll read for a while and then turn in early. Tomorrow's a busy day.

13

THE KIDS ARE ALRIGHT

After breakfast, Horvath washes out his gym clothes in the sink and hangs them to dry. He doesn't want to waste all his dough on dry cleaning.

Not that he has much left, even with what Lana paid him. The expenses are adding up.

Can't show his face around Paradise City, at least not for a while. So he gets a cab to drop him off six blocks away and snoops around the neighborhood. He asks around, but no one knows anything about the new owner, or the stooge who's acting like he runs the joint. No one's seen the thick-necks who chased him all over town, and no one's aware of any criminal organizations in the area.

No one knows anything, or maybe they're just not willing to talk. It's bad for your health.

He has a drink at a local bar and drops a few hints. Implies that he's looking for action, that he's a reliable and experienced soldier, but no one bites.

They've got this town sealed tight, he thinks. Everybody's running scared. Nobody's going to say a word, especially not around here, so close to Paradise City. Must be syndicate turf. Maybe they'll be more chatty on the other side of town.

He goes back to Smith's Tavern.

Dodgy place. Might not be connected to my case, but they're definitely cooking something up. I can feel it in my bones.

He orders a whiskey and sits by himself at the bar, hunched over his drink.

When the bartender shuffles by to top him off, Horvath drops a few names. Jaworski, Gilroy, the syndicate.

Nothing.

He asks about the guy who brought him to this dreary town, the guy he's trying to find.

Nothing.

Bartender shakes his head and keeps pouring. His arm doesn't shake. Doesn't even blink.

He asks about Rojak, or Kovacs, or Bill Worthington, whoever the hell he is. Lana's pal.

Nothing.

It's like he's speaking Chinese or something. This makes him think of Fang and the anthill she calls home. What a lady.

Or no, it's as if they're ghosts. Floating through town without leaving a trace. No one's ever seen their faces or heard their footsteps. No one even believes they exist.

He considers mentioning the young girls, and boys. Nothing too obvious. Just bring it up in a vague sort of way. Run it up the flagpole and see who salutes it. But no, just the thought of it makes him sick. Sometimes he wonders if he's really cut out for this business. He doesn't have the heart for it, or the stomach. And his eyes aren't too happy about it, either. The things he's seen.

But his fists are okay with it. They've never let him down.

Horvath sips the whiskey and thinks of a young man who had everything laid out for himself. Wife, house, car, professional job. Life was good. Nothing could go wrong.

Except it did. A few quick wrong turns and here he was, collecting information for the firm. He's not a bad guy really, and what he does isn't against the law. Not exactly. At least not most of the time. His life wasn't supposed to be like this. He's not prepared for child prostitutes or tossing a dead body into the garbage.

And he's not prepared for a woman like Lana.

But then again, no man is.

The bartender, a dozen yards away, is turning away from him.

Was he staring at me? Giving me the hairy eyeball? Maybe I asked one question too many. Now he's over by the telephone. Maybe he's going to drop a dime on me.

Horvath tosses back the rest of his drink and leaves, before he can find out.

Outside, the sun beats down like a hammer and he's the anvil.

Long day ahead and I'm already tired, he thinks. The booze is working through my veins. Need coffee.

He pops a few aspirin and walks back toward home, if that's what the Executive is. He'll find a diner somewhere along the way and sit down for a cup.

When he hears the bell ring, he looks over at a church made from heavy gray stone. Priest is standing outside in gold robes with purple stitching. Shaking hands, smiling. Inside, his men have collected money in wicker baskets lined in red velvet. The Catholics have it all figured out. They're in the protection racket, for your eternal soul.

Old pair of shoes, laces tied together and looped over the telephone wire.

A car backfires.

Nice family walking home from church. Cloistered in dark suits and bright yellow dresses. Ties, ribbons, good shoes. Hair just right. Like something out of a glossy magazine. He can't imagine raising a family in a town like this.

But then again, things are bad all over.

After a few blocks he sees an Italian deli. On the sidewalk, two iron chairs tuck their legs under a matching table. Old man in a long white apron stands outside the front door, hands on his hips. Broom leans against the side of the building. He's smiling, shielding his eyes from the sun and staring at something across the street.

Horvath remembers an Italian coffee he had once, in Newark.

They called it *espresso*. Very small and very strong. Like they sliced open your skull and jammed a cattle prod into your brain. Bitter, but it got the job done.

He steps inside and orders a double.

HE WALKS through town for a few hours, but doesn't learn anything new.

The espresso's doing its job. The first one was so good he ordered another, and then one more. Now he's wide awake and his mind is sharp as a knife-blade. He's got a million ideas, but they're all shouting at the same time.

After dinner he takes a bus across town and hops off on the east side, near the river. The plan is to look around for a warehouse, like the trainer said. Hopefully, he wasn't just telling stories.

He starts walking north.

To his left, a tall chain-link surrounds a car repair shop. Behind the gate, a squat hairless dog is tied to a stake with a thick metal chain. He bares his teeth and howls, drool dripping off his chin. Horvath almost jumps, but he manages to play it cool. A man in greasy coveralls comes out from a little hut and adjusts his cap, eyes locked on the stranger. He stands next to the dog and they both watch, like an old married couple. The man squints, mouth hanging open. A few of his teeth are missing, and he's no bathing enthusiast. He could use a leash, too, Horvath thinks.

Townhouses and apartments disappear, and buildings back away from the road. In the distance, at the edge of a forest, an old Ford truck turns to rust and crumbles into the earth.

He can smell the river and see trees leaning over the water. Sea birds circle high overhead before swooping down. The noise of the city is fading away. A few children play in an overgrown field surrounded by a wooden fence with a few missing slats. He thinks of the dog-owner's teeth.

The blacktop ends. There's only dust and gravel beneath his feet.

There aren't as many shops around here, no restaurants or bars. Empty lots, dead grass, broken bottles.

The end of a long road, and the end of town.

He can see a factory up ahead, looking out over the river. Clouds of black smoke hang above it and drift across the water.

The warehouse sits on a bed of concrete a few hundred yards to the right, past a green field. Big gray ugly block, a slap in the face to all this nature.

Small white clapboard building off to his left. The last structure before the gravel roads gives way to weeds, damp soil, wildflowers and emptiness. The warehouse is a quarter-mile ahead, maybe a little closer.

He walks toward the building. Tobacconist.

Inside, a wooden Indian stands guard.

"Can I help you?"

The lights are dim and, for a second, he thinks it's the Indian talking, but then a man stands up from where he was crouching in front of a low shelf.

"Sure. I need a few packs of cigarettes and some lighter fluid."

"Over here."

Horvath follows him through the shop. He's tall with a gaunt face and sharp cheekbones. Hasn't shaved in a few days, maybe a week.

"Here's our butane." He picks up a can. "This do it for you?"

"Yeah, that'll be fine."

"Cigarettes are up front. What brand do you smoke?"

"Lucky Strike."

The shop owner nods his way over to the till. "Anything else?"

"No, that should do it."

The man rings him up, and Horvath lays a sawbuck on the counter.

"Here's your change, sir."

"Thanks. Mind if I fill up?"

"Be my guest." He grabs a funnel from a shelf, pushes it across the counter.

"Thanks." Horvath takes out his lighter.

"Nice looking piece you got there. That's real brass, not one of those steel jobs."

He nods. "Friend gave it to me."

"That's some friend."

Horvath agrees, but he doesn't say anything. He just fills the lighter.

His name is engraved on the back. McGrath gave it to him when training was over, sort of a graduation present. The next day he got sent to the lions.

I could use his advice right about now. Maybe I'll get in touch with him next week. Once I get some solid answers. It's not protocol, but I need his take on a few things. I'm lost out here.

He puts the can of butane in his jacket pocket, flicks his lighter on.

"Good as new," the shopkeeper says.

"Alright if I have a quick smoke?"

"No law against it."

Horvath offers him a cigarette, but the man waves it away.

He lights up, walks closer to the door. "Say, what's that over there?"

The man walks up behind him. "Button Factory."

He points to the warehouse. "What about that?"

No answer. Horvath turns around.

The man shrugs. "Just a warehouse. Don't know what they got in there."

"Belongs to the factory?"

"Got me."

He nods, takes a slow puff. "Ever see anybody over there?"

"No, not really. Truck pulls up sometimes, or a van. That's about it."

"What about the cops? They ever snooping around?"

"Say, what's with all the questions?" The man hooks his thumbs behind his suspenders, looks at his customer's gray suit and pressed white shirt. "You with the FBI or something?"

"No, nothing like that." He forces a laugh. "Just curious, that's all."

"Well, you know what happened to the cat, don't you?"

"He didn't get promoted down at the bureau, did he?"

"No, sir. He's taking a dirt nap."

Horvath has one last puff and looks around for an ashtray. The man hands him an empty can of Chase & Sanborn coffee.

"Thanks." He stamps out the cigarette, hands the can back to the shopkeeper. "So you wouldn't recommend asking too many questions about that place?"

"No, I would not."

"I see."

"I got inventory to take." He scratches behind his ear, looks out a side window onto the street. "Can't set here jawin all day."

He looks around, but there's hardly any inventory to take. "Sorry, just one more thing."

"Go ahead."

"I'm new around here so I need to learn the ropes. Don't want to be a rube."

The man nods, picks his teeth with a matchstick.

"What are the cops like in this town? I hear they're not too keen on catching crooks."

A hollow laugh. "They couldn't catch a bus, know what I mean?"

"I do."

"They'd rather walk, anyway."

"Slower that way."

"Exactly," the man says. "They don't show up 'til the shooting's over."

"Saves them a lot of paperwork."

"You think those boys can read?"

"Wouldn't bet on it."

The man looks out the front door, to see if anyone's within earshot. "Look here, you don't mess with these guys. They may be slow and stupid, but they're not dumb. And they play rough. Let's say you got a restaurant and you don't pay em off? If you're lucky, the health department shuts you down, or maybe your beer distributor suddenly can't deliver the goods."

"What if you're not so lucky?"

"Bar goes up in smoke, or you wake up in the hospital with two broken legs and a busted jaw."

"Or you never wake up at all."

"You're not as dumb as you look, buddy."

He smiles. "I've got a few brain cells floating around in there somewhere."

"Good, you'll need em. But if you keep asking questions, you'll end up in the river over there. Duck food."

"I don't think ducks eat human flesh."

The shopkeeper turns and heads for the storeroom. "Depends how it's cooked."

Horvath is alone in the shop. Outside, the sky has gone from gray to black. The streets are empty and silent, but not peaceful.

He checks his watch. 8:17. The boys at the gym said things would get going at 9:15, 9:30.

A porch door slams shut in the distance.

Time to look around.

He walks to the end of the gravel road and across the field. Some of the weeds are tall enough to tickle his chin. After a few hundred yards the green turns to dirt and then to gray concrete. No cars, no people, no sounds. The warehouse doors are shut, and locked tight.

There's a row of high windows on the left-hand side of the building. He walks along the perimeter, picks up a wooden crate lying in the dirt, sets it on the ground underneath the windows. Not tall enough.

He walks to the end of the warehouse, looks around in the grass and weeds until he finds another crate. He grabs it, sets in on top of the first one.

Looks around, no one's coming.

Carefully, he steps onto the crates and puts his hands on the wooden planks of the building.

On tiptoes, he looks through the window but it's covered in years of dust and grime, more yellow than clear. And it's dark inside. He can't see a thing. He puts his ear to the window, but the place is silent as a crypt. He takes another look, tries to focus. Pallets, shelving, barrels maybe. Large square boxes or crates. He can see shapes but no colors or details. Nothing moves in the darkness.

"Whatcha doin, mister?"

Horvath turns, steps down. A small boy is standing there, red and yellow ball at his feet.

"Lost my cat. Thought it might have wandered over here. You seen it?"

"No, I haven't seen any cats. Couple squirrels, though."

He jumps off the crate, stares at the boy for a few seconds. "Where do you live, kid?"

"Back there." He points toward the road, the tobacconist, the edge of town.

"Your parents know you're playing over here."

"Yeah, they don't mind."

"It's getting dark."

"Yeah. I better get home soon."

He lights up, considers the boy.

"Ever see anyone going into the warehouse?"

"No, people don't come around here. This place is haunted."

"Right." He picks up one of the crates and tosses it back into the weeds. "You ever see a bunch of kids here? Going into the warehouse?"

"No, there aren't any other kids who live in this neighborhood. It's terrible."

He wants to laugh, but can't.

"You want to play ball with me, mister?"

"Maybe another time."

The boy's eager smile sinks down.

"Sorry kid, but I need to get home, too. Here's two bits." He hands him a quarter. "Buy yourself an ice cream and a comic book."

"Gee thanks, mister."

"Don't mention it."

The boy picks up his ball and runs off. Horvath is left by himself in the nightfall, with a pocketful of unanswered questions.

He walks around the other side of the building, but there's nothing to see.

He considers busting a window and sneaking in, but the place looks ordinary enough, and it's a pretty far drop from the window. Anyway, they'd know it was him. Too many people have seen his face snooping around.

They'll be here soon, he thinks. If I've got the right place. Need to hide somewhere.

He walks out into the weeds, crouches down, and waits.

By 9:15 his knees are screaming. He sits down on the moist earth and holds his knees.

He keeps waiting.

9:42. They're not coming. He stands up, brushes off the seat of his pants, and starts walking.

On his way back to town, he tries to fit the pieces together. Maybe it's just a warehouse. Nothing shady about it. The trainer could've been lying, or misinformed. Maybe they don't use it anymore, or maybe they're just not using it tonight.

Shopkeeper got real chatty all the sudden. What's his story? Is he just some regular joe, or is it more than that? Could be a look-out for Jaworski.

Horvath can still remember a time, years back, when he wasn't suspicious of everyone he met. He takes a good hard look at the man he used to be. What a sucker.

He keeps walking.

THE BOY WALKS toward the river. When he gets close, he kicks his ball into the reeds and pulls a pack of cigarettes out of his dungaree pockets. He lights up, takes a drag, and rolls up the sleeves of his sweatshirt. Burn marks cover his arms like freckles.

He keeps walking.

A bullfrog croaks, crickets chatter.

Something moves in the water.

He sees Mr. Jaworski leaning against a tree, and the orange glow of his cigarette. When he gets closer he can see the bulge in his jacket and the thick purple scar like a worm wriggling down the side of his face. The rowboat's been pulled up onto the muddy riverbank.

"How's tricks?"

"Everything's good, Mr. Jaworski."

"You ready?"

"Ready as I'll ever be."

"Good boy."

He gets into the boat first, and Mr. Jaworski follows. They row quietly through the darkness.

Soon, he'll tell Mr. Jaworski about the man who was looking through the windows. For now, he thinks about the other kids and what happens to them. It's bad, real bad, but there's nothing he can do about it.

14

WAITING FOR THE MAN

HORVATH DOESN'T SLEEP MUCH THAT NIGHT, AND IN THE MORNING IT feels like he didn't sleep at all.

He gets up, washes his hands and face, dries them with a thread-bare towel embossed with a gold *E*.

He gets dressed and heads downstairs.

Mr. Prissy is manning the front desk, as usual. His skin, lips and fingernails look extra shiny today, and so does the new royal blue suit. There's an extra quart of oil in his hair, too. Must be a special day.

Horvath walks up to the desk.

"Good morning, sir." The sarcasm and disdain have dried up.

"Morning." He pauses. "I'm at a disadvantage here because you know my name but I don't know yours."

"Gilbert." He says it like a Frenchman, *Jeel-bear*.

"So, Gilbert. Anyone ask about me?"

"No."

"Good. Anyone just hanging around the lobby, looking suspicious?"

"No."

There's something about his *no* that sounds a lot like *yes*. If he didn't know better, he'd think someone was holding a gun to the guy's head.

"Alright, thanks."

He walks through the revolving door and sunlight stabs him in the eye. But it's not as bad as it was yesterday, or the day before. The worst of it's over. Summer's dying.

Time to have a word with Lana over at Frank's, he thinks. Or Fran_'s. Need to check in, plan the next move. I'll stop for coffee and a donut on the way. Maybe throw back an espresso, a word that's probably Italian for *swift kick to the head.*

WHEN HE WALKS INSIDE, he sees her right away, sitting at the bar with crossed legs and her skirt hitched all the way up to the north side. Long sturdy legs poured into tight black stockings—makes him want to forget about his job, Jaworski, and all the rest of it.

She looks over, commits a crooked smile, and blows a smoke ring that hangs over her head like a halo. Fat chance. Lana's got a lot of good qualities, but she's no saint. Horvath knew that the first time he laid eyes on her.

He sits beside her at the bar.

The paper lies in front of her, folded in quarters, ballpoint pen off to the side.

He remembers the ditzy young waitress from the drugstore luncheonette. "What is it with women and crossword puzzles in this town?"

"We know a lot of words and we're not afraid to use them."

"Oh yeah, like what?"

"Like *missing friend, disappointing gumshoe* and *getting nowhere.*"

"Those are phrases, not words."

"What do you think a phrase is? Coupla words strung together."

He puts up his hands. "Alright, alright. Go easy on me. Haven't had breakfast yet."

"I can get you something. We've got a kitchen in back."

"Scrambled eggs and bacon, with crispy toast?"

"Sure."

"Will it be any good?"

"Probably not."

"Sounds perfect."

Lana turns her head, shouts. "Hey, Nick. We need two eggs—wreck em—bacon and a side of crispy toast."

"Coming up."

"And a pot of black coffee, extra bitter."

"Will do."

Horvath lights up.

She stubs out her cigarette and nudges the ashtray closer to him.

He looks around. Frank's is empty, but it's still early. Even the serious drinkers need to sleep in sometimes. "So how's the office?"

"Same as always. Long hours, no atmosphere, boss is a jerk."

"Got a question for you."

"Shoot."

"Few minutes ago, you said I was getting nowhere."

"Just pulling your leg." She leans over, rubs his forearm.

"But you're right. I'm at loose ends. How'd you know?"

She looks away quickly, shrugs, reaches for a silver cigarette case. "It's written all over your face."

Nick swoops in with breakfast before he can ask any more questions. He digs in while Lana pours two steaming cups.

"Thanks."

"Don't mention it."

She watches him wolf down the food. "You don't mess around, do you? It's like you haven't eaten in weeks."

"I need to bulk up. Try-outs for JV football are coming up."

"Aren't you a little old for that?"

"Yeah, but I'm immature for my age."

He mops up what's left with the last bite of toast, washes it down with coffee, wipes his mouth with a napkin.

"Ready to talk?" she asks.

"You bet."

He catches her up to speed, which doesn't take long: no sign of Kovacs and no one's talking.

"So you really are getting nowhere fast," she says.

"Feels like I'm running in place."

"You'll get there. Be patient."

"You got a photo of Kovacs?"

"No, sorry."

"It'd be a lot better if you did."

Her eyebrows twitch like terriers jumping over a short fence.

He tries to figure out what she's thinking, but comes up empty. A sip of coffee doesn't help. He stares at the bottles standing shoulder to shoulder behind the bar like crooks in a police line-up. "Time to be straight with me. What'd your friend do?"

"He—"

"—And don't give me that boy scout routine again. He must've been into something."

Lana glances at Horvath, looks away. She reaches behind the bar, pulls out a bottle of bourbon.

"Little early, isn't it?"

She looks at her watch. "Yeah, well, it's a little early for an interrogation."

He nods, finishes the coffee. She pours whiskey into their empty cups.

She takes a good long slug.

"Kovacs is from Denver, originally. Came to town a few years ago. Spent a lot of money, showed his face all over town. Flashy guy, always looking for a good time. Smile never left his face."

"And then?"

"Then he ran out of money, and the good times weren't so good anymore. Started asking around for a job. But there weren't any takers. Nobody could vouch for him. After a few weeks, things got desperate."

"He was with you at this point?"

She nods. "And he was willing to do anything."

"Let me guess, that's when a position became available down at the syndicate."

"You got it. They needed a bag man. Small-time stuff. Not much dough in it, but we were doing just fine."

"Until one of the bags came back a little light."

"Yeah, that's about the size of it."

"Someone got wise, and they snatched him up."

Lana finishes her drink. "That's all I got."

"Did you know he was skimming?"

"No."

He takes a long sip. The whiskey cuts through the donuts, espresso, breakfast, coffee and cigarettes like a samurai sword. So, he thinks. She finally spilled. But that doesn't mean she's being straight with me. Even if her lip quivered and her eyes did the Poor Starving Orphan routine. This may not be the truth, but we're getting closer.

"How about you?" she asks. "Find the guy you're looking for?"

"Not even close. Can't find a trace of him anywhere."

"We're just a couple of saps."

"Amen."

She holds up her whiskey and they clink fake porcelain cups.

"I've been looking into something else," he says. "Not sure how it's related, but..."

"What is it?"

He tells her about the gym, the children, the warehouse.

She makes a disgusted face, as if the whiskey was vinegar.

"My thoughts exactly," he says. "So this Jaworski's a big man in the syndicate?"

"Yeah." She uncrosses her legs, leans closer to Horvath. Her pencil skirt's more like a stub. "You don't want to mess with him."

"Understood."

"But you're going to do it anyway?"

"I go where the clues take me."

"It's your funeral."

"I want to be cremated."

"I'm sure that can be arranged."

"You know this Jaworski?" he asks.

"By reputation."

"Which is what?"

"Ruthless. Sick. Crazy. Likes to play with his victims before he kills them. More fun that way."

"Sure."

"He reports directly to Gilroy." Lana reaches into her handbag, takes out a lipstick, and starts painting. "You know much about his operation before you got to town?"

"Never heard of the guy, or his outfit."

But he knew it existed. Every town has a syndicate. Everyone's dirty. Even the men at the top, the pillars of society with white shiny teeth, expensive suits, and perfect hair, the ones who are always talking about cleaning up the town and getting rid of all the bad guys. Especially them.

"So what now?" she asks.

"Good question."

"The people you work for, they got ideas?"

"Yeah, but none of them are any good. I've been trailing this guy for weeks, across six states, but he's a ghost."

"What kind of leads they give you?"

"A name, an address, a license plate, a crash pad, an associate, another license plate, a bar..."

"Sounds like the guy's smart. Changes cars, hideouts, towns. He knows you're onto him."

"Maybe."

"You'll find your man. Don't worry."

He does. "I'd like to have another look around Paradise City, but it's too soon. They know my face and they're probably looking for me."

"Sounds like you need help."

"Is that an offer?"

When she turns to look at Horvath, he's staring at her. "Not a chance, slick. Too many people know me in this town."

"Alright then, got any bright ideas?"

She shrugs.

They don't speak for 20 or 30 seconds, which seems to last for an hour.

Lana shifts in her seat, almost imperceptibly. "I know someone."

"Who?"

"A guy."

"Is he reliable?"

Another shrug. She wears them like shoulder pads. "You can trust him, though."

"I doubt it."

"Why do you say that?"

"He's human, isn't he?"

"Yeah."

"You can't trust people like that."

Her smile slowly breaks into soft laughter. "You're a funny guy, you know that?"

"So they tell me."

"I need to make a call." She slides off the stool. "Get in touch with my unreliable, untrustworthy associate."

"Need a dime?"

"I've got a phone in the back office, no coins needed."

"An office with a private phone? You're a regular captain of industry. Got a secretary, too?"

"I wish." She turns, starts to walk away. "Now don't enjoy yourself too much while I'm gone."

Too late, he thinks, watching the gray pencil skirt wrestle with her curves.

Horvath lights a cigarette and asks himself if he's making a mistake. He's always worked alone, but now Lana's here. Somehow.

She's got some kind of hold over me. I can't think straight when she's around. Should I trust her? Does she know what she's doing?

Maybe I don't have a choice.

Lana steps from the shadows of the back hallway and walks across the room. He doesn't miss a step. The way she moves is better than Ginger Rogers, better than a boxer dancing in the ring. She stares him down, with the rumor of a smile on her small mouth, and walks almost as if no one's watching.

She sits down. "He's in."

"Good."

"He'll be here in a couple hours."

"I should get out of here."

"Yeah, me too."

She reaches for the bottle, and they keep drinking.

HE SHOWS up in the early afternoon. Lana and Horvath don't notice him at first. They're getting a little tight, laughing too loud at a stupid joke. Their barstools are so close together they're practically touching.

"Hey, I'm here."

They turn around.

Horvath pegs him at 5'2", 120 pounds soaking wet. Not a day over 17. Bright purple tie. Drowning in a pinstripe suit that's three sizes too big, like it's amateur day at Ringling Brothers. Fedora, tilted rakishly over the eyes. Chewing on a toothpick. It's the same all over. Every young punk thinks he's Al Capone, but most of the time they're just bed-wetters, soft and spineless as a jellyfish. Sometimes he feels like that, too.

"How old are you?" Horvath asks.

"Old enough," the kid spits out.

"Old enough for what? The merry-go-round?"

"Hey, cut it out." He grabs the toothpick from his mouth and points with it, a move straight out of the tough-guy handbook.

"You been practicing that one in front of the bathroom mirror, kid?"

He looks at Lana. "Hey, what gives?"

"Don't take it personal. He's just seeing what you're made of."

"Well, I don't need any lip from this mug. Got it?" The kid takes a half-step forward.

"I wouldn't push it," she says.

The kid's breathing hard, arms tense, hands balled up into tiny fists.

"I'd listen to the lady if I were you."

"You're not me."

"Okay. You're a real bruiser. I get it." Horvath looks at Lana, smiles. "What's your name, kid?"

"I'm no kid."

"Whatever you say, but what is it?"

"Jimmy."

"Your other name?"

"Milner."

"So...Jimmy Milner. Lana gave you the lowdown?"

"Yeah. You need me to go into a nightclub, look around, report back."

"Bingo. Think you can handle it?"

"Course."

"Good. Here's a little something to motivate you." He stuffs a five-spot into his breast pocket. "You'll get the other half when you're done."

"Meet back here at 9:00," Lana says. "And don't be late."

HORVATH GETS to Frank's early and sits at the bar. Place is nearly empty. He wonders how they stay in business.

Lana's nowhere around and the bartender's been polishing the same rocks glass for five minutes straight. The ashtrays are overflowing with butts, and empty beer bottles are lined up along the bar like soldiers in a parade. Frank's is a dump, but that rocks glass sure is clean.

She comes out of her office a few minutes later. The pencil skirt, stockings and stilettoes are gone. She's wearing a green pants suit, silky beige blouse, and sensible shoes.

She reaches for the bourbon. "Want a drink?"

"No, but I'll take coffee if you've got it."

"Sure." Lana puts the bottle down and walks toward the kitchen.

Horvath yawns. Too many drinks this morning, and not enough food. He tried to sleep it off back at the hotel, but he just wrestled with the bedsheets for an hour. Later, he sat up in bed and turned on the light. Read the western story until it was time for a shower and shave.

She comes back with two cups, carrying them like a professional. He tries to picture her as a waitress in some dive, taking orders and slinging food, but the picture won't hold.

"Thanks."

"Anything for you." She touches the small of his back, just for a moment.

But that moment's more than enough. Electricity shoots up his spine and down his arms.

"So you think your boy's up to the job?"

"Sure, why not? It's simple enough."

It always seems that way, he thinks. Until something goes wrong.

She grabs a sugar bowl, spoons a few lumps into her coffee and stirs.

"Thought you took it black, no sugar?"

"I need a pick-me-up. Not used to drinking so much, so early."

He has his doubts.

The spoon rattles when she sets it on the white saucer.

The kid shows up when they're halfway through the coffee. He's traded in the purple tie for a bright red number with a gold pin.

Horvath checks his watch. 9:06. The kid's late. His doubts are multiplying.

OUTSIDE, they grab a taxi and head for Paradise City. Jimmy tilts his head to the side and spreads his legs wide, like a two-bit goon. Lana is quiet and still, hard to read.

He stares out the window at the city rushing by. Men and women dressed to the nines. Tall buildings and small shops. Neon signs, telephone wires. Concrete and tar. Headlights, tires squealing, horns honking. Drunks stumbling out of bars. Shouts and laughter.

Working girl leaning into a car window. Office buildings dressed in glass and steel. Stray dogs skulking in alleys, sniffing at putrid trash. Veiled in darkness, you can't see the broken beer bottles or dead birds, the rusted out cars and potholes, bums in stained trousers with newspaper stuffed inside their shoes. At night, the city looks almost beautiful.

He likes it better on foot. You've got time to take it all in, to see every shop window clearly, every guy buttoning his coat and stepping onto the sidewalk, every woman glancing over her shoulder with a wry smile. Walking, you melt into the street and become a part of it. There's no space between you and the place you're in. But it's different in a car. You're set apart, a stranger, watching it all from the outside. You miss things that way.

"This is good." Lana taps the driver on the shoulder and hands him some folding money. "Keep the change."

"Thanks, lady."

They get out and walk north. The nightclub is six blocks away.

Ron Johnson's Paradise City. When the glowing sign is close enough to read, Lana points her head to the left and they step into an alley.

Red brick buildings rise up on either side. There are no lights here, no doors opening into the alley. This side of the street doesn't have any shops or bars so there's not much foot traffic. The flophouse to the left was condemned three months ago, so it's empty except maybe for a couple bums sleeping in the basement.

Lana did her homework. This is the perfect spot.

Jimmy starts to light up, but Horvath shoots him a look. The orange glow will give them away.

"You sure you can handle this, kid?"

"Easy as pie." He cracks his knuckles, shoves his hands into his pockets.

"Play it cool, okay? Have a drink, settle in, don't talk to anyone. Let someone else make the first move. And when they do, don't get too chatty. Just slip in a question or two, like you don't really care about the answers. Got it?"

"Yeah, easy."

"Mostly, just keep your eyes and ears open."

"Roger."

Jimmy stretches his arms wide as if he's about to dead-lift a barbell, and his elbow hits cold metal. A fire escape ladder slams down and he jumps, with a shrill yelp.

"Don't be scared, kid. Ladder hasn't killed anyone all year."

"I'm not scared. Just startled."

"Oh, is that it?"

"Alright, time to go in." Lana flattens his lapels.

"See you in the funny papers." Jimmy walks off, rolling his shoulders so everyone can see what a man he is.

"Got your best guy on the job, eh?"

"He'll do just fine," she says.

"Well, what's our backup plan, in case things go south?"

"You got a piece?"

"No."

"It'd be a lot better if you did." Lana unzips her handbag and pulls out a small pistol.

"What do you got there?"

"Saturday night special."

"Looks more like Wednesday afternoon."

"It gets the job done."

"I'd take a closer look," he says, "but I forgot my microscope."

"Real comedian, aren't you? But if it comes down to it, you'll be glad I've got it."

A woman who can handle herself. Not the kind you bring home to Mom, but still, his kind of lady. "Think he'll find anything useful?"

"I don't know. Maybe. But it can't hurt trying."

"Of course it can. He'll be lucky if one of those thugs doesn't wring his neck, or worse."

"Too late to do anything about it now."

They back away from the street and wait in silence at the dark end of the alley.

Here, they can have a smoke and think about things.

A gray cat slinks by, eyes on Horvath. Music slips like a thief from an open window. Two men shout at each other, several blocks away. Cars drive up and down the boulevard. A lady walks by with two bags of groceries, purse in the crook of her arm.

JIMMY WALKS past the alley 90 minutes later.

Lana and Horvath are standing closer to the street now, watching.

A minute goes by. Two minutes. No one passes by, on either side of the street. That means no one's tailing the kid.

They could've waited back at the bar, with a drink and somewhere to sit, but then they wouldn't know if anyone was following Jimmy. Better to play it safe.

Lana walks to the edge of the alley, casts a furtive glance both ways, walks off to the right.

A minute later, Horvath follows her to the Carriage House, a tavern that's been around since the 1890's.

The place is noisy, crowded with men. Old, middle-aged, a few younger guys. Plumbers, builders, cab drivers and electricians, mostly. A couple firemen and retired cops.

He orders a whiskey, takes a sip, asks where the bathroom is.

Along the way, he passes two heavy wooden doors with panes of smoked glass. Family Room. Women and children aren't allowed at the bar here, even nowadays when people are starting to scream for equal rights.

Lana and Jimmy sit at a long table, alone. Unless you count the dust. Looks like no one's used the room since Garfield was president.

He sits down, looks at her. "Good thinking. No one'll bother us in here."

"Women never come into this joint, because we know better."

"You're one smart dame." The kid flicks the brim of his hat so it snaps out of his eyes.

"Chandler or Spillane?" Horvath asks him.

"Huh?"

"Where'd you get your act?"

"I don't follow."

"Never mind."

Lana smiles into her drink. Jimmy looks confused, like someone told him the world wasn't flat.

Horvath raises his drink, tosses it back. "So, what do you got?"

Jimmy loosens his tie, plays with the fake ruby on his pinkie ring. "Not much."

"Not much, huh?"

"No. Place was nearly empty. I sat at one of the bars, but no one came anywhere near me. Even the bartender was standoffish. So I went to one of the other bars and stood near a couple guys talking loud, getting loaded. You know, businessman types."

"What'd you get from them?"

"Nothing. They was from out of town."

"What else?"

"Nothing. Look, I'm sorry, but—"

Horvath leans forward quickly, which makes the kid pull back. He almost falls off his chair. "Why you so jumpy, kid? You holding out on us?"

"No, I swear. I didn't get nothing cause there was nothing to get."

"You sound like a philosopher, kid. You should have that stitched on a pillowcase or something."

"Look, it's not my fault. That's just the way it is sometimes. Can't get blood out of a stone."

That's not what McGrath would say. There's only two things in this world, giving up or getting on with the job. If you want to get blood from a stone, then you beat the shit out of it until the red stuff starts dripping out.

He stares at Jimmy, wondering if the kid's holding out.

Jimmy stares back for a couple seconds, but then he looks away. "Look, I did my job. I don't need to put up with this." He stands up.

Horvath stands, too. Jimmy's staring at his chin. He has to lean back to look him in the eye.

"You sure you didn't hear anything?"

"Promise."

"And no one made you?"

"No way."

Horvath reaches into his pocket, pulls out a few bills, and stuffs them in Jimmy's breast pocket. "A put a little extra in there."

"What for?"

"To get your eyes checked. Maybe next time you'll see something."

Jimmy's about to speak, but Lana cuts him off. "Scram, kid."

They look at each other and finish their drinks. There's not much to say.

She leaves first and he follows, a minute later.

A taxi will be waiting at the end of the block. She'll throw the door open and he'll hop in. Lana has it planned down to the last footstep.

He lights up, leaves the family room, walks through the front door of the bar, and turns left. The cab is idling at the intersection. He looks over his shoulder at the reflection in a shop window. There's no muscle on his tail.

It's late, quiet. People are either home in bed or settling in at the bar.

Flicking his ash on the sidewalk, he doesn't see the shadow in a passing doorway.

But he does feel the lead pipe smack him in back of the head. For a few seconds, anyway, until everything goes black.

15

THE LOCKED ROOM

HIS MIND AND BODY ARE IN DIFFERENT CITIES, OR AT LEAST IT FEELS that way. The room is murky, shifting, blurred. His eyes are guppies swimming in a fishbowl.

Dry mouth, headache, lump on his head. Sitting in a chair.

Where am I?

Hands tied behind his back. Legs tied to the chair.

It's coming back to him. Lana, Jimmy, Paradise City. A lead pipe.

We blew it. Someone made the kid and followed him to the bar. They were waiting for me outside. Never saw it coming. They must be real pros.

Garbled voices. Fuzzy shapes on the far side of the room. Three men. Everything seems far away.

He's starting to come around.

A square room. Well lit and tidy, cool and damp. A basement. Thoughts are moving more slowly than normal, like a traffic jam in his head. Feels like it, too.

Table off to the side, and a small porcelain lamp. Black bag next to it.

The men look his way, laughing.

He tries to speak, but the words get trapped on his tongue.

Man walks over with a tall glass of water, puts it up to Horvath's mouth. "Here, drink this."

He tries, but most of water spills down his shirt.

"Let's try that again."

The man raises the glass, more slowly this time. Horvath drinks, carefully at first and then he gulps it down.

"Thirsty, huh?"

"Yeah."

"I'll bet."

The man turns around, empty glass in his hand. The other two are standing ten feet back. One of them walks over and takes the glass.

He looks at the guy standing in front of him. Older, maybe around 55. Thick brown hair, swept back and flecked with gray. Medium height, medium build. Thick scar on his cheek. Nice suit, white shirt, tasteful tie. Expensive shoes, long camelhair coat. Did I sleep all the way through to winter?

"Ready to talk? You awake now?"

"Not quite. Maybe if you gave me a good slap across the face."

The man laughs, thinly. "Yeah, we just might do that."

The other guys laugh like it's the first joke they've ever heard, but the man turns around quick and they shut up even quicker.

Horvath is alert now. He was seeing double a few minutes ago, but he's got that down to about one-and-a-half. The two guys are big, and they don't look like they're in the Book of the Month Club. He recognizes one of the thick-necks. It's Goon #2, who tailed him from Paradise City. The other guy is twice his size and four times the Neanderthal. He's almost perfectly square, like a fresh hunk of granite but with a few little features carved out. The sculptor must've got bored halfway through and stopped, so he doesn't look very realistic. Square head, square jaw, square chest. Little square hands. No thumbs, probably. He's not that evolved. His black hair is so short it looks painted on. Small crooked mouth, and eyes to match. Wide flat nose like a vacuum cleaner attachment. The teeth are small and sharp.

The older man's staring at him.

"You got any aspirin?"

"Sorry, kid. Maybe later."

So now I'm the kid? It's not my lucky day.

"Time to talk, princess." The man snaps his fingers and one of the heavies brings over a chair. He sits across from Horvath. "I hear you been looking for me?"

"Maybe."

"Maybe I'll have my guys work you over."

He looks at the muscle. "Better get some new lackeys. These guys are a little soft."

"Good one, kid. I like your style. Marco?"

He considers saying *Polo*, but his mouth is too dry for extra words.

The larger guy waddles over and, mid-stride, punches Horvath in the side of the face. Then he turns around and stand next to the other guy. No pause, no words, no extras. He's been trained well.

"Again."

Marco waddles back and lands a kidney punch, then a left to the kisser.

It takes him a few seconds to realize that he got knocked out. The man is still sitting there, legs crossed, picking lint off his coat. The smaller goon snickers in the background. Marco is perfectly still and lifeless, a new exhibit at the science museum.

How long was I out? Just a few minutes, he guesses.

He tastes blood and looks down at his white shirt, action-painted with red. One-hour martinizing won't take care of this, he thinks. He stares at a small white object on the floor, by his left foot. A tooth.

The man follows his line of sight. "Want me to pick it up and save it for you?"

Horvath looks up. "No, I've got more where that came from."

"So do we, pal. So do we."

Marco grins very slowly, as if the mechanism needs oil.

"You ready to talk now?"

He smirks through the blood. "Like I said, this guy's a pansy. He needs to take his skirt off and show me some muscle."

"A real tough guy, aren't you?"

"Maybe."

"Not when I'm done with you. You'll be singing like a bird."

"What kind? Are we talking about a pigeon or some type of warbler...?"

"So we're going to dance, huh?"

"Yeah, slow dance. Nice and close."

The man yawns. "Look, I can barely understand you with that mouthful of blood and broken teeth. And I think your tongue must've swelled up or something."

Marco cracks his knuckles.

The smaller thug walks over to the table, opens the black bag, and starts taking out a series of objects. Screwdriver. Awl. Monkey wrench. Box cutter. Electric drill. He looks over at Horvath and smiles like a rabid dog.

"He's drooling," Horvath says. "Somebody get this punk a bib."

"You should go to Las Vegas," the man says. "Do your routine at the Tropicana."

"Maybe I will."

"Sure, if you're still breathing when we're all done here."

"What, you're going to awl me to death?"

"Good one, kid, but you don't want to joke around about Nicky's bag of tricks. Trust me." He pauses, uncrosses his legs, and leans forward. "So, you were looking for me. What gives?"

"You Jaworski?"

"That's right, Einstein. You been asking about me all over town."

"So you know about that?"

The goons laugh.

"Are you a dimwit, or what?"

"Some people think so."

"Look, pal. I know everything that happens in this town. You take a shit on the north side, and I smell it downtown."

"You should look into getting a window fan, scented candle, something."

"Enough!" Jaworski points a finger at Horvath. His face is red, forehead wrinkled with anger.

"I've been patient with you, but I'm sick of the comedy act."

Marco's licking his lips. Nicky strokes the flat blade of a chisel.

He doesn't have the strength for a snappy comeback, and he can't afford to lose any more teeth.

"Okay, yeah. I've been snooping around, asking a couple questions."

"Why?"

He tells Jaworski about the man he followed to town, and the guy Lana asked him to find.

"Never heard of em. What do they have to do with me?"

"I don't know. Heard your name somewhere and thought maybe you were involved."

"Well, I'm not. Where'd you hear this?"

"I forget."

"Nicky, pliers."

The goon selects one of two pairs lying on the table. He walks behind Horvath, grabs his left hand, pinches the nail of his index finger with the jaws of the pliers.

Horvath's been in this position before, but he still has all his nails. He turns his head to the right and sees a low rectangular table with a bowl of fruit on top, and flowers in a pale green vase. Seems out of place here, like running a whorehouse out of a convent.

"You're in over your head, kid. Tell me where you heard my name, or you lose a nail. After that, the real fun starts. Believe me, it'll get messy."

"Alright, alright."

"I figured there must be a brain in there somewhere." Jaworski looks at Nicky, who backs off.

"I overheard some guys talking in a bar."

"What bar?"

"I don't know the name. Walked in off the street."

"Who were they?"

"No idea. Never been there before, and I don't know them from Adam."

He doesn't want to give up the two guys at the gym. If he did, it might lead back to the trainer, who seems like a decent guy.

"So where was this bar?"

"Downtown." He names the cross streets, a few blocks from Smith's Tavern. The place is dirty, and he knows it. No big loss if a few of the boys over there get worked over.

"Describe the place."

"A real dive. Dark, dirty. Long bar in the middle, wood cracked and faded. Wobbly tables. Bathroom was a cesspool. Ceiling fan was busted so it was hot and humid. Bartender didn't do much. I've seen people in comas move quicker. Place didn't smell too good, either. Like stale beer and broken dreams."

"You're a regular poet. And I see your memory's improved." Jaworski gives him a handkerchief. "Clean up, will ya? I can't stand looking at that bloody face anymore."

He takes the handkerchief, mops up as much as he can.

"That's better. Now keep talking."

"So...I was walking toward the bathroom when I heard two guys by the payphone."

"Describe them."

"They had their backs to me so I didn't see their faces, but one was tall and thin and the other guy...medium height, little husky I think, dark hair...that's all I remember."

It seems like a reasonable description. Not too specific, not too vague. Could be anyone, or no one.

Jaworski stares at him, nods. He's not sure if he believes him. "Sounds like Smith's Tavern. That ring any bells?"

"No, sorry. Like I said, I was in the neighborhood and just walked in."

"Just happened to be strolling by, huh? That sound plausible to you, Marco?"

The goon shrugs.

"Yeah, I don't know either." Jaworski moves his chair a few inches closer. "What were you doing in the neighborhood?"

"Had some time to kill so I was browsing in a record store."

"Browsing, huh?"

"That's right."

"Buy anything?"

"Some Lester Young. *Laughin' to Keep from Cryin'.*"

When you're lying, keep it as close to the truth as possible. Another move from the McGrath playbook.

Jaworski leans closer and stares hard. "So you like jazz?"

"Yeah, what about you?"

"Crooners."

"Like who?"

"Russ Columbo, Rudy Vallée, Val Anthony..."

"Vic Damone?"

"He's okay."

"Sinatra?"

"Overrated."

Horvath nods. "You're right about that."

Jaworski's smiling now.

That was Horvath's plan—take control of the conversation and start asking *him* questions. Lighten the mood.

"I know the record shop you're talking about. Guy who runs the place is a real charmer. Snide, flamboyant, thinks he's the Sheikh of Araby or something. Smith's is right down the street."

He leans back, turns his head, whispers something.

Nicky starts packing his bag.

Marco doesn't move an inch.

"Here's the deal. You don't seem like a bad fella, you been straight with me more or less, and I'm in a good mood."

"Why, your wife out of town?"

"Don't push it, Horvath."

"You know my name?"

Jaworski frowns. "Course we do. Don't be a chump."

The thick-necks are staring at Horvath. Nicky has a big dumb smile on his face, but Marco's expressionless glare makes the Mona Lisa seem overexcited.

"I'm feeling generous," Jaworski says. "Stop nosing around and leave town tomorrow morning, bright and early."

"What's in it for me?"

"My boys won't break your legs."

It's a fair deal, but he doesn't say anything at first. He wants to make his surrender look real.

"What do you say?"

He stares defiantly at Jaworski, then drops his eyes. "Okay, you win."

"Good boy."

"I do have one question, Mr. Jaworski."

"Yeah, what is it?"

"How'd you know?"

"Your little friend? He stuck out like a bastard at a family reunion. Too slick, too loud, too obvious. Kid's got no idea how to operate. We had him pegged the moment he walked in."

"So you kept your eyes on him?"

"What else could we do? Had two of my boys follow him to the meet, wait outside, then politely introduce themselves to you when you came walking out later."

"I didn't see anyone, and I was looking hard."

"They're professionals, Horvath."

"These guys?" He pointed to Frick and Frack.

"Them? No, they don't do subtle. I have other guys for that."

"Well, they sure know what they're doing. Give em my regards."

"Will do."

"One more question."

"Sure, but make it quick. I got places to go, people to shake down." He smiles at his own joke.

"Why'd you come after me, and not the kid?"

Jaworski looks over at the bowl of fruit. "He was hardly worth it. Anyway, he probably had to be home for bedtime. And we weren't going to rough up a girl."

"No, I guess not."

"So that left you." He shrugs. "Alright boys, gag him."

Marco takes an old sock that smells like it's been hanging around the gym for a few weeks, and shoves it in his mouth. Gag's the right word. Nicky wraps electrical tape around his mouth. Marco unties his arms and lifts him up.

Nicky walks over to the table and grabs his bag.

Marco lets go of Horvath for a second and he gets lightheaded, starts tipping over. Smiling, the goon grabs him by the back of his jacket and props him up like a puppet.

"You'll be fine after you sleep it off and get something to eat." Jaworski walks over to the door, unlocks it, steps outside into the alley.

Marco ties his arms again and drags him outside like it was nothing. Nicky follows. He turns off the light, shuts the door, and locks it.

Horvath is wide awake now and he's trying to remember everything for later.

It's night, though he thought it would still be daylight. He wonders if they slipped him something.

Jaworski gets into the back seat of a long black Lincoln. Nicky sits beside him, closes the door.

There's no one around. It's quiet. The buildings on either side of the alley have no windows.

The trunk is open. Marco tosses him inside like it's opening day at Yankee Stadium. There's no tire iron, he notices, no jack. No crowbar or baseball bat. Nothing he can surprise them with when they let him out. Smart guys.

Marco slams the trunk shut, gets in the driver's seat.

It's a long, bumpy ride. They're driving in circles so he won't know where he's going or where he's been, and it works. Horvath has no sense of direction. His stomach lurches and he wants to throw up. It's not like the movies. The good guy, if that's what he is, needs more than guts and instinct, and his hunches aren't always right

Nice roomy trunk, he thinks. That's class. Bet it's a Continental.

But what do I know about cars? I don't even own one.

He scoots to the back of the trunk and puts his ear against the divider, but he can't hear anything. The trunk is a thick steel trap and the car's making too much noise.

Hold on. Music. A man's voice.

The music's getting louder.

It's Frank Sinatra. He's singing "The Best Is Yet to Come."

Somehow, he doubts it.

HE MUST HAVE DOZED off for a while because the next thing he knows the car's parked and the trunk is open. He can see a quarter moon and a long line of trees. The three men are standing outside in a cloud of cigarette smoke.

Marco whispers something to Jaworski, who turns around.

"Time to get up, kid. School bus will be here any minute."

Nicky giggles and Marco does his best impression of a frozen mime.

"Get him."

Marco grabs his torso and Nicky holds the feet. They pick him up and start walking away from the car.

Jaworski flicks a cigarette butt into the dirt and gets back in the car.

It's quiet, he realizes. Too quiet. The sky is as black as a preacher's Bible. There are no streetlights or neon signs, just stars.

A wolf howls, or maybe a fox. He's a city boy and doesn't know the difference.

A seagull looks black against the moonglow.

They're walking through a bog now. He can hear the squish of their shoes in the damp soil. Cattails, reeds and tall grasses rise up on either side, instead of concrete, steel and brick.

He starts to worry when he hears Marco's shoes splash in the water. Maybe they are going to kill me. Thought Jaworski was being straight with me, but I guess if he can sell kids into the sex trade, he can tell a few lies.

"Ready?" Nicky asks.

"One, two—"

He doesn't hear anything else. Time slows down and stops, but it's also racing forward more quickly than he can process. He's struggling to breathe. Panicking, swallowing water. He knew the end would come some day, but he didn't think it would be like this.

His mouth is filled with mud, brackish water and something like seaweed. They say it's peaceful, drowning to death, but it doesn't feel that way. He's face-down, sinking, wondering how deep the water is and what it feels like to die.

But he isn't moving. He's already at the bottom.

It isn't easy, but he manages to turn over. His face is covered in water, but if he arches his back he can breath through his mouth, around the gag.

They didn't toss me in a lake to drown. They threw me in a shallow bog to put a scare in me, to humiliate me, and maybe for a laugh. Jaworski's one funny guy.

Horvath gets to his knees, stands up. Turns around.

He's all alone. Even the birds have called it a night.

There's a shadow in the distance. A large gray block. It's the factory, and that's the warehouse next door. He looks out over the water. I'm at the edge of the river. The tobacconist should be right over there. It's a long walk back to the city, but at least I know where I'm going.

And I'm not dead yet.

He starts walking.

By the time he gets back to the city limits, he's untied the rope. Marco didn't make the knots very tight. He takes off the tape and gag. The thick, polluted city air never tasted so good. He takes in a deep breath of car exhaust and bitter fumes from the brewery.

Feels like I'm running in circles, he thinks. Using a lot of energy but getting nowhere.

He checks his pockets, but the aspirin's gone. If he's passes a drugstore, he'll buy some more.

16

BLOOD, PUS & BREAKFAST

MAYBE THE HEADACHE WAKES HIM UP. OR THE CUTS AND BRUISES. Hunger, thirst. Hard to say. The hotel room is filled with so many loud, angry characters. It could any of them.

The first thing he has to do is peel the pillowcase off his face. It's stuck to the blood, which might as well be Elmer's glue. He counts to three and rips it off in one go. Hurts like hell, but now it's over. When he looks down at the pillowcase, there's a large patch of pus and bloody skin. It's all over the sheets, too.

They're going to charge me for this.

He's in a hell of a lot of pain but he's felt worse, plenty of times.

Horvath gets up, drinks from the sink, lights a cigarette.

He feels better already.

Life isn't so bad after a sleep and a smoke. They can solve all your problems, or at least make you forget about them for a while.

He sits on the edge of his bed, looks down at his feet. Heels are red and sore. There's a blister on the ball of his right foot. It's so big and pink, looks like someone stuck five sticks of gum in his mouth and blew a bubble. He needs a bandage and aspirin.

But the real emergency is food.

He washes his face in the sink, carefully so he doesn't open the wounds. Afterward, he blots himself dry with a towel and gets dressed.

HE'S ALONE in the cramped elevator, but it feels like a dozen people are crammed inside, everyone smoking at least four cigarettes. He remembers being stuffed in the trunk of the car, gagged with an old sock, tossed in the bog. Maybe I should retire, move out to the countryside, give up smoking.

He's laughing when the doors open. The fresh air would kill me.

As he passes the front desk, Gilbert looks up from his ledger and raises an eyebrow.

"You don't look so good yourself, pal."

"Of course I do."

He laughs.

"Have a nice day, sir."

"Seems unlikely."

When he turns for the front door, he sees Lana sitting by a window in the lobby. Her hair's down, caressing her long pale neck. Hat and lipstick are the same shade of red as her slinky dress.

He stops walking so he can see her like this, in a frame of sunlight. Horvath doesn't know squat about fashion, but he does know one thing. Whoever made that dress really knew what he was doing.

"I've been looking for you." Lana stands up on her six-inch stilts. "Where've you been?"

"Relaxing at a health spa."

"That right? Next time, tell em to take it easy with the facial massage. Looks like they were a little...strenuous."

"That's all part of the program. Gets the blood moving. Supposed to be good for you."

She unclasps her handbag, takes out a pair of dark glasses. "Where you headed?"

"Breakfast. Want to join me?"

"Sure, but it's lunchtime."

"Even better. Let's go."

He holds out his arm and she takes it. They walk into the sunshine.

No one speaks for a few blocks. He walks slowly, to have more time with her.

"Where are you taking me?"

"I need some things at the drugstore. They've got a luncheonette in back. That okay?"

"Sure, but let's not make it a habit. You'll spoil me."

He holds the door for her. "That would be impossible."

"Good answer."

Lana follows Horvath through the store. He grabs nail clippers, a large bottle of aspirin, cigarettes, and a pack of band-aids.

"You have a boo-boo?"

"Something like that."

"Need Momma to kiss it and make it better?"

He laughs, wishing it wasn't a joke.

She checks her watch. He stops by the rack of novels.

"What are you looking for?" she asks.

"Mystery, detective story, something like that."

"Cops and robbers, huh?" She picks up a cheap paperback and reads the title. "*Hammer of Justice*. This your kind of thing?"

"It's not bad."

She looks at the cover. Man in a dark alley, casting a long shadow by streetlight, holds a hammer above his head. Another man cowers at his feet. There are smaller pictures, to the side. Buxom blonde in a hayloft. Smoking gun. The scales of justice.

"Doesn't look very realistic," Lana says.

"It isn't. None of them are."

"Then why do you read it?"

"Because it's not very realistic."

She shakes her head. "Pick one already."

Date With Death. The Missing Casket. Destiny Carries a Revolver. The Lady in 2-C.

Without thinking, he grabs the last one and heads for the register.

He pays and they head back to the lunch counter.

Lana wipes off the red vinyl stool before sitting down. Horvath doesn't.

The ditzy young waitress from last time catches his eye and lopes over. "Hey, haven't I seen you somewhere before?"

"I don't think so." He's in no mood to reminisce.

"Are you on TV?"

"Yeah, I'm Secretary of State. Maybe you saw me on the news."

"No, that's boring. I like Jack Benny."

"We can all use a laugh sometimes."

"Tell me about it." She walks over, leans down, and rests her chin in her hands. Then she looks up at him like she wants a psych consult.

"Hey, I've got an idea," he says.

The waitress perks up. "What?"

"How bout you take my order."

She frowns. "Oh, okay. What'll it be?"

"Scrambled eggs, bacon, sausage, home fries, two orders of crispy toast, and strong black coffee."

"That all for you?"

"Yeah."

"Must be hungry."

"You catch on fast."

She looks at Lana. "Anything for you?"

"Coffee."

The waitress skulks back to the kitchen to get the order wrong.

She lights up. "You broke her heart."

"It was like that when I found her."

He pops a handful of aspirin and swallows them dry.

Lana stares at him with small hard eyes, like he's an advanced chemistry textbook and she's in the wrong classroom.

"Sure you're okay? Your face doesn't look so good."

"It never did."

"Nonsense. You've got a lovely face."

He raises an eyebrow.

"You seem to be missing a tooth."

"I've got others."

The waitress comes by with two coffees. There's more in the saucer than the cup.

"Bring the pot, will you?" he asks.

"Sure thing."

"So," Lana asks, "you going to make me ask or what?"

Horvath tells her about the sleepover with Jaworski and his lackeys.

"Poor boy."

"I'll live."

She looks away. "I'm sure you will."

No one speaks for a minute.

"Sorry I got you into this mess," she says.

"It's got nothing to do with you."

"Do you need more money? I'm flush."

"No, I'm fine."

"Let me know when my bill's due."

"Sure." He pauses. "Jaworski told me to split town or else."

"Or else what?"

"Or else they'll break my legs and I'll never dance again."

"You dance much now?"

"Not really."

"Then it's no big loss."

He smiles, sips his coffee. "You're looking as fresh and beautiful as ever."

"You're spoiling me."

"So Jaworski's boys didn't stop by for a chat?"

"Nope."

"They didn't rough up the kid, threaten him...?"

"Not from what he told me. Want me to call him up and ask?"

"No. If they messed with the kid, you would've noticed the trembling legs and piss stains on the carpet." He pours coffee from the saucer into his cup. "So they grabbed me and left the two of you alone."

"They're hardly going to slap a woman around," she said. "Or some dumb kid."

"Yeah, that's what they said."

Lana stamps out her cigarette and lights a new one.

"I'm glad they didn't touch you."

He doesn't say anything else, but she can hear it all in his voice and in the eyes looking down at the counter. "You're sweet."

The waitress brings over his breakfast, lunch, lunches. Whatever this is.

He attacks the food.

Lana watches, impressed and slightly repulsed. Is he a man or a vacuum cleaner?

"You took a beating for me." She strokes his arm. "Toughed it out like a man."

"Yeah, I didn't break. Just begged a little and cried maybe three or four times. Barely sucked my thumb."

"My sweet little tough guy."

"I used to box, you know?"

"Yeah?"

Why did I say that? I sound like a jerk. "It's no big deal. Just a few amateur fights."

She takes his right hand, looks at it, turns it over. "Small hands."

"I know." He makes a fist, relaxes it. "But I can move in the ring. Good legs."

"I'll bet." She leans over and kisses him on the mouth, soft but passionate. "I'm glad they didn't mess up your face too much."

"*Too* much?"

"Well, you do look a little rough, but I like it. Gives you character."

"My face has more than enough character already."

She kisses him again, longer and slower this time.

When she pulls back, he looks into her pale green eyes. The ring of gray around the outside is disconcerting, like a stranger squinting at you from the edge of a family picture. There's something lurking there that he can't see, behind her eyes and words. He doesn't know what it is and he doesn't want to.

17

ONE LONELY NIGHT

THEY LEAVE THE LUNCHEONETTE AND STAND ON THE SIDEWALK, WITH nothing much to say.

"Frank's won't run itself," Lana says.

He nods.

She squeezes his hand and leaves without another word.

Won't run itself? Horvath isn't so sure about that. Those old drunks will keep rolling in, no matter what, the bartender will keep pouring, and the cook will keep churning out the slop. Once you flick the switch, everything keeps going no matter what. Arms and legs moving without a thought. The conversation never changes. The people are androids who don't need eyes, brains, hearts or old-fashioned human feelings. Just like a science fiction story.

He watches her march down the avenue, hoping she'll turn around and smile but knowing she won't. The shops turn and stare as she passes by. The streetlights whistle and the blacktop makes an off-color remark.

He walks back to the hotel to think.

The city is heavy and threatening. He quickens his step and lowers his head to avoid the danger. Buildings are crouching down, reaching out with arms of steel and hands of concrete, ready to pounce.

He's a city boy. The suburbs and countryside have always seemed unreal and vaguely foolish. But sometimes it's too much. The angry streets, the crowded shops, the noisy bars. The grime and muck and filth. The crime, corruption and violence. You can't trust anybody here, least of all yourself.

Horvath needs to get inside and pull the covers over his head, escape for a little while.

Bookstore across the street. Red brick, green awning, big shiny windows. Inside, the books are lined up in tidy, even rows. Alphabetical order, by subject. Everything is new, orderly, pristine. Nothing's as fresh and clean as those pure white pages that no one's ever soiled with greasy fingers. Not a fresh mountain stream or a young girl's soul.

The window display is simple, clear and inviting. The latest thriller from Suzanne de la Franchette. Lady writers are making a killing this season.

The hotel's still a few blocks away and he needs to get off the fetid streets.

I'll buy a book, he thinks. Even though I just got one an hour ago. Probably finish it by morning. I should get a library card. Spending too much on books. I wonder if this dump even has a library.

He ducks inside.

It's quiet and peaceful here. Like a church, but without the old men in gold robes telling you what to do and why you're going to hell. If they could see what I've seen, they'd know hell wasn't so bad.

"May I help you, sir?"

Horvath looks down at a mousy young man hiding behind thick glasses and a tattered cardigan sweater.

"Sure. Do you have any Richard Yates?"

It's quick, almost imperceptible, but the clerk gives him a second look.

"Yeah, the book's for me."

"Oh no, sir. I didn't—"

"—It's okay. I know I don't look like much of a reader, but I appreciate a good story. Went to college and everything."

"I'm sorry, sir. There may have been a mis—"

"—Don't sweat it, kid."

"Okay."

The clerk worries his fingernails.

Guy lives with his mother, Horvath thinks, and he's afraid of his own shadow. But he probably sleeps like a baby. "So, about the book?"

"Oh, right. Yates. Let's see...I know we have his new collection of stories. *Eleven Kinds of Loneliness.*"

"Sounds like a good laugh."

"It isn't."

"I know, kid. I was being sarcastic."

"Oh. Right. Sorry."

"Got his novel? I heard it was good."

"I'm...I'm not sure."

The poor kid is green around the gills. Horvath almost feels bad for him.

"Let me check with the owner. Just a minute, please."

"Take your time."

The clerk shuffles off to the back while Horvath soaks it all in. Dim lighting, dark wooden bookcases, thousands of books, a few chairs hiding in soft corners. A man could get lost in here and never come out. He can't stop smiling.

A minute later, the clerk comes back with the owner. It's a one-man operation and that man is a woman. Tall and thin, all sharp elbows and pointy features. She's got dark brown eyes and a small ironic mouth. Slacks and a white blouse, hair tied up like she's French. Not his kind of woman, but she looks good in her own way.

"You were looking for Richard Yates?"

"Yeah, you got him tied up in back?"

She laughs and gives him the same look as the clerk. Must be related. He didn't think he was that easy to read. The kind of man he's become must be written all over his face, like the blurb on a cheap dime-store novel.

"This is his only novel, *Revolutionary Road*." She hands it to him. "You'll enjoy it."

"I'm sure I will."

"He'll ring you up."

"Thanks."

She smiles coyly, turns, and walks back to her office. She moves slowly, like she knows he's watching. Even lady bookstore-owners know how to work it.

HE SLEEPS FOR TWO HOURS, gets up, and cracks open the new book. *Revolutionary Road* is slow, grim and depressing, but it's also beautiful and sometimes even funny. Cops and cowboys are fine, but sometimes he needs a bit of real life. Six-shooters don't always hold 40 bullets.

When he starts getting tired, he reaches for his bookmark, the Do Not Disturb sign. The staff at the Executive knows better than to knock on his door without a good reason.

He looks back over the past three or four weeks. All the towns and cities, the cars and hotels, busses and trains, dives bars and seedy hotels. Gary, Indiana. Peoria, Illinois. Joliet, Chicago, Milwaukee. He's been all over, but is it worth it? Is he getting anywhere? Does the guy really matter that much?

His name is Van Dyke and every time Horvath rolls into town, he's just missed him. The failure is like clockwork.

He sets the book down, lays back, and stares at the ceiling. He's sifted through the details 100 times before, but maybe 101's the charm.

Van Dyke was an accountant for the firm. Still wet behind the ears. Couldn't be more than 23, 24. Fresh out of college. He joined the outfit, kept his head down, and did good work. Or so Horvath was told. He never met the guy. Van Dyke worked out of the Detroit office.

He was well-groomed, neatly dressed, reliable, always smiling and attentive. A real go-getter.

Got to work early and stayed late. His work was immaculate. Respected by his colleagues, and reasonably well liked. Smart as a whip. In fact, thought he was the smartest guy in the room. Rubbed a few people the wrong way because of that, though no one made a stink about it.

Too smart for his own good, apparently. Started embezzling from the firm. A little at first, and then he got more reckless. 65 grand in all. Thought a bunch of crooks would be too stupid to notice. But Wilson, his boss, knows everything that goes on and he counts every dime. Plus, there's a whole team of bean-counters because sometimes you need an accountant to keep the other accountants from stealing.

Wilson got wise to the scam. Instead of settling Van Dyke's balance sheet right then and there, he played it cool. Had a few trusted men keep their eyes and ears open. McGrath was one of them. Kept tabs on the young man for two weeks. Followed him down the city sidewalks. Watched him across dark smoky bars. Sat outside his apartment late at night, waiting.

But then one night he never came back.

Wilson was furious, and the higher-ups were breathing down his neck. It wasn't a lot of money, not by the firm's standards, but they had a reputation to protect. They couldn't let some nobody steal from them and get away with it. And how did he manage to skip town, with so many eyes on him? That was next to impossible.

And where'd he get the guts to steal from the firm? Horvath was a solid boxer, and he's still got pretty quick his hands. But he's only a collector. Information, people, ideas. Whatever they need, he goes out, finds it, and brings it back. But he isn't the real muscle. Those guys, now they're tough. They enjoy the work and they're good at it. Some of them will snap your bones in half just to hear the sound.

Van Dyke. Such a quiet and unassuming young man. So clean-cut and ordinary. There's more to the story. Has to be. But he's got no idea what it is, not even after following him all over the country. McGrath passes along whatever information he has, but it's not much.

Horvath doesn't have a clue where he is.
The guy's a ghost. No one's seen his face or heard his footsteps.

18

MONEY

HE'S RUNNING OUT OF CASH.

A few dollars in the billfold, a little more in his shoe, 20 under a floorboard in the closet. He'll be dead broke by the end of the week.

After breakfast he walks six blocks uptown until he finds a phone booth. It's on the corner, by the newsstand. The phonebook's been ripped out, but there's a dial tone.

He dials the number.

"Yeah?" It's not a warm voice, or a familiar one.

"Horvath. I'm looking for Ungerleider."

Silence.

He smacks the receiver to make sure it's still working.

"Ungerleider's not here."

"Who's this?"

"Lourette."

Name doesn't ring a bell.

"You find our guy yet?" the man asks.

"No."

"So why you callin?"

"Running low on scratch."

Lourette says nothing, but the way he says it is filled with disappointment and frustration. Horvath doesn't like being jerked around by some guy he's never heard of.

"I'll send somebody. Two days."

"Good."

Lourette names a time and a place.

Horvath can't wait to get off the phone.

Lourette pauses. The phone's away from his ear.

He can hear something in the background. Static, or maybe a radio playing in the next room.

"Hold on, somebody wants to talk to you."

Uh-oh, he thinks. Hope it's not Kvasnika, that slovenly prick. Or Wilson. I'm in no mood to get dragged on the carpet. It's not my fault I can't find this guy. He's slippery as an eel. And it better not be Atwood. Once the big man wants to talk to you, you're already dead, even if you know it yet.

"How's it going, pal?"

"Oh. Hi."

It's McGrath. He couldn't have asked for anything better. Surprising, though. McGrath's getting older. These days, he doesn't hang around the office too much.

"You still on his tail?"

"Yes and no. I'm looking everywhere, but I'm not finding much."

"You will. Keep sniffing around."

"Alright."

"Come on, man. Buck up. You sound awful."

"Sorry."

"You doing alright?" McGrath asks.

"Yeah, yeah. No, I'm good. Just frustrated. The trail's gone cold."

"When that happens, forget everything you know, or think you know, clear your mind and start over. From the very beginning."

"I remember. That's rule #36, right?"

McGrath laughs. "Something like that."

Horvath stares at his shoes, feeling chastened. McGrath's his favorite person in the world, but something about the guy makes him feel like a kid in the principal's office.

"Don't think about it too much," McGrath says. "And don't look for clues. Let them find you."

HE FEELS LIGHTER NOW, walking back to the Executive. Stronger and more alert. Van Dyke is still in the wind, but at least they're sending more cash. And the firm isn't angry. If they were, Wilson would've called him back home, or sent a couple guys to sit him down for a long talk.

And he got to hear McGrath's voice. Always so calm and soothing, like the father he wished he had.

He thinks about his old man. That sack of air in a gray flannel suit. An insurance adjuster. Whiskey for blood and a balance sheet where a heart should be. Came home from work. Changed out of his suit into a another suit. Read the paper, went to bed. Never broke the law but he never had time for me, either. A real prince.

Of course, McGrath's right. I'm tired, worn out. Losing my focus. I see everything more clearly when I don't try so hard. I need to stop. Big steak dinner, couple whiskeys, a few more after that. Sleep in. Walk around the city, then walk some more, no particular place to go. Don't look for anything at all. I'll get there. I'll get there.

Horvath barely registers the fact that he's walking through the front doors of the hotel. He doesn't see the people in the lobby, the clerk behind the front desk, or the tired bellboys trying to look busy.

Up in his room, he takes off his shoes, throws his jacket over the back of a chair, sits on the bed.

He picks up the Yates and starts reading.

He drops the book 30 minutes later and pretty soon he's fast asleep. Dreaming of elevators with no walls, rivers of blood, monsters with two heads, large scary men chasing him through dark forests, high rooftops, and winding corridors that never end.

TWO DAYS later he goes to the corner of 11th and Pine. There's an Anglican church on one corner and a hardware store on the other.

He lights up, stands by the lamppost, and waits.

A quiet part of town.

Mailbox, car parked down the block.

Teenage girl walks down the street with her mother, both of them pretending to be prim and proper.

That's about it. Horvath expects to see a tumbleweed any second.

Late-model Chrysler drives slowly down the street, pulls over to the curb, parks.

Man rolls down the window, hangs his arm out. There's a ring on his finger with a bright red stone.

Horvath drops his cigarette, stamps it out, walks over to the car.

The man reaches out the window with his other arm, hands him an envelope.

He slides it into one of the inside pockets of his coat.

The man drives off without a word. No eye contact. No smile. Not even a wink. A real pro.

One of McGrath's men, I'll bet.

He's semi-retired now. What a shame. The firm won't be the same without him. But he is getting old. Will he get out of the game for good? Horvath wonders how it works and if they ever let you go. Probably not. The firm is for life. Once they get their hooks in you, they don't let go.

19

JAGGED SKYLINE OF CAR KEYS

HORVATH IS FLUSH. HE HAS MONEY NOW, BUT STILL NO LEADS.

He's been lying low, asking no questions, keeping himself out of trouble.

The cuts are almost healed, and the bruises are fading from deep purple to a dull greenish yellow.

Eating, sleeping, walking, reading.

Drinking, watching, popping aspirin, changing bandages.

It's a simple life. Lonely, raw and simple. Monastic, but he likes it. No complications.

Then he thinks of Lana. Those legs, that neck, the kiss.

She's a complication he can live with. When he thinks about her, he starts to rise up and float away from the ground beneath his feet. He doesn't have size or shape anymore. No weight to speak of. He's a frail leaf blowing wherever the wind takes him.

He shakes his head almost violently to kill the thoughts. He's got work to do, back here on earth.

Hasn't seen her in a few days. Last time he dropped in at Frank's, she was out and the bartender couldn't tell him when she'd be back.

A letter came this morning. Someone slipped it under his door.

Gilbert, probably. The fancy young man at the front desk. Not a bad guy, actually. Horvath is warming up to him.

His first thought was Jaworski. A death certificate with his name on it. Something witty like that.

But it was just an address.

436 Cantrell.

It's on the north side. So far uptown it was practically on the southside of the next city. He doesn't know the street, but it's a bad neighborhood. Even for a town like this.

The letter was from Wilson, or possibly McGrath. When you don't know where do go, who to talk to, or what to do, this is how they respond. A license plate, a bar, an address. That's it. The rest is up to you.

HE WAITS for sundown and then walks toward the subway.

The streets are empty, too empty for a Friday night. The sidewalks are clear, most of the shops are closed, and the restaurants only have a few customers each. He looks through the window of a steakhouse and sees a waiter leaning against the bar, arms crossed, and a filthy white rag over his shoulder. A car drives by and two people whisper on the street corner, but other than that the streets are dead.

Where'd everyone go? They're acting like rats when a storm's coming.

He looks over his shoulder but no one's there.

Turns right, crosses the street, stops and glances in a store window. There's no one on his tail. No one suspicious hanging around.

It's been like this for days. He feels someone watching, hears footsteps on the pavement, senses a pair of eyes tracing his movement. But when he turns around, no one's there. Not a sound. Not a breath. Not even a shadow reaching out from a doorway.

Maybe I'm just being paranoid.

But no, someone's been watching me. I know it. One of Jaworski's men. Or maybe the firm is keeping an eye on me. They like to do that. Keep us on our toes.

He takes a deep breath and keeps walking.

Office buildings rise up in the distance. Tenements, water towers, electrical pylons like steel skeletons. At night, everything has the same dark gray color, but in different sizes and shapes. The city looks like a jagged skyline of car keys.

He thinks about the day he met McGrath. Middle of the afternoon at Eddie's, a poolhall in Newark. His wife was gone, his job and his house. Everything he thought he wanted. All he had left was an old pair of boxing gloves, couple suits, and a bad taste in his mouth. McGrath bought him a beer, told him things he didn't want to hear, and turned him into a new man. He picked him up, got him back on his feet. Gave him a new job and a new way of seeing the world.

I owe him everything. He made a man out of me, made me better than I ever thought I could be.

The elevated subway platform is just ahead, looking down over the street. Below, there's a bodega, car service, coffee shop, Chinese takeaway where you can play the numbers. A crumpled newspaper blows across the street and sticks to a chain-link fence. A small garage is wedged between a barbershop and a Russian bakery, with a stack of old tires outside. A busty woman with too much make-up stands on the corner, looking for a date.

Horvath climbs the metal staircase, drops a token in the turnstile, and waits for the train.

A few minutes later it shudders into the station, slows down, and comes to a stop.

He gets on and takes a seat.

The train rattles off.

Three other passengers in the car. They sit there like corpses, pale and sickly in the yellow light. Grim faces, eyes downcast. No one talks, no one moves. The people get tossed back and forth like ragdolls by the motion of the train, but they don't bother holding on.

He stares out the window, but it's hard to see anything through a veil of dead flies and golden sap, dirt and ash, traces of blood maybe, unidentifiable grime he'd rather not think about. The city sleeps under a blanket of darkness like a hulking child with neon night-lights in its bedroom, keeping watch. It looks almost peaceful from up here.

The train picks up speed, plunges down into the tunnel, runs beneath the city and, in the blink of an eye, everything goes dark.

20

DARK END OF THE STREET

HE GETS OFF THE TRAIN.

The platform is empty, and pitch black. There are two street-lamps, but the bulbs have been smashed.

He takes the stairs two a time.

On the street, a bum holds out a tin cup for change. Horvath gives him three quarters.

A pair of young hoods stand on the corner, looking tough. Collars up, dungarees, motorcycle boots. Switchblades and brass knuckles on display. The leader turns toward Horvath, but quickly looks away. No time for squares. And anyway, the guy has greasy hair to comb.

He puts his head down and walks north, then cuts left.

A bad neighborhood in a bad town. The streets are filthy, trash piles up on the sidewalk. Rusty shopping trolley on its side, like a passed-out wino. Men drinking in their shirtsleeves outside a grocery store. Broken bottles and crushed tin cans. Boarded up windows, burned out houses, iron bars and barbwire. Young kids with no parents around. Cars with missing hubcaps and slashed tires.

An old lady in a housecoat shouts from an open window.

Kids throw a spaldeen against a brick wall. Playing butts-up, probably. Or maybe slapball.

A dented Cadillac crawls down the street. Guy in the passenger seat gives him the stink-eye.

This is no place to be walking around on your own. Not without a piece. He moves faster and stays alert. Even tough guys get scared, no matter what they tell you.

436 Cantrell.

Maybe I'll get lucky. Van Dyke's just sitting there on the sofa, watching television. Shoes off, no gun at his side. Maybe.

302. One more block.

It's a red brick apartment house. All the lights are out. Overflowing trashcans lined up out front, like nightclub bouncers. A guy is smoking on the stoop. He could use a haircut. Girl walks out the front door and sits next to him. Bums a smoke. She's wearing old pants and a man's sweatshirt. Artist? he wonders. Or maybe a junkie. It's hard to tell the difference.

He looks up at the building. Some of the bricks are crumbling like feta cheese and others have fallen out, an old man with missing teeth. A few windows have been smashed, fixed up with cardboard and electrical tape.

This must be 436, but the numbers have been ripped off. Horvath just hopes there's something inside for him. The firm's been getting sloppy with its leads, ever since McGrath started taking time off. He ran a tight ship, but now it's a leaky rowboat.

He mounts the concrete stairs, but the smokers don't seem to notice he's there. Hell, they don't notice each other, or themselves. Pale gray skin, dead eyes. Junkies.

There's no doorknob so he sticks his fingers in the round hole where a knob should be and pulls the door open.

It's hot, humid. No ventilation. Place feels like a morgue.

Five-story walk-up.

He'll go to the top first, then check out each floor one at a time.

The staircase is narrow, dark and airless. He thinks of the elevator back at the Executive, the car trunk he took a ride in. It's a steep climb but his legs are strong and he likes it. Walking's good for your character.

Horvath stays close to the wall, in case he meets someone coming down. He can't see more than a few inches in front of his face.

He stops to take a breath on the fifth floor landing. He opens a door and walks down the hallway. Can't hear a thing. Most of the doors are closed, and there's nothing to see. He stops and listens. Nothing.

At the end of the hall, he turns around. He looks through an open door, but no one's inside. A little trash. Something in the corner. Bedding maybe, and a small cluster of objects. It's too dark to tell. Maybe someone's sleeping here.

He peeks inside a few more apartments, but they're all empty.

Before going downstairs he tries one of the closed doors. Locked.

He tries another one.

The hinges creak so he opens it as slowly as possible. There's light coming in from the window. Blinking white light and a lot of red. Must be a strip club next door.

A noise so faint he almost doesn't hear it.

He turns to the right, behind the door and all the way against the wall.

Horvath flicks on his lighter. A small, lumpy man in a tweed coat stands very still, holding a wooden yardstick. Glasses, beard, baggy pants. A professor type. Soft all over. He remembers them from college. They've read a million books and know everything there is to know, except how to live.

But this guy hasn't seen the inside of a classroom in a few years, if he ever has. Ripped pants, no shoes. Shirt buttoned all the way up, but no tie. His eyes are flat and dull but they seem to glow in the darkness.

Behind him, a small girl sits on a tall stool. She's wearing a pointy hat.

He looks from the professor to the girl, trying to work it out.

No, it's not a hat. It's her head. Long, tapered, misshapen. *Bullum head*, they call it. And she's no girl. 30, 35 at least. Wearing a pristine white dress and ragged black boots.

He takes a step closer. There's a rope tied to the woman's ankle.

No, a leash. It snakes across the floor and the other end is tied to a radiator.

"You okay, lady?"

She doesn't say anything, or even look at him.

"You okay there?"

Now she turns, and starts grunting.

"You're upsetting her," the man says.

He reaches out with his yardstick and touches her arm, near the shoulder. He pats her three times and she calms down. "She can't talk."

Horvath looks down at her ankle.

"For her own good. She gets away, runs wild through the streets."

"Sure..."

"It's not safe out there."

He's right about that.

"She's a looner," the man says.

"Looner? What's that?"

"It means she's not all there. More animal than woman."

"You her father?"

"Uncle. My sister and her husband, they ran off and left her."

"Some parents."

The man shrugs. "It was too much for them."

"But not you, huh?"

"I do what I can."

The girl hops up and down in her seat, barking.

He's seen a lot in his time, but not this. "So, what are you doing here?"

The man was staring absentmindedly at the floor, but he snaps his head up and stares hard at Horvath. "What do you mean? We live here."

The man looks insulted, and not so soft anymore.

Horvath looks around but doesn't see much in the way of furniture, possessions, or life. He wants to ask questions, but he can't find the right words. "I'll leave you to it then."

She should be in a lunatic asylum, he thinks. But maybe that wouldn't be any better than this.

A few seconds later, he walks out.

The fourth floor is a graveyard. Nothing to see, nothing to hear.

He takes the staircase down.

The third floor is alive. He can hear rats scritching inside the walls, scurrying along the baseboards. Roaches tapping across the tiled floor. The place smells bad, even from the hallway. Old food, sweat, stale beer, dirty clothes, dark corners used as toilets. Maybe a dead animal or two. A flophouse for bums, dopers, crooks and runaways.

He pokes his head into a few rooms, but there isn't much to see, except trash.

At the end of the hallway he almost steps on something. The carcass of a large fish. Must be two feet long, eight inches wide. The flesh has been eaten, or rotted away, but the bones are still intact. The ribcage is round and full. Looks like one of those small wooden ships people make, and then shove inside a bottle.

The rooms are all empty, except for a man sleeping in a corner under a pile of newspapers and tattered sheets. Horvath leaves him alone, tiptoes out the door.

Second floor.

Voices.

He moves cautiously down the hall, stopping outside the room where the noise is coming from. The voices are louder now, and more urgent. He looks inside. A middle-aged man in a sleeveless t-shirt is yelling at a woman in a short skirt, wrinkled blouse, heels dangling from her right hand. Her hair's a tornado and she's crying, mascara running down her face. She's young, maybe 20 or 21. But she's done a lot of living in those years. His wife? Girlfriend? Daughter? Maybe a business associate.

He keeps going.

End of the hall, a door is open a few inches. He pushes inside.

His eyes have adjusted to the darkness. Over by the window, two men sit on the floor, leaning against the wall. They don't speak or move. One has a smile on his face and stares at nothing. The others are asleep, or nodding off.

Laughter.

He turns around. Two kids, a boy and a girl, are running down the hallway. No older than nine. They look inside the apartment and laugh. At the junkies? Horvath? They keep running, dart into the stairwell. He listens to their feet pound the hard steps. No one is innocent.

Horvath follows the kids down.

The main floor has one apartment, the manager's office, a supply closet, and the super's room. All locked.

What was I supposed to find here? Or who? How's it related to Van Dyke?

Under the stairs there's another door, leading to the basement.

He goes down.

There's no railing, no light.

Horvath smells smoke and ash, but there's no fire, no light. He stops and listens. Nothing.

He keeps going. Holding his breath, trying not to make a sound.

When his foot reaches the floor, he hears a faint splash of water. It's even hotter and more humid down here. The walls are sweating, and it drips off the ceiling.

A large room with a low ceiling. Size of a basketball court, maybe bigger.

Stone floor, brick walls. A dozen boxes against the wall, cobwebs and a busted chair, but that's about it. Empty space. Exposed pipes run across the ceiling, like blood vessels.

There's an arched doorway at the far end of the room.

He walks closer.

The water on the floor gets deeper.

Something moves. Maybe a rat.

Closer. Closer.

It's a bit cooler over here. The rumor of fresh air.

Back to the wall, he stands near the doorway, inches forward. Looks around the corner.

He squints. Pinpoints of light cut through the darkness.

It's a long narrow hall, only wide enough for one person. The back door's at the end, and an iron gate. Door must be open, letting in sunlight.

He feels it before he hears anything.

A second or two later, the ringing in his ears is a maelstrom.

And then he feels soft and warm all over, as if someone wrapped him in a thick blanket. There's liquid on his arm, up by the shoulder, like he's swimming in a heated pool. But he isn't doing laps down at the Y. He's been shot with a .45 at close range.

There's no pain, at first. But then it grabs him by the throat and won't let go.

Another gunshot, bouncing off the brick walls.

He can't sees anything except for a shadow, rushing toward him.

This wouldn't be a bad time to pack a gun, he thinks. But McGrath wouldn't hear of it. We're not animals, he'd say. We're not dirty thugs.

He can see the man's face now. Jaw clenched, teeth bared. He's raising the pistol again.

Horvath swings at him, uppercut to the nose, but the guy bobs left and the punch glances off the side of his face. He's a big man, but slow. He swings and misses. He swings again, but Horvath ducks. The guy steps forward and Horvath runs at him, smashes his head against the bricks. He drops his piece on the floor and reels back. Horvath lands two quick jabs to the gut and he doubles over, groaning. Horvath puts everything into another punch, but his tank's on empty. The guy barely flinches when the fist connects with his jaw.

Both men are eying each other. Horvath has lost a lot of blood, and the big guy is no fighter. He runs at Horvath, knocks him over, and keeps going.

Horvath leans against the wall, breathing hard. He feels even warmer now, and so tired.

Maybe I'll sit down, he thinks. Just for a second.

21

ALL TOO HUMAN

WHEN HE WAKES UP, HE HAS NO IDEA WHERE HE IS.

He sits up, leans back against the wall, fishes a cigarette out of his pocket, and lights up.

It all comes back to him, and that goes double for the pain.

He looks at his arm. He'll live, but the suit's on life support. Ripped, soaking wet, covered in blood.

Too weak to move, he finishes the cigarette first.

As soon as he stands up, he feels lightheaded and starts to stagger. He leans against the brick wall for a couple seconds.

He flicks on his lighter, looks around. The gun is still on the ground, half submerged in the grubby water. He picks it up, takes out the bullets.

The back door's unlocked. He walks into the sunlight, which is a dagger to his skull.

The alley is all jagged red bricks, like the basement where he just spent the night. He reaches into his pocket, pulls out the little bottle. He takes an aspirin, and then one more, and then another.

He walks down the alley, turns right, and he's back on Cantrell.

The streets are empty. Back to the subway.

On the next block there's a trashcan on the corner, in front of a

Puerto Rican bodega. He drops the bullets inside and stops for a smoke.

He's tired, dead tired after a short walk. But he feels strong enough to make it back to the hotel.

The street toughs are still there, standing around doing nothing. One of them looks over and laughs, without joy.

He looks down at his soiled clothes. They must think I'm a bum or a doper.

An old woman walks by, across the street, humping a 40-pound sack. Can't be more than five feet tall, 90 pounds. She holds it with one hand over her shoulder. Grocery bag in the other arm, cigarette dangling from her mouth. Tough old broad.

He starts crossing the road. "Need help with that?"

She shakes her head. "I'm good."

He's on the sidewalk now, a few feet away from her. "Fang?"

She stops and turns, sees who it is. "You look like shit."

He laughs. "I do, you're right."

Fang puts the bag down.

"What you got in there, rice?"

"Potatoes. You know, we don't just eat rice all the time. We like noodles, yams, all kinds of food."

"My mistake. What are you doing around here?"

"Buying potatoes, stupid, what do you think?" She flashes that 100-watt smile. "I'm going back to Chinatown now."

"Chinatown? Didn't know they had one in this dump."

"Well, it's not so big. More like China block." She looks at his arm. "You okay?"

"Yeah, I'm fine. Just a minor gunshot wound."

She nods. "Thought so. The blood was my first clue."

Horvath sniffs a laugh. "Hey, I got a question. See that building over there?"

He points, she looks.

"You know anything about it?"

"Yeah."

"What?"

"You should stay out of there."

He dumps ash on the sidewalk. "You're probably right."

"Come on, I know someone. He'll take care of you real good. Cheap, too."

"Is he a doctor?"

She shrugs. "Close enough. But it's not like you have a choice. A real doctor would ask questions."

She picks up the sack, tosses it over her shoulder, starts walking uptown.

Horvath drops his butt and follows her.

It's hard to keep up with Fang, even though she's a small elderly woman carrying half her weight in potatoes. After a few blocks she turns around and sees that he's lagging 30 feet behind.

"Come on, slowpoke. I don't got all day." She glares at him, but slows down.

"How much farther?"

"Close, close."

They keep walking. It's not close.

The streets get narrow and more congested. There's life here, and the place is clean. Everybody's moving. No one's standing around on the corner trying to look hard, staring off into space, or drinking from a brown paper bag. No, they're too busy for that. Good hard-working people with large families and small apartments. Chinese, Poles, Armenians, Russians, Jews. A few Norwegians with square shoulders and solemn expressions. The shops are small and cramped, but tidy. Jeweler, butcher, baker, cobbler, hatmaker, plumber, electrician, pawn shop, haberdasher. A city within the city.

He doesn't know where he is or where he's going, but he feels a little better already.

A middle-aged woman in an apron waves to Fang, who yells something at her in a language Horvath doesn't recognize. She's picks up a few dirty glasses from a sidewalk table and brings them back inside her café.

Fang stops in front of some kids on the next block. She puts the sacks down, reaches into her grocery bag, and pulls out some candy. The kids each take a piece and run off.

He catches up to her. "Close, huh?"

"Almost there. Promise."

She crosses the street, walks half a block, and stops in front of a Chinese restaurant.

"Wait here."

Fang goes inside and comes out a couple minutes later.

They keep walking.

After three more blocks Fang stops by a metal door on the side of a gray stone building that takes up half the block. There's no sign or indication what's inside. She opens the door and steps in. He follows.

They take a metal staircase to the seventh floor. Fang doesn't breathe hard or slow down. Her muscles don't strain under the burden. The stairwell is cool and their footsteps echo on the metal.

"Here." She stops on the landing, opens a heavy door, walks through.

A thin filet of blue carpeting in the hallway, florescent lights over-head. White walls and wooden doors. The space is tidy, orderly, spare.

"Where are we?"

"Doctor's office."

She turns right, walks down the hall, stops in front of what looks like a broom closet. No sign on the door, no number or nameplate. Horvath wonders what kind of medicine man he's about to see. He hopes it not one of those quacks that sticks little needles in your skin and makes you drink shark-fin soup.

Fang knocks once, waits a beat, opens the door.

A husky Chinese man with large black glasses and a white lab coat sits on a squat wooden stool. He looks at Fang and then at Horvath's bloody arm, but the guy doesn't flinch. He's seen it all, twice.

She barks at him in Chinese. He barks right back. Horvath wonders why other languages always sound like an argument. Are they really shouting, or is it just my stupid foreign ears?

"Hi, Doc."

"He doesn't speak English."

The doctor looks at Horvath, nods slightly. His face wears its favorite expression, which is no expression at all.

She speaks to the doctor in quick, fervid bursts while Horvath scans the room. It's a broom closet. Or was one. Now it's a doctor's office. The walls are blank. No desk, no operating table, no sink, no fancy equipment. No icebox to store medicine. Just a countertop, cabinets, one shelf, a few supplies. One lamp, two stools. A simple operation.

"He'll fix you up," Fang says. "Take off your shirt."

He removes his jacket, shirt and undershirt. The doctor smiles and says something to Fang. They both laugh.

"He says you're a big strong boy."

"Well, at least you two are having a good time. Don't worry about me."

The doctor flaps his hands impatiently, then grabs Horvath by the wrist and pulls him down to the other stool. He speaks more quietly now, eyes fixed on the bloody arm. Fang opens a drawer, takes out a bottle of alcohol and some gauze, hands them to the doctor. He pours alcohol on the dressing and grabs Horvath above the elbow with his left hand. His grip is strong, but his hands are small and wrinkled. He blots at the gunshot wound, gently at first.

The doctor waits to see how his patient reacts, but the white man doesn't blink or twitch. Pleased, he cleans the wound more quickly and forcefully.

Horvath doesn't cry out or jerk his arm away.

The doctor looks up at Fang, says something.

She nods. "He says you're a good patient. You stay very still and quiet. Like Chinese man."

"Like a Chinese man, huh? I'll assume that's a compliment."

The wound is bleeding again so the doctor blots it with gauze. He says something to Fang, who moves behind Horvath.

The doctor reaches into a cabinet, pulls out a bottle of whiskey, holds it up with a questioning air.

Horvath nods. The doctor pours a few fingers into a graduated beaker.

He drinks it down.

Fang grabs him by the shoulders. The doctor picks up a pair of tweezers, pours alcohol over them, and leans toward Horvath. He grabs his bicep and holds it in place. Horvath remembers the bench vise in his old man's workshop, growing up.

The doctor narrows his eyes, leans forward, inserts the tweezers into the gaping hole in his upper arm. He's got a light touch, but the pain is sharp and severe. Horvath closes his eyes, takes a deep breath, and floats away. He's trained himself to step over the pain and walk into the next room.

The doctor pauses, rests his working hand for a second, then goes back in. He fishes around for a few moments, clamps onto the bullet, and slowly extracts it. He shows it to Horvath and smiles, like he just pulled a plum out of a pie.

"Nice work, Doc."

The doctor drops the bullet into a small wastebasket that sits at his feet like the family cat. He mumbles something to Fang, who cleans the wound again, wraps it in gauze, and secures the bandage with thick white tape.

"All better now." The doctor shows off one of his six English phrases. Three are curses.

Fang pats him on the shoulder and he looks up at her. When he turns back to the doctor, the man's holding a long needle.

"What's that?"

"Medicine, stupid. What do you think?"

"Your bedside manner could use some work, Fang."

"Don't blame me. You're the one who got yourself shot."

She has a point.

The doctor jabs him. Horvath wonders why the shot didn't come before the operation, but he doesn't complain about it.

"Thanks again, Doc. You know, you run a pretty tight ship over here. You deserve your own clinic. Or at least a bigger broom closet."

Fang translates this.

The doctor throws his head back and laughs, loud and long, slapping the countertop and stomping his feet on the ground. Then he pats Horvath on the arm several times. "Good man. Good man."

He gets dressedwhile Fang and the doctor clean up.

When they're finished, the doctor stands up and turns to Horvath.

He takes a few sawbucks out of his billfold and hands them to the man. "Will that cover it, Doc?"

The man nods, bows.

Fang picks up her sack of potatoes.

They turn and walk out of the office, or broom closet, and the doctor sits back down on his stool.

OUTSIDE, the sidewalks are busy and the sun's working overtime. Horvath shields his eyes with a meaty right hand, but the bright lights don't seem to bother Fang.

"Feeling okay now?"

"Better, yeah, but I'm a little tired."

"Sleep it off."

He nods. "What was in that medicine, anyway?"

"It's just medicine. Don't ask so many questions."

He wants to ask her about the apartment building on Cantrell. When he brought it up earlier, she seemed to know something.

As if reading his mind, or maybe the worry lines on his face, she broaches the subject herself. "Ever heard of DiLorenzo?"

"No."

She drops the potatoes, reaches into her shirt pocket for a cigarette, and lights up. "Fiorello DiLorenzo. Owns a big chunk of the north side. Apartments, mostly. Slums. Bad man. He's got office buildings, too. Laundromats, construction company, taxies, dry cleaners, clip joints, massage parlors."

"Sounds like a class act."

"Pillar of society. Has lunch with the mayor twice a week."

"Really?"

"I don't know. Maybe it's three times."

"Sounds about right."

"One of the richest men in town. Police are in his back pocket. City Hall, Chamber of Commerce, everyone."

"Lemme guess, DiLorenzo gets all the city contracts?"

"Most of them." Fang yawns, stretches out her arms. "He owns the racetrack, too. That's where most of his money comes from these days."

"Where's that?"

"Outside of town. 15-20 miles. Most days, that's where he hangs out."

"He's with the syndicate?"

"Not exactly. He's got his own operation, but they have an understanding. You know who Jaworski is?"

"Name rings a bell."

"Gilroy runs the syndicate, and Jaworski's his right-hand man."

"They have any legitimate businesses?"

"Few bars and nightclubs, but mostly it's girls, dope, graft, extortion, murder, armed robbery, gambling..."

"The seven cardinal virtues."

Fang tips her ash, looks around.

"So what's all this got to do with that empty rat's nest on Cantrell?"

"DiLorenzo tried to torch it last year, for the insurance money, but somebody stopped him."

"How?"

"He sent over a couple guys with gas cans and a book of matches, but when they got there some people were waiting for them."

"Gilroy's men?" he asks.

"Probably. No one knows for sure."

"So what happened?"

"They started a fire in the storeroom. Paint, turpentine, old rags. To make it look like an accident."

"Sure."

"And the fire started alright, but then these other guys came out of the basement and gunned them down."

"Anyone see who it was?"

"It was late, but there were people around. Bums, dope fiends, streetwalkers. It's not Fifth Avenue, you know? People stay up late around there."

"But nobody finked, right? Nobody was willing to name names?"

"No. They might have been threatened, or paid off, or maybe no one saw their faces. But people heard gunshots, saw a few men run out and jump into a car."

"Is that it?"

"Fire department put out the fire. Insurance company wouldn't pay up. Few weeks later, two of Jaworski's men were killed."

"That's some understanding they've got."

"Tell me about it."

"How'd they die?"

"Strangled, then tossed in the river." Fang pauses. "But you didn't hear any of this from me."

"Course not."

"Any more questions?"

"Yeah, where's the subway?"

She picks up the sack of potatoes. "Follow me. It's real close."

22

BLOOD AND GRITS

Horvath sleeps for 12 hours.

He wakes up with a terrible headache, as if someone's drilling on his skull from the inside, and his arm hurts like hell. But at least he's not stuck to the bedsheets. Fang wrapped him up good.

He reaches over to the nightstand and grabs a cigarette from the pack. Lights up, rolls onto his back and smokes, staring at the ceiling.

He's got a million questions but not much else.

Ever since he rolled into town, he's been running into bad guys, crime, violence and death, but no answers. None of it adds up.

Who was the guy with the gun? How'd he know I was coming? What was I supposed to find on Cantrell? If it was Van Dyke, then where is he? The guy who shot me—maybe that *was* Van Dyke. He knows the firm is looking for him, wants to bring him back home. Or bury him in a shallow grave. He knew I was coming. Waited for me and took his best shot.

But no, that guy was too big. Too strong. Van Dyke's a milquetoast, from what I hear. Skinny guy with glasses. Doesn't want to get his hands dirty. He's the type of guy who'd pay someone else to do his dirty work.

There's a lot of people like that.

Aspirin. Water. Shower.

Horvath gets dressed, takes the elevator down, leaves through the back door.

He walks east until he finds a new place to eat. Grecian Corner, a diner the size of a toll booth. He has a club sandwich, French fries and coffee.

Calls Lana at the bar. Plans to meet her bright and early the next day.

Stops at a drugstore for bandages and medical tape.

Goes back to the Executive, reads for a while, and drifts off to sleep.

IN THE MORNING, he feels pretty good. Whatever the doctor jabbed into his arm, it did the trick.

He gets dressed, looks at himself in the mirror.

Yesterday, his face was smooth and clean. Today, it's a mess. Scars and wrinkles wind across his skin like interstate highways on a road map. Bruises, cuts, scratches. Worry etched deep into the flesh.

I'm getting too old for this.

Horvath's running out of clean clothes. He grabs a suit and two shirts for the dry cleaner. The suit he wore yesterday is covered in blood. It lies on the floor in a crumpled mess, like a dead body. It'll have to be tossed in the bin.

Downstairs, he looks at Gilbert, who nods faintly.

Walks through the front door, heads for the dry cleaner.

The sun is assaulting him, all over again.

He drops off his clothes.

Afterward, he stops at a five and dime. Cigarettes, candy bar, dark sunglasses. Paperback, small enough to sleep in his coat pocket. Another jar of aspirin, just in case.

Back to the Greeks for breakfast.

Feels like trying something new. Grapefruit juice. Hotcakes.

Bacon. Crispy toast. And a side of grits. He doesn't know what they are, but he's always wanted to try them.

The coffee's strong and hot. Add that to the nicotine, and it's a sharp jab to the solar plexus. Not even Fang's doctor has such good medicine.

I can take on the world now, he thinks. All by myself. I'll find Van Dyke, maybe even that Kovacs character. Go ahead and shoot me up all you want. Take your best shot.

The waitress brings his meal. He digs in.

The food is good and he feels happy. Happy to be alive, happy to have a full stomach and, though he doesn't completely understand it, almost trembling with excitement. He hasn't seen Lana in a few days.

The grits are okay. Greasy, rich, fatty. Not bad on a bed of crisp toast. He probably won't order them again, but not bad. The rest is perfect. Those Greeks really know how to make American food.

Man walks through the door. Too fast, nervous eyes. Avoids looking at Horvath.

A few bites left, and half a cup of joe. He stamps out his cigarette in the cheap metal ashtray.

The man walks toward the counter, stopping when he gets close to Horvath. His eyebrows twitch as he reaches inside his coat.

Horvath's gripping the table, ready to duck or stand.

A red carnation blooms on the man's chest. He must be a magician because Horvath didn't see the boutonniere when he walked in.

But it's not a flower, of course. It's a bullet hole. Outside, an engine revs and tires spin on the blacktop.

The man collapses onto Horvath's table. The juice glass and a small white plate smash to the floor.

The place is quiet, for a moment or two, before a waitress screams and a man walks his wife out the front door.

The cook looks over, spatula in hand. He scratches himself, takes a puff on the cigarette hanging from the corner of his mouth, and ashes onto a bread plate.

Horvath opens the man's jacket to see what's in there. No gun, no blade. Was he reaching for his wallet? Pack of smokes? Breath mints? Before he can search his pockets, the body rolls onto the floor.

He looks down. Blood and grits on the checkered tiles.

The cook reaches for a telephone.

He looks across the room at a small hole in the window and broken glass scattered across the table.

The screaming waitress collapses onto the floor. *Why'd I ever move to this crummy place?* she asks herself.

An older waitress walks over, refills his coffee. She's Greek, probably married to the cook. "Want me to clean up this mess?"

"You should probably leave it for the cops."

"I meant the plates, smartass."

He grins. "Oh, sure. I'm finished."

There are a few drops of blood on the counter. Horvath wipes them up with a napkin. He chugs the coffee, leaves a few dollars under the juice glass, steps carefully over the body, and leaves.

Outside, Horvath looks down at his suit. No bloodstains.

He smiles. It's his lucky day.

ON THE WAY to Frank's he tries to put the pieces together.

First, who's the stiff? Second, why was he killed?

Third, was the bullet meant for me? Maybe it was just bad luck. Poor sap stepped in front of a bullet that had my name on it.

And who shot him? Was it the same guy who shot me the other night, or was it somebody new? What does all this have to do with Van Dyke? And Kovacs? Or is it just one of Jaworski's men reminding me to get out of town?

Maybe it's got nothing to do with me. Maybe it's just a coincidence.

Fat chance.

Horvath sees the dead man's face. The hole in his chest. Blood wriggling out like an earthworm. The still pool of his eyes. Body dropping to the floor like a sack of potatoes. The more he sees, the less he knows. Dead men tell no tales, it's true. In fact, they don't say anything at all.

WHEN HE WALKS through the door of the bar, she's sitting there in her usual place. Cup of coffee at her side. Legs crossed, green dress riding up her leg. Her hair's down today. She's done something different with it, but he's not sure what.

His heart's beating fast and he can't stop the smile from spreading across his face like blood pooling under a dead body. What the hell's wrong with me? It's like I'm 16 again. Get a hold of yourself, man.

She's looking down at a ledger with little glasses perched on the end of her nose. When she sees Horvath, she takes them off quickly and shoves them in her handbag. This just makes him like her even more.

"Pretend you didn't see me like that, okay?"

"*Boys don't make passes at girls who wear glasses?*"

"Something like that."

"But you look even more gorgeous with them on."

"I'll bet." She takes a sip of coffee. "So what do you know?"

"Not much." He sits next to her. "But I've had a busy morning."

The bartender brings over a cup, saucer, and a fresh pot.

He massages his neck.

"You okay?" When Lana touches his elbow, electricity runs up and down his arm. If she kissed him, he'd probably faint.

"Yeah, fine. Just a little sore."

Horvath tells her about breakfast, the building on Cantrell, DiLorenzo, the racetrack, Fang and the doctor.

Lana doesn't say much, at first. In fact, she acts as if she's barely listening. She finishes her coffee, eyes Horvath, and signals to the bartender, who takes her ledger and stashes it under the counter. "Fang, huh? Sounds like a real maneater."

He laughs. "She's one tough broad."

"Should I be worried?"

He thinks about it for a few seconds. "Well, she's about 80, maybe older. So no, you've got nothing to worry about."

"Yeah, well maybe that's your type. What do I know?"

"Good point."

She leans over and kisses him on the mouth.

"Want to take a drive out to the country?" he asks. "Play the ponies?"

"Sure."

"You got a car?"

"58 Thunderbird. You man enough to let a woman drive?"

"Long as she has a license."

"I do, and my picture's not half bad. Find anything new on Kovacs?"

"No, sorry."

"That's okay. I owe you, though. Three days plus expenses." She takes a roll of dough out of her purse.

He puts his hands up, leans back. "I can't take your money."

"Why not?"

Because it feels wrong. Because McGrath wouldn't approve. Because we're an item, or getting there. "Because I haven't gotten anywhere, and I don't even have a lead. Anyway, I've been working my own case most of the time. Haven't had time for yours. And lately, I haven't been working much at all. Just been getting knocked around and sleeping it off."

She nods, puts the money away. "Well, what if I want to buy you a beer and a couple hot dogs at the track?"

"I could live with that."

She kisses him again. This time, he pulls her close and gives her lips a good workout.

After a few minutes, she comes up for air. "Slow down, tiger. You'll pull a muscle."

"I just wanted you to know I was here." He touches her arm, softly.

"You're sweet, you know that?"

"I have my moments."

She takes out a small mirror, checks her lipstick, adjusts her hair. "So what's the plan? At the track, I mean. What are we looking for?"

"I don't know."

"But we'll know it when we see it, huh?"

"Maybe not."

"Sounds like you've got it all worked out."

"Yep, every detail." He sips the coffee. "We'll keep a low profile. No use use asking questions. No one talks in this town. Just keep your eyes and ears open, see what happens." He pops the lid on the aspirin and tips a few into his mouth.

"Go easy on those things, big boy. You don't want to get hooked."

"Too late for that."

"Well, maybe the country air will sort you out."

"Maybe."

"Give me a few minutes," she says. "Then we can go."

"Sure, take your time."

Lana gets up, walks to the back. Horvath can't take his eyes off her. Even on a stake-out he's not this vigilant. Everything she does is so poised, elegant and charming. Even the way she turns to the side when someone passes by in a narrow space. He watches her go around the bar and down the hallway toward her office.

He finishes the coffee, wipes his mouth with a napkin, walks off to the men's room.

As he passes by her office he slows down and, just for a moment, and puts his ear to the door. Not a sound. There's nothing wrong with love, if that's what this is, but you still have to be careful.

SHE TIES a scarf around her hair, puts the top down, starts the car, and crawls through the city. It's not easy walking all over town with bruises up and down your body and a finger-sized hole in your arm. For once, he's glad to be driving.

Once they pass over the bridge and onto the open road, she works through the gears and makes the Thunderbird earn its keep. He looks over at Lana. A little fast, but she knows what she's doing. The engine growls and the tires kiss the black pavement.

There are factories and storehouses on the edge of town, but they quickly disappear. The houses and shops spread out, give each other room to breathe. No more tenements, bars, restaurants or poolhalls.

The countryside comes quickly.

Trees, wooden fences, farmland, grassy fields, hay rolled up in fat bales.

Water tower, silo, rolling hills, a creek winding through the valley.

Nice big house sitting all by itself on a hilltop. It's got a white porch, a rocking chair and everything.

Cows, a woman on horseback riding parallel to the road.

Clouds, meadows, black birds and wildflowers.

He looks up at the sky. Out here, away from the smog and filth, away from the shadows of hulking factories, the sky is blue and the clouds are white. He forgets that sometimes.

They don't speak.

The drive is longer than Fang said. Horvath wonders if she's ever been outside the city limits.

The billboards let them know that the Sunday drive is almost over.

Gas, food, lodging.

The racetrack is two miles on the left.

Lana slows down, takes the exit, merges onto the smaller roads.

They drive through a hick town toward the races. Horvath is always amazed at how different things are once you get a few miles outside the city. The way people talk, and walk, and dress. The kids are well behaved and people stop to chat with strangers. No one locks their doors. Everyone's got a big smile. The streets are neat and clean, and people look so calm and happy. Something about it makes him nervous.

She pulls into the parking lot and finds a space.

"Ready?" she asks.

"More or less."

"Any sign of Jaworski in the past few days?"

"Not unless you count the gunplay."

"Do you think he knows you're still in town?"

"I don't think so. Haven't seen any of his men following me around."

"Well, maybe they're just good at not being seen. That's the whole point of tailing somebody, isn't it?"

She's right, but Horvath's too busy thinking to put any of his thoughts into words.

23

LONGSHOT

THEY WALK THROUGH THE FRONT DOORS, UP A RAMP, AND INTO THE concourse. It's early, so the place is relatively quiet and peaceful, like a church where they worship money.

Like a regular church, in other words.

Horvath buys a racing form from a kid standing behind a makeshift wooden counter. He tips him a dime.

"Thanks, mister."

"Don't mention it."

"Where do you want to sit?" she asks. "Grandstand?"

"Too much trouble. The walk to the bar, bathroom and betting window's too far."

"All the important B's, huh?"

"You catch on quick. I like to stand outside, by the rail."

"Better view that way."

"The view from here's pretty good, too." He touches the small of her back and guides her through the glass doors.

Outside, an old wino in a stained suit and crumpled hat stumbles around, or maybe he's dancing with an invisible partner.

"Little early, isn't it?" Lana asks.

"Not for him, apparently." He points to an empty bench, a few feet back from the rail. "I would've thought you ran into a lot of morning drunks in your line of work."

"Not at Frank's. I run a respectable joint."

"Oh, do you now? Hey, I've been meaning to ask, who's Frank?"

"No one. It's just a name."

He takes a seat on the bench. She wipes it with a handkerchief before sitting down.

The ground is covered with old newspapers, losing tickets, heartache and broken dreams.

He studies the form.

"You an expert?" she asks.

"I know a thing or two."

"Oh yeah, like what?"

"Like don't bet more than you're willing to lose. And there aren't any real winners here, except for the house. You know what vig is?"

"No, what?"

"It's the juice, the money they take off the top. It comes out of your winnings."

"So even if you win, you lose?"

"Exactly. Bookies take a cut, loan sharks, the track, all of them. Even banks, but they call it interest. You can't do anything in life without somebody taking a piece of the action."

"Sounds like you know your way around a track."

"Just enough not to lose my shirt."

"What's your system?"

"I only do straight bets. One horse to win, nothing fancy. No hedging my bets. And I don't bet on the favorite. That's for suckers."

"How's that?"

"Let's say you put $5 win on the six horse, a heavy favorite at 1/9. Your payout's only going to be about $5.50. Chump change."

"So you should go for a longshot, right?"

"Well, they're called longshots for a reason. They rarely win."

"So what do you do?"

"I look at the horses with the second through fifth best odds. See what it says about them in the form. How long the race is, the track conditions, who the jockeys are. Couple other factors. Then I wait until a few minutes before post-time. Look at the board and see if the odds are changing."

"Why do you do that?"

"The real gamblers, the pros, they don't bet unless they've got a hot tip. Maybe the race is fixed and they know it, or they've got some kind of inside information. They wait until the last second to place their bets, after all the suckers have gone. If I see big money going on a horse right before post, that's who I bet on."

"Sounds like a good system. Does it work?"

"Hardly ever."

She laughs, with her head back and her mouth wide open. Horvath wants to hold her and never let go.

"I do bet on a longshot sometimes. Couple dollars on a 60/1, 70/1... If the horse comes in at those odds, you walk out of here with a lot of cash."

"Maybe today's your lucky day."

"Yeah, maybe." He checks his watch. "First race is coming up soon. I better start reading the form."

"Go ahead, professor. I'll be in the ladies room."

"Don't you want to take a look?"

"I've got my own system."

He watches her walk away, which is even better than the racing form.

The racetrack is getting crowded, and noisy. Horvath can feel the life, the energy, the excitement. He looks around. Their eyes are filled with hope, expectation, joy. Hats at rakish angles. Shaking hands, slapping backs, laughing. Mouths are practically watering. In a few hours they'll be half-drunk, broke, angry and bitter. He knows that. But for now he feels good because they feel good.

The loudspeaker crackles. Five minutes to post.

He studies the board. The three horse looks good. It's moved from 4/1 to 2/9.

Horvath goes to the window, places his bet, goes back outside.

His bench is taken. An old lady with a bagful of yarn and knitting in her lap. Something for one of her cats, he guesses.

Lana's standing by the rail, watching the ponies line up.

He stands next to her. "Place your bet?"

"Course. What do you think I'm doing here?"

"What's your system?"

"I pick the rider with the best-looking silks."

"That's as good a system as any."

They're off. A hundred voices scream, a hundred bodies lean forward and press against the rail.

Two minutes later it's over.

Tickets carpet the ground. Everyone walks off, heads down, quiet. The people look smaller now, and empty, like balloons with a slow leak. A few people cheer and hug, but the losers avoid looking at them. The big winners don't say a word. They wait until later to cash in, and don't draw attention to themselves. You don't want someone following you back to the car with a long knife and empty pockets.

He pulls the form out of his coat pocket. "Round two."

Lana's smiling.

"What are you so happy about?" he asks.

"My horse won."

"Must be your system, or color scheme, whatever you call it. How much did you bet?"

"Just a few dollars, but it was 5/1."

"Not bad."

"Hot dogs are on me."

"Throw in a couple beers and you've got a deal."

"Thought it was too early for you?"

"A beer or two won't hurt, but it's a little early to foxtrot with an imaginary woman."

"Lucky for you I'm not imaginary."

The way she smiles at him is even better than how she looks, better than her hands on his arm, her lips on his. Where is this going? he asks himself. It feels good, sure, but watch yourself. You don't need any complications.

They order two beers and two dogs at the snack bar, walk them over to one of the tall round tables scattered throughout the concourse.

"No seats?" she asks.

"This ain't the Ritz, honey."

"Guess not."

They eat and drink standing up. For dessert, they both light up and smoke.

"Time to have a look around?" she asks.

"Almost forgot this was a business trip."

"What's the guy's name, DiLorenzo?"

"Yeah. This is his clubhouse, from what Fang tells me."

"Fang again. The other woman..."

"You're the only woman in my life."

"I better be. So what's the plan?"

"Place our bets, watch another couple races, then see what happens. Maybe have a look in the grandstand, or over by the stables. We'll play it by ear."

She nods, tips her ash.

Horvath looks across the room at the bar. A fat man chewing a big cigar is laughing too loud. Couple of working girls are sizing him up. One's already got her hands on his knee, eyes on his wallet. Their pimp is standing a few feet away, trying to look inconspicuous. Someone's getting rolled tonight.

Lana follows his eyeline. "I thought people were different out here in the country? Good Christians who followed the golden rule, the 10 Commandments, and all that?"

"Yeah, I thought so too. But I guess people are the same all over. Around here, they just speak more slowly and know how to skin a deer."

AN HOUR LATER, he's sick of losing and tired of reading the form.

"C'mon." He takes Lana by the arm and steers her around all the rubes standing in front of the betting windows. "Time to work."

They go outside, turn left, make their way to the end of the rail. The track is to their right and the paddock is straight ahead. Horses, grooms, jockeys, trainers. They're all here, in a small grassy field, preparing for the next race. The horses are moving around, stretching, getting ready to run. There's a wooden fence around the paddock. The men are talking strategy, odds, making plans for the evening. Gamblers eye the horses.

The sixth race is coming up and the crowd has started to thin out. It's always the same, this time of day. The excitement has died down. Money's running out. Beer and whiskey are bedtime stories that have made everyone a little sleepy.

They stand in front of the rail, along with a dozen people gawking at the horses.

"What are we looking for?" she asks.

"Anything suspicious. If the horse looks doped up, or the rider. Jockey's tired, hungover, smiling too much, seems like he's had a few."

"That happens?"

"These guys really like to tie one on."

"Learn something new every day."

A two-year-old turns around, whinnies, takes a crap a few feet away from Lana.

"There's that, too. Now he'll run faster. Not carrying as much weight. The good money's on him."

"It's a filly, Horvath."

"Oh, right." He gets a better look. "Thought you didn't know anything about horses."

"I know the difference between a male and a female."

"Okay, well, *she* should run faster now."

"Thanks for the tip, but we're working here, not making bets."

"You've got a pretty sharp tongue, lady."

"And you like it."

He's got a comeback, but decides to keep it to himself. Instead, he leans over and whispers. "This is where all the big shots hang out. Guys who own the horses, high rollers, organized crime bosses, all the men who run this town."

"We're not in town anymore, remember?"

"These guys run the whole state."

Lana considers this. "You should be careful then. Jaworski might see you."

"Not a problem. I brought sunglasses."

"Anyone ever say you were a genius?"

"No."

"Big surprise. Look, I need to call the bar, check in. I'll be a little while."

"Take your time."

"Should I pick up a few beers on the way back?"

"Well, I'm not going to say that's a dumb question, but a cold one is always nice."

"Now who's got the sharp tongue." She pinches his cheek, then caresses it.

Horvath leans on the rail, looks around. He doesn't see anyone he recognizes, or anything suspicious. No Jaworski, no thick-necks. No one with a telltale bulge under his jacket.

What he does see are fat men wearing expensive suits, pointy shoes and self-satisfied grins. They've got young women on their arms. Too young. And they're surrounded by yes-men. Three-four guys usually, with greasy smiles and short tempers. Laughing at the fat man's every word, telling him what he wants to hear.

And then Horvath sees him. One of the guys from the gym. The taller one, who first mentioned Jaworski, a night out with young girls and boys. *Anything goes.*

He wishes he had that beer, to wash the rotten taste out of his mouth.

Now he sees the other guy, his partner. Couple of no-account wise guys, but they might lead him somewhere.

Horvath takes the sunglasses out of his pocket and puts them on. Not much of a disguise, but it's better than nothing.

He looks around, bends down, quickly steps under the rail.

A man turns and looks at him so Horvath lifts his chin, smiles and waves to someone across the paddock.

He gets closer to the two men, but with a horse in-between so they can't get a good look at him. A jockey's standing there, holding his crop. He's talking to a trainer, who's brushing the horse and telling a dirty joke about a donkey and an exotic dancer from Juarez.

Horvath holds up the form and pretends to read it. He looks over the horse at the two wise guys. They're smoking, checking their watches. Waiting for someone. A few seconds later, a big guy comes over. He doesn't say anything, or smile, but he indicates with a faint nod that they should follow him.

It's Marco, Jaworski's giant goon.

They're moving away from Horvath.

He follows, head down, walking off to the side.

They join a group of older men.

One of them looks familiar, but he can't place him. The short one's in charge. He can tell because everyone looks at him and listens whenever he opens his mouth. He's talking to the two men from the gym. He hands the taller one a business card.

Horvath stops next to a couple gamblers in white suits and loud ties.

Too far away. He walks along the rail toward a group of laughing women. He stands behind them, face hidden in the racing form.

Marco looks around the paddock with small hard eyes.

He turns his back to the men and moves a few feet closer until he can hear what they're saying.

Friday night. Party. Important business.

He'll be there.

Mayor's townhouse. 9:00.

He turns to get a better look at the man who's speaking. It's Peters, the Chief of Police. He saw his picture in the paper the other day. Apparently, he's cracking down on crime. Horvath wonders if his English isn't as good as it used to be. *Crack down* means *stop*, doesn't it? Or does it mean *aid and abet* these days? So hard to tell. Words are as slippery as people and twice as devious.

Marco's looking over at him, so he turns to one of the women and asks what time it is. He laughs, like she said something funny, and moves a step closer to her. Satisfied, Marco turns away.

The women give him a dirty look but they don't say anything.

Two plainclothes cops stroll across the paddock and stand behind Peters. A minute later, he leaves with them. Marco waddles off on his own, and the little party breaks up.

Horvath slips back under the rail. The mayor and the police? He's no boy scout, but dirty cops really get his goat. They're supposed to serve and protect, but most of the time they're just like everybody else. Taking their cut and looking out for themselves. You can't trust anyone.

Horvath checks his watch.

A few minutes later, Lana comes back with two cold beers.

"Took you long enough," he says.

"You timing me?"

"I just missed you, that's all."

She smiles, hands him the drink. "Well, I told you I'd be a while. And I had to put my face on."

"You don't look any different to me."

"That's because I know what I'm doing. Clowns like to slather make-up all over their faces, so you know it's there." She takes a sip. "But not women."

"I'll keep that in mind."

"You do that." Lana gives him a ironic smile. "So, you see anything worth talking about?"

"Not yet."

24

THE AUTOMAT

HE SHAKES THE RAIN FROM HIS HAT AND WALKS INSIDE.

The public library.

He needs to know where the mayor lives and what the layout's like. Address, cross streets, alleys, adjoining buildings, rooftop access. If he finds a set of blueprints, all the better. He could try asking someone, but most of the people around here are too scared to talk. And word keeps getting back to the bad guys. He needs to keep quiet, so no one finds out what he's looking for.

The reference section. Looks pretty well stocked, even for a rinky-dink library in a mid-sized town. He's got to hand it to the city fathers. Libraries are great institutions. Thousands of books and loads of information, all for free.

He flips through the card catalogue.

A tall leggy redhead walks by, stack of books pressed against her chest.

He can't help but notice, and stare. These places are even better than I thought.

She flirts with her eyes, crosses the room. "Can I help you with anything, sir?"

"You the librarian?"

"One of them." She flips her long straight hair over her shoulder. "You don't look like our usual customer."

"No? I'll take that as a compliment."

She smiles, looks down, sets her books on the scarred wooden table. "So what are you doing here?"

"Just looking something up."

"Need any help?"

"No, I should really do it myself."

"Too bad. I'd love to help."

She's young, he thinks. Too young. And she's got bad taste in men. She needs someone with a car and a steady job.

"What do you do?" she asks.

"Cause trouble, mostly."

"I'll bet." She inspects her fingernails, like there's a clue hidden under there.

He doesn't bite, so she picks up her books.

Horvath goes back to the card catalogue.

"Well, if you need anything, I'll be over there." She points to the reference desk, smiles, walks away.

He pulls the mayor's card from the catalogue.

The guy hasn't written any books, but he's in the Subject file under Childers, William.

Childers? Rings a bell.

It's the name of the guy who runs Smith's Tavern. Horvath could tell, soon as he walked in, that the place was shady. Coincidence? Not likely. Probably the mayor's brother, or maybe one of his cousins.

Mayor Childers has been mentioned in local and regional newspapers hundreds of times. Twice in national magazines. There's also one hit for a book. James McAfee, assistant professor at the state college, wrote a history of Franklin County.

Horvath takes notes, gathers his material, and starts reading.

He opens the book first. The city's been around since colonial times and it lies in the dead center of Franklin County. Childers has two lines in the index, but when he turns to the relevant pages he doesn't learn much. As far as history's concerned, the guy's nothing but a footnote.

The periodicals are more useful.

William A. Childers, the city's 14th mayor. This is his third term in office. He graduated from Vanderbilt University, where he played shortstop for the baseball team. He's married with two children, one of each. His friends call him Bill. He enjoys fishing and numismatics.

That's coin collecting, right? Is that a cute way of saying he's a graft enthusiast?

Every year or two, there's a corruption scandal. The mayor denies any and all involvement or knowledge of the alleged crimes. In the end, not much comes of the allegations. The evidence is weak, circumstantial, or it disappears. So do the witnesses. If the public needs a scapegoat, somebody gets fired. End of story.

The street address is easy to find. It's right there in the phone book.

He finds a large map of the city, spreads it out on the table, and studies the neighborhood.

Mayor Childers lives in a four-story brownstone over on the west side. It's a polite and safe part of town. Trees, parks, nice shops, the whole nine yards. No drunks wobbling around on the street corner. No pawn shops, bond bailsmen or tattoo parlors. The men tip their hats when a lady walks by.

Horvath can't find any blueprints, and he doesn't want to ask. Might have to call the City Architect, or whatever he's called, for something like that, and Jaworski probably has him on the payroll. Too dangerous.

But he still wants to get into that house. He needs to. Everything points to Childers. Jaworski and his goons, dirty cops, a seedy bar, DiLorenzo and the racetrack. Scandals that come around every year, like the flu. So far, not much has added up, but this does. His townhouse is where the answers are, he's sure of it. That's what his gut's telling him and his gut's never wrong, except for all the times when it is.

I'll have to play it by ear. Show up early, see who's going into the party, find a way in.

He puts everything away, nice and neat. Like McGrath always says. Cover your tracks. Leave no clues behind. They should never know you were there.

Horvath grabs a few books at random and scatters them on the table he was using. That'll throw them off, he thinks. In case I've been followed and someone comes snooping around. They'll never know what I was looking for.

On the way out, he sees her behind the counter, stamping a date in purple ink on one of those index cards. Then she stuffs the card into its little sleeping bag inside the back cover of the book. She does her work well, without even looking. Her eyes are watching him instead.

She puts the date stamp down, bites the nail of her little finger.

He nods with a blank face and walks outside. No use encouraging her.

It's still raining. Harder now, like he's being strafed with bullets.

Two kids in raincoats and rubber boots walk home from school, holding hands.

A dog hides under an Oldsmobile and whimpers, like somebody's beating it.

There's an automat down the block. He heads there and steps inside for something to eat, and to keep dry.

He gets in line, grabs a tray, and shuffles along with everyone else.

The room is large, quiet and fairly empty, which makes him think of the library down the street. The customers are mostly single men eating a meal in silence, or hunched over a cup of coffee. Working men, for the most part, or guys who used to work and haven't gotten around to it in a while. A few of them wear neckties and clean white shirts, but Mayor Childers and his crowd wouldn't be caught dead in a place like this. They probably go to one of the big hotels for lobster and champagne.

He stops in front of the coffee machine, puts in a dime and a nickel, opens the cabinet, and takes his drink.

After this, he keeps moving. The sandwich locker doesn't look very promising, but he drops in a few coins and grabs a ham on rye.

Horvath finds an unoccupied table. He takes off his coat, drapes it over a chair, sits down.

There's hardly any conversation, except when someone asks the clerk for change. And then its all whispers. No one laughs here, but sometimes a chair leg screeches against the slick floor. This isn't a library, he thinks. It's a funeral parlor.

The sandwich is dry and tasteless, but it beats starving. Barely. The coffee is hot and strong, so that's something. Next time, he'll eat in a bar or pick up something from a deli.

He thinks about the mayor and his party. All the important players will be there. Maybe even Gilroy, Jaworski's boss. He runs the syndicate, but no one ever sees him. Likes to keep his hands clean. He's got hundreds of foot soldiers to do his work for him, and he likes to keep out of the spotlight. But he just might show up for a party, especially if they've got business to discuss.

He still isn't sure what Van Dyke has to do with any of this. Or Kovacs. But one thing's for sure. If you're into anything dirty around here, the syndicate's involved. One way or another. So that's where he needs to look for clues.

When he finishes the coffee and sandwich, he has a smoke, and then one more. He doesn't think too hard about everything he knows, but just lets the facts roll through his mind like a set of early-morning waves at the shore.

Time to go. He stamps out his cigarette in the empty mug, gets up, puts his raincoat on.

Outside, the rain has stopped and sunlight is stepping out from the shadows.

A car backfires and a woman locks the front door of a duplex.

Two men argue on the corner, with inflated chests and insistent forefingers.

He walks back to the hotel.

· · ·

THE PROBLEM, in a swank neighborhood like this, is there's no place to sit and wait.

No café, no bar, no newsstand or bodega. You can't just stand around on the corner and have a smoke or take a few slugs from a brown paper bag. You can't stand around at all, unless you're a doorman or some rich guy wearing a top hat and tails. Anyone lurking on the street will arouse suspicion. Before you know it, the police will be in your face asking a lot of nosy questions. Or if it's not them, some private muscle.

He has a few days before the party, so Horvath stakes out the neighborhood. There aren't too many options. Pretend to be a street cleaner or a delivery man. Set up a shoeshine stand on the corner. He can't come up with a good plan, and he doesn't spend any time with Lana. Mostly he just lies in bed, stares at the ceiling, and has a good long think.

On Thursday, he enters an apartment building across the street from the mayor's townhouse. It isn't as classy as the other buildings on the block. Not much of a lobby, and no doorman.

There's a small counter of polished wood, but no one's standing behind it waiting to help the residents.

There's a hallway to the right of the elevators. He takes it to the end.

On his left, two steps down, a small alcove. There's noise coming from behind a locked door. Manager's Office.

As soon as he knocks, the voices and laughter stop.

A few seconds later, someone opens the door six inches and looks out. "Yeah, what do you want?"

"I'm looking for Tony," Horvath says. "You guys seen him around?"

"There ain't no Tony around here. Now get lost."

There were at least three guys inside the room, sitting around a desk playing cards. It was mid-afternoon, but they were already drinking pretty hard.

Horvath comes back a few hours later.

This time, it's quiet. The door is halfway open so he walks up, clears his throat, and steps inside.

A swarthy man sits behind a cluttered desk. He looks like he hasn't slept in a while, at least not very well. He could use a shave and a clean shirt.

"What do you want? Hey, aren't you the guy from before?"

Horvath nods. "I need a room."

"For how long?"

"Just one night."

"We only rent by the month, fella."

"I'll make it worth your while." Horvath drops a few bills on the desk.

"This is a respectable joint."

"Yeah, I can see that."

"What are you going to be doing up there?"

"Just keeping an eye on someone."

"You a private eye?"

"Something like that."

"You carry a piece?"

"No."

The building manager sizes him up, decides it's worth the risk. He lost his shirt playing poker so he could use a few extra bucks. "No girls, no booze, no drugs. Nothing like that."

"Not a problem."

"Don't make any noise up there, and leave everything just the way you found it."

"I'll be quiet as a church mouse."

"Good, so what's your name?"

"Tom. Tom Lassiter."

"Alright, Tom. Now look, wear a suit and tie, don't talk to people in the building, and don't mention our little deal to anyone."

"Will do."

They shake hands, and Horvath leaves.

．　．　．

So that's where he is on Friday night. Second-floor apartment across the street from the mayor's house. pair of binoculars in his hand.

9:00 comes and goes, but so far no one's shown up.

Two valets stand around in black pants, white shirts, burgundy jackets, and little white gloves, waiting to park cars. They've cleared out all the spaces in front of the building, but that's just so the drivers have somewhere to pull over and drop off the guests.

Horvath wonders where they'll take the cars. Not much parking around here. Maybe the mayor owns a lot nearby. Or Gilroy's letting him use one of his.

He sits on the window ledge with a fresh pack of smokes and a steaming cup of coffee from a bodega. He takes a sip, puts down the paper cup. Picks up the cigarettes, slowly removes the cellophane.

Coffee, smokes...If I didn't have them around, I wouldn't have any friends at all. He laughs, but wonders how much of a joke it really is. He tries to recall the last time he had a friend, a real friend. He thinks of McGrath, who's almost 20 years older than Horvath and more like a father. He wonders how much time you have to spend on the road, by yourself, before you lose your mind.

He lights up and forgets all about his problems. That's what cigarettes are for.

9:12. He looks through the binoculars again.

A long black car pulls over to the curb, and a tall man with thick gray hair steps out. He bends down and offers his hand to a woman with a fur stole and a little crown in her hair. Must be the Queen of England.

A few minutes later the street's blocked, like an artery clogged with fat. Everyone's showing up at the same time, as if responding to some unspoken signal.

Here they come, all the swells and toffs. The men wear tuxedos and the women have wrestled themselves into evening dresses and heavy jewelry. He can practically hear the gemstones rattle. Everyone's dressed to the nines; some of them might even be in double digits.

The street's choked with cars and the sidewalk is screaming with bodies.

There are more valets now, and an older man to supervise them.

By 9:30 the scrum has cleared.

The guests are inside, and most of the valets have disappeared. They're probably out back somewhere, shooting craps or sharing a bottle.

Nothing happens between 9:36 and 9:50.

At 9:51 a black Lincoln drives slowly down the block, almost misses the townhouse, then stops. The driver backs up and parallel parks.

Two men get out of the back seat, one on each side. They look around, button their jackets.

Horvath adjusts the focus and presses closer to the windowpane.

Marco and Nicky. He'd recognize those overgrown toddlers anywhere. Revolvers bulging out of their suitcoats. That's not the way you're supposed to play it. Stupid and indiscreet. With those big swollen lumps under their clothes, everyone knows how tough they are. But tough guys don't need heat. McGrath taught him that.

A few seconds later, Jaworski gets out of the car.

He leans down, talking to someone who's still inside the Lincoln.

A small, neat man steps out onto the sidewalk. He's very slender with pale gray skin and not much hair. Jaworski says something to him and the man looks angry. Jaworski stares at his feet.

Must be Gilroy, he thinks. The man in charge.

Everyone else is in black, but he's wearing a fitted dark blue suit and thin blue tie. He looks nervous and uncomfortable, like a kid about to have his school picture taken. He isn't used to appearing in public, and he doesn't like it much.

Horvath waits until 10:15 before leaving the apartment and taking the back stairs down to the first floor.

He drops the key off with the manager, who's pleased as punch. *I made a little scratch*, the manager thinks. *And there weren't any problems from that Lassiter guy.* He lights a cigar, leans back in his chair, and smiles because he's the smartest guy around.

Horvath walks through the revolving door, stops and turns right.

He goes to the end of the block, crosses the street, turns left, and slowly approaches the mayor's townhouse.

There are no cars pulling up, dropping off, or idling at the curb. The valets have gone off somewhere and all the guests are inside.

The house is set back 20 yards from the street. A knee-high stone wall separates the sidewalk from the mayor's property, with a black metal gate in the middle. Iron lampposts stand on either side of the gate, like bodyguards. Around here, he thinks, even the walls and grass need a little muscle. Not a bad idea.

It's a red brick house, four stories plus a basement. Flat roof, bay windows, two modest columns flanking the front door. The place is plenty old, but still in good shape. Real class. Horvath wonders how many houses the mayor has, and how often he stays here in town.

He opens the gate and walks through. He doesn't have much of a plan, but he knows one thing for sure—he needs to get inside. That's where the answers are.

There's thick green grass on either side and a brick walkway down the middle. It takes money to have a lawn this good and people to care for it.

Flower garden, maple trees, birdbath, ivy climbing the brick walls. It doesn't feel like the city.

The drapes are closed but plenty of light is sneaking out.

There's no way he's going through the front door.

He walks across the grass, under the shadow of an oak tree, and around the side of the building. There's no door here, though, and the windows are shut tight. There's a thick hedgerow around the backyard, with space to walk through. He edges around the side of the house and peeks around the corner. The valets are standing in a tight circle, smoking and talking. There's no way he could get past them.

He goes around the other side of the townhouse. The setup's exactly the same—no doors, locked windows, hedgerow sealing off the backyard. A rake leans against the building and a wheelbarrow, scarred with concrete, is parked next to it.

It's dark but his eyes are adjusting. There's a black railing next to the brick wall, behind a row of shrubs. No one's watching. He walks quickly across the lawn and through a rock garden with bonsai trees and a green Chinese lantern. He has to duck and turn sideways to make it through the shrubbery.

The iron railing surrounds a concrete staircase. Four steps down with a drain at the bottom and a heavy door.

The door's locked. He looks through the window, but it's too dark to see anything.

He walks back up the stairs, looks around the side of the building. Valets are still there. Someone from the kitchen, too, wearing a stained white apron. He's telling a long, complicated story and everyone's listening.

A young man stands by himself at the edge of the property, staring over a tall wooden fence.

Horvath thinks about it for a minute, takes a deep breath, and walks through the opening in the hedge.

Someone looks his way, but no one turns around or says anything.

He decides to play it cool. If you act like you know what you're doing, people believe you. If you act nervous, they get nervous too.

He doesn't say anything to the valets but heads straight for the back door.

He walks up the brick staircase, opens the door, and goes in.

The kitchen. A dozen people are busy chopping vegetables, carrying trays, wiping sweat off their faces, yelling at each other, worrying skillets, looking into ovens and under pot lids. No one pays attention to the man in a gray suit.

He smells cinnamon, garlic, lemon.

Petit fours are stacked on a silver platter on top of a white doily.

There's a door to his left. He smiles and touches the knob.

"Excuse me?"

It's a question, not a statement, and that's what worries Horvath. He turns around. "Yeah?"

A man in a dark suit is standing there. White shirt, pristine spit-shined shoes, yellow tie, pink flower in his buttonhole.

"Where are you going, sir? Are...you a guest?"

"I'm heading into the party and yes, I'm a friend of Mayor Childers."

"You are?"

"I worked on his last campaign. Joe McDevitt."

"Very good, sir." The man's trying hard to strike the right balance. He needs to be polite but he also has to keep out the reporters and riff-raff. "Stay here for a moment while I check the guest list."

"Of course."

"I'll just be a moment." The man bows slightly and hurries toward a side room.

Horvath turns around and heads for the back door.

Outside, he picks up the pace, walks across the lawn, turns right at the sidewalk, and gets lost in the night.

25

THE MOVING TARGET

AFTER BREAKFAST, HE TRACKS DOWN A NEW PAYPHONE AND CALLS WORK.

Never use the same phone twice in a row.

Don't believe anything people tell you.

When you go out somewhere, come back using a different route.

You don't want people to think you're a thug, so dress like an insurance salesman.

Don't sit with your back to the door.

THE RULES ARE CONSTANTLY REPEATING themselves in his head, but the words move so fast they've nearly lost all meaning. He thinks of the old ladies at 6:00 am Mass draped in black veils, saying the rosary. *OurFatherwhoartinHeavenhallowedbeThyname.* They spit out the words in one long rapid stream as if they're not talking to god but calling an auction.

He dials the number. It rings.

"Yeah?"

It's Lourette, his new contact. He misses Ungerleider.

"I need some cash."

"How bad do you need it?"

"I can manage for a few days."

Horvath is given a date, a time and a place.

That's settled, he thinks. But the mayor's house isn't. I need to get in there.

He decides to case the joint.

The first time he passes by he's wearing a hat. He slows down, stops, and lights a cigarette, keeping an eye on the house. Two men wearing business suits walk in.

He lingers for a moment, crosses the street, keeps walking, ducks into an alley.

The second time he passes the house he's wearing sunglasses and no hat. He slumps his shoulders and moves with a more shuffling gate, to seem like a different person.

A woman comes down the walkway and turns right. Someone on his staff, a housecleaner maybe. Two more guys walk inside. Muscle.

Horvath walks past a few more times, in different variations of glasses, coat and hat, then he hides out in the alley for 20 minutes.

He's going in, somehow.

A cigarette for courage, then he walks to the townhouse, goes through the gate, and around the side of the building, head down. He cuts through the rock garden and goes down the concrete steps.

He listens at the door and looks inside. Nothing.

The door's unlocked. Must be his lucky day. Horvath was prepared to wrap his fist inside his coat and punch his way in.

He opens the door, slips inside, and stands still. The basement is dark and dank. He doesn't sense anyone lurking in the corners.

He flicks on his lighter.

Cobwebs, a boiler, boxes stacked neatly against the wall.

Two broken chairs.

Wooden pillars run from floor to ceiling.

He moves forward slowly, careful not to make any noise.

It's cool but humid down here. The floor and walls are concrete. There are no windows, except for the grimy yellowed glass in the door.

Double sink against the wall to his left. A bar of lye in a metal dish.

A wooden cart next to the sink. Fels-Naptha. Distilled water. Bleach. Old rags. Scouring pad. Steel wool.

There are five or six drains in the floor, spread evenly throughout the room.

Straight ahead, a string hangs from the ceiling next to a single lightbulb.

On the other side of the room he sees a bundle of old newspapers bound in twine. Metal shelving stacked with work gloves, blankets, towels, fertilizer, gardening trowels. A workbench with wrenches, screwdrivers, pliers, sandpaper, hammers, mallets, drill bits, a plane and auger. Washers, nuts and bolts in an old coffee can. Hedge clippers hang from the wall. Everything nice and tidy. The mayor runs a tight ship.

Cans of paint lined up against the wall to his right. Brushes, rollers, drop cloths, paint thinner, shellac. Two five-gallon buckets.

He keeps looking but doesn't see anything suspicious.

I need to find his office, he thinks. Search through the desk.

He hears a sound. The door is creaking open and the weight of a large body makes the staircase groan.

The man stops and says something.

Horvath tiptoes over to the boiler, creeps sideways behind it, and crouches down.

Now two bodies are coming down the staircase.

He sees three large hooks on the wall. A pile of heavy chains curled up on the floor below. Handcuffs resting on top.

This is a dungeon. Or at least a holding cell.

Horvath keeps very still and very quiet.

The men walk down the staircase and stop at the bottom. They start talking, about everything and nothing. Horvath can't see them and he can't hear what they say, not clearly. He closes his eyes and takes long slow breaths.

After a minute, the men move over to the shelves and start picking things up. He can hear the metal clang and ding.

They exchange a few words.

He hears feet shuffling across the concrete floor.

One of the men is at the workbench now. Heavy objects are picked up and put back down.

Silence. Horvath pictures him holding a large hammer or monkey wrench, feeling the weight in his hand.

The men are suddenly quiet. They don't move.

Do they know I'm here? Am I about to be attacked with a claw hammer? His body grows tense, and he's ready to fight. Sweat drips down the side of his face.

A loud stomping echoes through the room.

"You get him?"

"Yeah, fucking cockroach."

He hears a shoe scraping the side of a wooden pillar.

"You ready?"

"Yeah, let's get out of here."

He waits a minute before standing up.

Horvath creeps out from behind the boiler, dusts himself off, wipes the sweat from his forehead. Close call.

He grabs a mallet from the workbench, just in case.

Before heading upstairs, he waits another three minutes.

He looks up the staircase at the closed door, wondering what's waiting for him on the other side. This could be it, he thinks. Early retirement.

It's now or never. He takes one step, to hear how loud and angry the staircase is. He takes another, and another. If he walks carefully, one foot on the far end of each step, they don't have much to say.

At the top of the staircase, he puts his ear to the door. Nothing.

He grabs the knob and turns it, opens the door and steps through.

A long, narrow hallway. He can't hear voices or footsteps.

It's an old house, from the mid-19th century he guesses. Back when they were built to last. Not like these modern places, cheap and flimsy. He looks around. Thick walls, solid construction. Wood, concrete, copper, brass and marble. You can't hear whispers on the other side of a wall, or a child's footsteps through the ceiling.

He walks down the hallway, turns right.

Closets, sitting room. Another hallway.

He turns left.

The corridor empties into an open space. The foyer.

Wide staircase to his left. Short hallway and vestibule by the front door. Rooms off to both sides.

He hears footsteps, and a woman's voice.

Soft laughter, and another voice.

He takes the stairs, quickly. The landing is carpeted and U-shaped. He peaks over the polished wooden banister.

Two women are at the foot of the stairs, holding laundry.

There are six rooms up here. He slips into the first.

It's empty. He leans back against the door, his heart beating so loud he can hardly think.

A guest bedroom, probably. There are no personal touches, no socks in the corner, no jacket over a chair, no signs that anyone's been sleeping here.

The women's voices get closer. He hides in a closet.

Her can't hear anything. The door's made of thick walnut and he's drowning in clothes hanging from a metal rod. Furs, long woolen coats, evening clothes, sparkling gowns. A cocktail party for ghosts.

Horvath waits five minutes before getting out of the closet. He listens at the door. Nothing.

He opens the door and steps onto the landing.

There's a door at the end of the hall. Looks like an office to me, he thinks. Or it might be the can. Who knows.

A furtive glance over the banister. No one's there. He walks down the hallway, stops and listens. No voices, no footsteps, no sound or movement of any kind.

Deep breath. He waits a beat, then opens the door.

Bingo, it's an office.

But he's not alone.

A young tough sits back in a big plush chair with his feet up on the shiny oak desk. He's polishing his gun and chewing on a toothpick, just like some cheap hood from one of those old movies with Bogart or George Raft.

For a second or two he just sits there, staring at Horvath. Then he turns to an older, bigger goon across the room. He's standing next to a bookcase, head tilted sideways, looking at the titles printed on the spines. As if he can read.

No one speaks or moves.

Horvath grabs the doorknob, slams the door shut, and races down the staircase.

This was a bad idea, he thinks, hoping he doesn't slip on the staircase. What was I thinking? Walking right into a house in the middle of the day, with no plan and no back-up. McGrath wouldn't be happy about this.

But at least I've got a mallet.

There's a young woman standing in front of the vestibule by the front door, and she looks scared. He doesn't want to knock her out of the way so he turns to the right and bolts down the hallway back to the basement.

He can hear the goons chasing after him, calling out to their colleagues for help. Time slows down and he can see every moment clearly, as if trapped in a photograph. He stands outside himself and watches what he's doing. He hears someone shout, but he can't hear what. He's got blisters on his heels, again, and he can feel a headache coming on, a bad one. His hamstrings are sore, but he runs faster. He hears the sound of a pistol being cocked, or that might just be his imagination.

The hallways are empty. His heart beats so hard it feels like it's going to rip through his chest.

He turns down the last corridor and makes for the basement.

A side door opens and a man with a wide-brimmed fedora steps out. He's holding a pistol.

Horvath almost runs him over, but he slows down just in time to stop a few inches away.

He stares at the Colt double-action revolver pointed at his chest, and then at the man holding it. Probably his service pistol from the war. When he came back from Europe, he found a new way to use it.

"Drop it."

He doesn't know what the man's talking about at first, but then he sees the mallet in his hand. He bends down to put it on the floor.

A voice speaks up from behind the man. He turns his head, just an inch or two, and his eyes forget about Horvath.

He swings at the man's left kneecap.

As the gunman starts to buckle and keen, Horvath swings the mallet up and knocks the gun out of his hand. It's pure luck, but that's okay. Lucks counts, too. You can't get by without it.

He opens the basement door and runs down the rickety wooden stairs.

The voice follows him so he runs faster than he should.

The last step isn't a step at all. It's the floor. He trips, falls onto the unforgiving concrete, rolls over, and smacks into one of the wooden columns.

He's knocked out, but only for a second or two.

The voice becomes a pair of soft feet moving slowly down the staircase so Horvath has time to get to his feet. A broken rib or two, he guesses, and a lot of pain tomorrow morning. But nothing serious. Nothing time and a few glasses of whiskey can't fix.

His eyes adjust to the darkness and the voice has now become a man, standing right in front of him. He's around 6'4" and at least 250 pounds, none of it brains. He's not a politician or an aide, that's for sure. He's not on the city council and he's no civil servant. This guy's muscle, pure and simple. He's a big boy, but the eyes give him away—strong, but not tough. Once you've stepped into the ring a few times, and brawled in the street, you know the difference.

The goon takes a step forward and throws a meaty right hand, but Horvath ducks out of the way.

He jabs the guy in the ribs, but he doesn't even flinch. He's got too much muscle to feel a little punch. Horvath can see him smile in the dim gray air.

The goon fakes a left jab then lands a right to Horvath's temple.

Feels like an anvil just fell on his head. While he's still thinking about how hard the guy punches, he lands another blow to the jaw. Then he tries to get Horvath in a headlock, but he wriggles away.

He grabs a screwdriver from the workbench, lurches through the darkness, and drives it into the guy's shoulder.

The goon doesn't cry out in pain, but moans low and deep like a wounded rhino.

There are voices at the top of the staircase, and then footsteps.

The goon pulls a long thin blade out of his waistband.

Horvath punches him in the nose, which has twice the force because he's still holding the screwdriver.

He can feel the cartilage split in two. Blood gushes from the guy's face and runs over his hands.

The back-up muscle is still halfway down the stairs when Horvath slips through the door, runs across the lawn, and hits the sidewalk.

He crosses the street, sprints two blocks, ducks into an alley, and hides behind a dumpster. There's a fire escape on either side, and an open window two stories up on the right. If the mayor's men find him here, that's his escape route.

His hands are bloody but his suit's clean. More good luck.

He thinks of the chains lying on the cold floor, steel hooks bolted to the wall. Knives, guns, a small army of foot soldiers. Why would the mayor need so many thugs hanging around? Same reason he's got a torture chamber in the basement. Because he's dirty.

Horvath closes his eyes and thinks. What did I learn from all this? Not much. The mayor's a bad guy. He's involved with Jaworski and the Thin Man, who's probably Gilroy. Something's going on at his townhouse. Something bad. You don't have chains and handcuffs when it's just fun and games.

But I don't have any concrete facts. I'm still shooting in the dark here, no closer to finding Van Dyke or Kovacs. And I don't know anything about the dead bodies, the children, or anything else.

He pops a handful of aspirin and swallows them down.

There's a newspaper folded in quarters lying next to the dumpster. He grabs the front page and wipes the blood off his hands. His knees are aching so he stands up, drops the newspaper. He's tired, sore, hungry and needs a drink.

He waits 40 minutes in the alley.

It feels safe now so he puts on his sunglasses and walks back to the Executive, moving in the opposite direction at first, then looping back through alleys and side streets.

He stops in a dive bar and has two glasses of rye. He orders a third, but the pain is building up faster than he can drink them down. While the bartender pours the whiskey, he wonders why he ever went to college. Intro to Psych didn't prepare him for all this.

BACK AT THE hotel Gilbert's busy with a guest, so Horvath stands back and gives him space.

He looks around the lobby. An old woman with white hair and a crooked back sits near the window alone, staring at the people who pass by. A clean-cut man with thick glasses and an overcoat draped over his arm walks through the front door. He goes toward the elevator, pushes the button, and waits. Two bellhops joke around in the corner. Nothing seems out of place.

Gilbert's free, so Horvath approaches the front desk.

"How's it going, sir?"

"Still got all my limbs. And they're in working order, more or less."

"Glad to hear it."

"Look." Horvath leans over the counter, speaking softly. "I'm in a bit of a jam. Things are getting hot."

"I don't want any trouble here."

"Neither do I, but what can you do?"

"Skip town."

"Not in the cards, I'm afraid." He pauses, looks around. "We may not be able to avoid trouble, but we can try to manage it. That's why I'm giving you a heads up."

"How can I help?"

"Anyone comes around asking for me, tell him I checked out."

Gilbert nods.

"One more thing. If you see me coming, and somebody's waiting for me, give me a signal."

"Like what?"

"Just a little nod. No words, no smile, no gestures."

"Will do."

"And I'll take the back stairs from now on."

"Good idea." Gilbert reaches into the pocket of his blazer and pulls out a metal ring with two keys. He slides it across the counter. "Big square key's for the service elevator. Other one's for the basement door, in case you need it. Leads to an alley where we take out the trash."

"Thanks."

"But you didn't get it from me."

"Understood." He takes out his billfold, peels off a few dollars, sets them on the desk.

Gilbert slides the money back toward Horvath. "No need. It's all part of the job."

He pockets the money. "You know something? You're a pretty decent guy."

"Tell me something I don't know."

Horvath laughs, turns, and makes for the stairs.

THE NEXT DAY he gets up early, walks down to the Italian butcher shop. He throws back a double espresso, and then one more.

Time for another money drop.

A different corner, a different street. Never stick to a pattern.

He checks his watch, lights a cigarette, and waits.

Always get there early. Never be late. Live by the rules. They're all you've got.

Horvath isn't paid to think. His job is to watch, follow and locate. But sometimes he can't help it. There are so many questions and so few answers.

They're always one step ahead. Maybe someone's keeping tabs on me, reporting back to Lourette and Wilson.

Lana? Fang? Gilbert?

The whole damn town, it seems like.

But I've been following this guy for weeks. Hell, it's probably months by now. Long before I met any of these people. And none of them would have any way of knowing I'd run into them. The hotel wasn't planned. I ran into Lana by accident. Fang, too.

No one knows where I'm going, not exactly. Not even the firm. No one knows what my next move is, not even me. How could they betray me if they don't know where I'm going or what I'm about to do? It's not possible.

Horvath starts to wonder about something else.

How long are they going to bankroll this job? It's costing them an arm and a leg to track down Van Dyke. Hell, pretty soon it might cost me an arm or a leg.

Forever, that's how long, They don't care about losing money. They just don't want to lose face. If you steal from the firm, they'll hunt you down until they find you. Then they'll bring you home and make you face judgment.

A car drives down the street a few miles an hour under the speed limit.

He drops his butt and stamps it out.

The car slows down, pulls over to the curb.

Horvath knows a thing or two about cars, even though he doesn't own one. It's a 1957 Chrysler New Yorker, and the owner takes good care of it. Washed and waxed. The engine purrs like a kitten settling in for a long nap.

He crosses the street and walks toward the driver's side window.

The driver turns off the car. That's not part of the plan.

He slows down and gets ready to run or fight.

A tall, broad-shouldered man steps out of the Chrysler. McGrath.

They shake hands.

"Didn't expect to see you here," Horvath says.

"Well, I didn't expect to come."

"So why did you?"

"Thought you might be getting lonely. You've been out in the cold for a while now."

Horvath admires the clean whitewalls and shiny chrome bumpers.

"Speaking of which, I brought a few friends along." McGrath hands him a thick envelope. "I'm sure you'll have a lot in common."

"If they like whiskey and scrambled eggs, then yeah. We should get along just fine."

A car with two missing hubcaps drives by, and a stray dog sniffs at a corner trashcan.

Two bums walk out of a bar. One crosses the street and sits on a bench. The other turns and wobbles uptown.

A popular song drifts from an open window.

McGrath yawns, stretches his arms, looks around. "So, you going to show me around this dump, or what?"

"Sure. What's first?"

"Breakfast. You know a place?"

"I know lots of places."

"Hop in."

They drive to a nearby diner and order enough to feed a basketball team. McGrath's been driving for hours, through the early morning darkness, and Horvath is just being himself, always hungry.

"Not bad," McGrath says, after a forkful of hotcakes, sausage and maple syrup.

Horvath nods, takes a sip of coffee, wipes his mouth with a napkin. He can't think of a better way to start the morning. A nice big meal with his old friend. But he also wonders why he's here. Maybe they're not happy with my work. I'm taking too long, not getting results. They've sent him to check up on me. Give me a deadline. Maybe take me off the case, if I don't wrap it up soon.

They eat and talk. Sports, jazz, women, people back home. The cruel things that time does to a man's body.

It's nature, not humans, who invented torture.

When they're finished eating, McGrath snaps his fingers for the waitress. She brings over a fresh pot and fills their cups.

They light up and drink coffee, quiet now.

"Not a bad little spot." McGrath turns and stares at the waitress walking across the room. "So how you doing? Is this town alright?"

"I've seen worse."

"You found things to keep yourself busy?"

"Yeah." He thinks of Lana, and a stack of dime-store novels. "I don't mind it here."

"Good."

"How's everything back at the office?"

"Same as always. Wilson won't get off my back. Houlihan's useless. Mr. Atwood sticks to the top floor, never comes out of his office."

"You ever seen him up close?"

"Sure, few times. But he's never spoken to me."

"Has Wilson...mentioned me?"

"Sure. He asks how the case is coming along."

"What do you say?"

McGrath shrugs. "I say it's coming along." He lights a new smoke from the dying one, leans back against the vinyl booth. "What else can I say?"

Horvath was leaning forward, elbows on the table, but now he leans back too.

"Is he upset?"

"Hard to say. You know how Wilson is. He's angry even when you get a result. Always yelling, face like a boiled tomato, veins in his neck popping out. Never seen a guy sweat so much. He'll have a heart attack one of these days."

"Probably why all his hair fell out. Too much stress."

"Yeah, probably."

"But no one's talking about replacing me, or firing me. I mean, I've been on his tail for, what?, five or six weeks?"

"Seven."

"Seven weeks, and nothing to show for it..."

"You're fine, relax. Just keep doing what you're doing. It'll all work out."

"I hope so."

"Don't sweat it. You were my best student. If you keep digging, you'll find the answers. You always do."

For weeks, something has been eating at him, hounding him, following him through the streets at night. Failure. Weakness. The idea that he's running in circles, chasing his own tail. He feels slightly better now.

"Some people just don't want to be found," McGrath says. "Nothing you can do about it. Sometimes it takes a while, and not every case gets solved. That's just the way it is."

"Yeah, I guess."

"So." McGrath pushes his empty cup out of the way. "Give me the rundown."

Horvath tells him everything that's happened since he got to town. McGrath cuts in a few times to ask a follow-up question, but mostly he just listens, staring out the window and nodding every once in a while.

When Horvath is finished speaking, McGrath doesn't say a word. He just sits there, as if he was alone.

The waitress drops off the check, face-down in a film of water. Both men think of a dead body lying in a pool of blood.

McGrath takes out his billfold, counts off a few dollars, lays them on the table.

"So, you going to take me out for drinks tonight? And something to eat?"

"Sure, whatever you want."

"I don't need to get back right away, so I thought we'd go out on the town, scare up a little trouble."

"Sounds good." Horvath fights back a smile.

McGrath slides out of the booth, and Horvath does the same. They walk outside.

"Look," McGrath says, "I've got some other business in town."

"Does this business have red hair and long legs?"

"Something like that." McGrath smirks. "You can find your way home alright?"

"Yeah, sure."

"Good. Meet you here at 7:00 pm sharp. And clear your dance card. I plan to tie one on."

He watches his friend get in the car, start the engine, and complete a three-point turn. McGrath drives out the way he came in, no matter what the rules say.

At 6:53 Horvath is standing on the same corner waiting for the same man, as if time has stood still. He's going over some of the rules in his head:

Wind your watch.

Never be late.

Stick to the schedule—it's your Bible.

McGrath arrives at 6:56. Horvath opens the passenger side door and gets in.

A big band is playing on the car radio. Horvath prefers real jazz, but at least it's not one of those lightweight singers, like Brenda Lee or Andy Williams. Listening to that crap is like eating cotton candy dipped in horseshit.

"You ready?"

"Always."

McGrath revs the engine. The Chrysler, with eight cylinders and 325 horses, is a bass drum holding the band together.

"Where to?"

"Go down to the corner, make a right."

McGrath puts the car in gear, checks his side mirror, and steps lightly on the gas. He drives cautiously through the city.

They're silent for a few blocks.

Horvath tells him when to turn.

"Where are we going, anyway?"

"Thought we'd try an Italian place I know. Nice and quiet."

McGrath nods.

Two seagulls floats down to the curb and peck at a brown paper bag and the remains of a hoagie.

A heavyset woman walks up her stoop and yawns, reaching into her pocketbook for the housekeys.

They keep driving.

HORVATH HAS BEEN to Rossino's a few times for lunch, but not dinner. The host who greets him inside the front door is a surprise. Balding, small mustache, middle-aged. Dressed like the waiters but with a cheap black blazer.

"We'll sit in back." McGrath points to a corner table away from the window. "Right over there."

They sit, and the host hands out the menus.

"Glad I'm not a few inches taller," McGrath says. "Or my head would be in the rafters."

"*Intimate* is what they call it."

"Sorry, I thought it was small and cramped."

"Look, McGrath, it's dark, quiet and cheap. And the food's alright. They hit all the marks here."

"What's good?"

"Meatballs, chicken parm, ravioli. The cacciatore looks good, but I haven't tried it yet."

The waiter comes by a few minutes later. They order dinner and a bottle of Chianti.

McGrath scans the room with those lasers of his. He's careful and vigilant every second of every day. Nothing gets by him. Horvath wonders if he ever relaxes. Must be a nervous wreck. Or maybe he's trained himself so well that he doesn't have to think about it. His eyes and hands do their jobs without him, independent contractors. They do all the work and he just sits back and cashes the paycheck.

When the food comes, they dig in right away. McGrath is so

hungry he nearly keeps up with Horvath, but not quite. The human vacuum cleaner is more machine than man.

They don't talk much over dinner. Afterward, Horvath throws down a handful of aspirin and washes it down with red wine.

"Still popping pills?"

"Bit of a headache."

"Aspirin? You're the most pathetic junkie I ever met."

"I've been knocked around a few times since I got here."

"Looks like it."

"Sometimes I wouldn't mind a gun."

"You know the rules."

"Yeah..."

"And anyway, if you carried, you would've used it by now. And then you'd be in the cooler or hiding out from the cops. Either way, you wouldn't be able to do your job."

"That's why you have the rule," Horvath says.

"Bingo."

He leans forward, whispering. "Before, at the diner. I was doing all the talking."

"Yeah?"

"So you didn't tell me what you know."

"About what?" McGrath asks.

"The syndicate, Jaworski, Gilroy, all of it..."

"Never been to this town so your guess is as good as mine. We sent you all the leads we had."

"Yeah, I got them."

"No good?"

"I've had better."

McGrath shrugs. "Sorry, but you know how it is."

"I sure do."

"Don't look so down." He puts his arm around Horvath's shoulder. "We'll get to the end of it all one of these days. Then you can come back home and catch your breath. Take it easy for a while."

"When?"

"Soon."

"I hope so."

"Trust me." McGrath gives his neck a squeeze. "We're through the worst of it. Goal line is just a few yards ahead."

"Aright." Horvath laughs, for no good reason.

"Now let's finish this wine and then go somewhere for a real drink."

"Good idea."

McGrath smiles and that's the end of the conversation. He's said enough.

26

KISS OF DEATH

THE NEXT DAY HE WAKES UP LATE WITH A HEADACHE LIKE A COUPLE RATS fighting in his head. His stomach doesn't feel so good either.

11:52.

He lights up and glances at the stack of books on the end table. No, too tired and groggy for that.

They closed down the bar at 2:00, 2:15. McGrath and the bartender were trading shots, to see who passed out first. They both lost.

It was a swell time, as far as he can remember. McGrath is great with people. Telling jokes, buying drinks, dancing with all the women. He has a way of making you feel like you're the center of the universe.

A cockroach climbs up the end table, sniffs at one of his books, then skitters away as if he's unimpressed. Doesn't like science fiction, Horvath guesses.

Time to eat. He washes his face with cool water, takes a double-dose of aspirin, and gets dressed.

He listens at his door, opens it, and looks down the hallway. All clear.

Service elevator, back door, hit the streets.

He stops in a drugstore for two packs of smokes and a candy bar. Breakfast is still 20 minutes off and he needs something to hold him over.

Toothpaste, razers, aftershave, Vitalis.

He wants to buy something for Lana, but he's not sure how she'd feel about it. Or how he feels about her. There's not much here at the drugstore. Nail clippers? Bunion pads? Epsom salts?

He goes over to the book aisle instead.

His eyes skim the shelves and a title jumps out. *Death Rides a White Horse.*

A man in a long coat holds a smoking gun. In the background a stallion rears and a death's head floats in a gray sky. He's not sure if it's supposed to be a western or a crime novel, but either one is okay.

He pays for his things, walks out, and eats the candy bar on the way to the coffee shop.

Crossing the street, he turns his head to look for passing cars.

In the reflection of a shop window, he sees a man turn away quickly and look down at the sidewalk. Twitchy shoulders, watchful eyes, hat pulled low over his face.

He's being followed.

Never let them know you're onto them. Rule #14.

Horvath keeps walking.

He enters the coffee shop, sits down, and orders breakfast.

On the way here, he passed a phone booth. He walks outside, goes to the corner, and drops a dime in the machine.

"Frank's." It's Lana.

"Hey. It's me."

"You stopping by today?"

"Maybe."

"What's the good word?"

"Someone's tailing me. I need a place to hide out."

"It's not safe here. Too many people in an out. But I know a place. Meet me here in an hour."

"Better make it two. I want to make sure I lose this guy first."

"He may have friends so keep an eye out for them, too."

Lana's no dummy. That's one of the things he likes about her. "Will do."

"My car's parked around back. There's a blanket in the front seat. Crouch down low, pull the blanket over you."

"Thanks."

"Don't mention it."

What a girl. Should have bought her those Epsom salts.

He takes his time over breakfast, as though he doesn't have a care in the world. Afterward, he settles up and then strolls outside toward the phone booth.

His tail is across the street, buying a newspaper from a metal rack.

He grabs the receiver, stops, puts it down, pats his pockets. He pretends to think for a few seconds, then he walks back inside the diner.

The waitress glances over but doesn't say anything. He left her a 40% tip, so she won't spill.

He walks through the kitchen and out the back door.

The alley smells like spoiled milk and rotting fish. Stray cats lean up against the brick wall like prowlers.

Horvath walks briskly down the alley, turns right, goes one block, turns left.

He increases his speed but doesn't swing his arms. That's a dead giveaway. Nobody's following him, at least not that he can see.

Elevated subway platform.

He takes the metal stairs, head down.

Uptown train is coming.

He gets on, takes a seat in the middle of a crowded car. There's a wrinkled newspaper on the bench. He holds it up so no one can see his face.

Four stops later, he gets off and takes a downtown train.

He gets off, crosses the platform, hops on a different line. The G train, eastbound.

Three stops. They're underground now, in the center of town.

He gets off, waits for the next train.

When it rattles into the station and the doors open, he steps onto the car, sits down, and waits.

Horvath can hear it, the sound of train doors getting ready to close. Quickly, he stands up and jumps through the doors a second before they close.

Frank's is just three or four blocks from here. He walks quickly down the platform, takes the stairs, turns left at the sidewalk.

Before he takes a side street, he makes sure no one's following him. The coast is clear.

One more block, turn into the alley. Good, he thinks. The car's there, just where she said it would be.

He looks around, slips inside, and hides under the blanket.

Two minutes later, Lana comes out, gets in, and starts the car. For three blocks, they don't speak.

"You alright back there?" She looks in the rear view. Horvath is a plaid lump on the floor.

"Couldn't be better."

"We'll be there soon."

"I hope so. You check the mirrors?"

"No one's on us."

Six turns and 18 minutes later, Lana pulls into a gravel driveway. Tires crunching over small rocks always makes him think of broken bones and grinding teeth.

"It's safe. You can get out now."

A detached clapboard rowhouse with a small yard in front. White with black shutters. Two-stories, shingle roof. No flowers or shrubs, but the grass is green, thick and tidy. Narrow porch with a white railing.

They walk inside. She drops her purse and keys on the sofa, walks into a side room. Comes out a few seconds later without her hat.

He looks around. The air is stale. No one's been staying here, at least not for a few weeks. The living room is furnished, barely, but there's not much living going on. Chair, sofa, chair, table, lamp, table, standing ashtray. One picture on the wall. A small red boat in the harbor, bouncing on blue waves.

She goes into the kitchen.

He looks up at the light fixture on the ceiling. It's yellow with age, filled with dust and dead flies.

Dining room is small, kitchen's in the back. Small room off to the side. Coat closet. Bedrooms upstairs. No basement. The curtains are drawn.

Lana walks across the room, stops in front of Horvath. "This alright?"

"Yeah, fine. Thanks." He pauses. "It's safe here?"

"No one knows about this place."

"No one?"

"Kovacs, but he's missing."

Horvath nods, takes off his coat, throws it on the sofa. "Your house?"

"No, but I stay here sometimes. Belongs to a friend."

He wonders what kind of friends she has. And why they lend her houses.

"I'll be honest with you, Horvath. You don't look so good."

"No, wouldn't think so. Been folded up in the back of your car, and I've got a nasty hangover."

"Poor baby."

"And a few days before that, I got into it with a few local boys."

"You're always causing trouble."

"It was just a misunderstanding."

"As in, they wanted you dead and you disagreed?"

"Something like that."

"Who were they?" She lights a cigarette, blows smoke toward the ceiling, cradles her right elbow with her left hand.

"I don't know. Just some cheap hoods."

He isn't going to tell her everything. You never know. Always hold something back, just in case.

"And before that I was shot at, introduced to a few dead bodies, took a beating or two."

"Beating or two, huh? So how bad did these hoods rough you up?" She takes a step closer.

"Not bad. I can still walk."

"Well, that's something."

"But I'm sore all over." He massages his jaw, where the hired muscle got in a good one. "Could use some painkillers."

"Fresh out of opium."

"How about some whiskey?"

"That much I can do. Ice?"

"Neat."

She walks into the kitchen. He can hear cupboards open and close, liquor run from the bottle into two glasses.

Moments later, a beautiful woman crosses the room holding two whiskeys. He doesn't remember dying but this is starting to feel a lot like heaven.

"Here's to recuperation," she says.

"Amen."

She takes a sip and he drinks the whole thing down.

"Feel better now?" she asks.

"I could still use something."

"Oh, yeah?"

Horvath steps forward, wraps his left arm around Lana's waist, pulls her close. They kiss, long and slow. His left hand is on the small of her back. He's got the whiskey glass in his other hand, but he wraps the arm around her body.

He puts the glass down and they kiss some more.

She makes a quiet noise so he lets his hands off the leash.

"Let's go upstairs," she says. "I'll give you something to dream about."

"One more drink, first."

"I'll meet you in the bedroom."

Horvath steps into the kitchen and pours himself another whiskey. He can hear the high heels crossing a wooden floor above his head, stabbing at it. The bed groans and her shoes drop. He drinks the whiskey, and then one more for good measure.

He puts the glass down on the kitchen counter, loosens his tie, and walks up the staircase.

. . .

SHE WAS RIGHT. As soon as it's over he rolls off, falls asleep, and dreams of being stuck in an endless building. Climbing ladders, slipping across doorways, crawling through heating ducts, pipes and secret passageways, discovering hidden rooms. Never making it out. Always moving through the darkness, never stopping for rest. Always tired, hungry, thirsty.

He wakes up an hour later, well rested but disoriented. It takes him a few moments to remember where he is.

Lana walks in from the hallway bathroom in a black silk robe, smiling. "Feel better now?"

"I do." He sits up. "But I could use some more medicine."

She sits next to him, kisses him on the lips, neck, rubs his bare chest. "Not yet. You get a new dose every six to eight hours. Doctor's orders."

He thinks of Fang's doctor, if that's what the man was.

She slips on a pair of long satin gloves and then starts rolling her stockings up her legs. He remembers asking his mother about this when he was a boy. The gloves are to keep your fingernails from snagging the silk stockings.

"What time is it?" he asks.

"5:45, 5:50."

"I'm starving."

"Of course you are."

"What can I say. I'm a growing boy."

She raises an eyebrow. "You felt like a man to me."

They kiss some more.

"You know, Horvath. You never told me exactly what it is you do?"

"I look for things, people, information."

"That all?"

"When I find something, I report back."

"Sounds simple enough."

"It is."

"So how'd you get into this racket, anyway?"

He can see the man's face, clear as day, as if he's standing in the corner next to the bedside lamp. Tall, thin, dark blue eyes, thick head of hair. Fake smile pasted on his face, like a preacher or used car salesman. He lived down the block and drove a brand new Chevy. Horvath's wife wasn't happy and she hadn't been for a while. He knew this, but he never thought she'd run off with that jerk. Six years later and it still hurts, thinking about her. She took his car and his money, but left him with all the anger and bitterness in the world.

He started drinking, showing up late for work, or not at all. His suits weren't pressed quite as well as they had been. He was getting sloppy. Losing papers, forgetting names, skipping meetings. He was a wreck.

After a few months he got his act together, but he was a different man. He didn't trust anyone, he couldn't make small talk around the water cooler, and he didn't like the idea of working hard for 30 years to make someone else's fortune, all for a gold watch and a measly pension.

Once he snapped out of his funk, Horvath had a closer look at all those papers he was shuffling. Something wasn't right. He studied the contracts, the companies involved, the industry, the regulatory body and its policies. His colleagues, his boss, the men at the top who sat back and counted all their gold coins.

They were dirty, but when he spoke up they pinned it all on him. Called him a no-good drunk who'd lost his mind when his wife left him for another man. They weren't half wrong.

That was the last straight job he ever had. He had to cut loose and run before he got locked up. If McGrath hadn't found him when he did, well, Horvath didn't like to think about that.

"Hey, you hear me? I asked how you got into this racket."

"The usual way. I just sort of fell into it."

"You're quite a talker, aren't you?"

He shrugs.

"That's okay. I don't trust a man who can't keep his mouth shut."

"Neither do I."

Lana's getting a bit gabby herself, he thinks. Lots of questions, all the sudden. Maybe it's because we slept together. Questions and answers are the price of admission.

There's a round mirror mounted to the wall above the chest of drawers. She's standing in front, putting on lipstick.

Does she think we're an item now? He studies the faint lines hiding in the corner of her eyes, but he can't find the solution. He's not even sure what his own answer would be.

"What about some dinner?" he asks.

She shakes her head in mock-disapproval. "Don't you ever get enough to eat?"

"Rarely. And right now I need to refuel." He throws her his best suggestive leer, which isn't very good.

"Is that right?" Lana puts away her lipstick, blots her mouth with a tissue. "Well, I could probably put a meal together, but let's wait an hour or two."

"Sure."

"What's your plan for today?"

"I need to lay low until tomorrow, at the very least."

"And then?"

He shrugs. "Keep looking around, asking questions. Other than that, I just make it up as I go along."

"And that works for you?"

"Sometimes."

"Then maybe you need a new plan."

He doesn't have an answer for this, either.

She fixes her hair, then sets a pillbox hat on her head at just the right angle.

He's happy to sit and watch.

She sits on the edge of the bed, far enough away so he can't paw at her.

He starts scooting over, but she sticks out her palm like a crossing guard. "Back off, mister. I'm all made-up."

He answers with raised eyebrows.

"Tell me this." Lana crosses her legs. "If your job is to collect things, then why do you keep stumbling over dead bodies and tossing them in garbage cans?"

"That only happened once. But the thing is, I'm also supposed to tie up loose ends."

"So a stiff is a loose end?"

"As loose as they get. Whatever mess they leave behind, I'm supposed to clean it up."

"I get it. So you're a janitor?"

"Something like that."

"And by *they*, you mean the syndicate?"

"I mean whoever's involved."

"Well, the way I see it. If something stinks in this town, it always leads back to the syndicate. One way or another."

"You're probably right."

"So when you stumble onto a murder or a stick up, how do you know it's got anything to do with the guy you're looking for? How do you know it's a loose end and not just a few crumbs."

"I don't."

"But you have to clean up those crumbs, anyway."

"Bingo."

She takes a silver cigarette case out of her purse and lights one.

Horvath gives her a look, so she lets him have a drag.

"But still and all," she says, "no Van Dyke and no Kovacs."

"True, but we've covered this all before, haven't we?"

"I'm just thinking out loud."

"Give me one of those."

Lana takes out another smoke, hands it to him.

He sticks the cigarette in his mouth and she lights it. The perfect team.

THERE'S NOT enough food in the pantry to make dinner, so Lana has to go out and shop for a few things.

She comes back an hour later and makes beef stroganoff.

Coffee, cigarettes, washing up. They're like an old married couple.

Whoever's following him is going to want answers and, when they don't find any, they'll get tough. Horvath thinks about Gilbert back at the hotel. He hopes they don't rough him up.

It's a long evening with nothing much to do. No books, no radio.

He finds a deck of cards in a kitchen drawer. After dinner they play a few hands of gin rummy.

Later, when they're lying in bed, Lana catches him staring at her.

"You're not falling in love with me, are you?"

"No."

"Good, because it's not the smart play."

"I may be falling in like, though."

She smiles, strokes the side of his face. "I guess that's okay."

When she turns out the light, it feels as if his feet are floating and his body's made of feathers. He can't stop thinking about her. His aches and pains don't ache. She's a drug.

And I'm a dope fiend, he thinks. Sedated, out of my head, not thinking straight.

He's not floating anymore. His feet are anvils and he comes crashing back down to earth.

Something doesn't add up. Frank's is always empty, except for a few old drunks. But she's got a nice car, fancy clothes, a house somewhere. She's always flush with cash. And somebody lets her use this crash pad.

Where does the money come from? Who are her friends?

She's connected to all this, somehow.

Horvath doesn't want to think about it, and he doesn't want to believe what he knows. He doesn't want to ask the hard questions, but he can't afford not to.

IT'S NOT CALLED WAKING up if you don't sleep first.

What Horvath does is get out of bed.

He throws on some pants and makes his way down to the kitchen.

Lana's fully dressed, made up, and strapped into her stilettoes.

Every hair's in place. Eggs and bacon are cooking on the stovetop. Percolator's whistling.

She turns around, smiles. "Take a seat. Breakfast'll be ready in a minute."

He sits at the round wooden table crammed into the corner.

She takes the percolator off the hob, sets it on the counter, scares up two cups and two saucers. Pours the coffee. Turns off the bacon and eggs, plates them. Brings the food and coffee to the table. Goes back to the counter, takes one last puff on her cigarette, stamps it out with one hand while she unties her apron with the other.

Horvath likes watching her work. Quick, precise and efficient. As if she works in front of a stove somewhere, or waits tables, instead of running a bar. Maybe that's closer to the truth.

He digs in. Lana made breakfast just the way he likes it, right down to the crispy toast.

Afterward, he sips the coffee.

"Need anything else?" she asks.

"No, I'm good. Thanks, it was delicious."

She clears the table.

"Tell me more about this Kovacs character, will you? Anything at all."

"I don't know much about him really. I already told you everything I know."

"You hadn't known him for long? When he went missing, I mean."

"No. Just a few weeks. Maybe a bit longer. Two months at the most."

"Did he have any enemies?"

"Not that I know of."

"Right."

Horvath picks a hairclip off the table and twirls it in his fingers. He stares at the creamer and a white sugar bowl with baby blue trim.

Next door, someone revs a V-8 engine and races off down the street.

Lana has the apron back on, and a pair of rubber gloves. She sticks a clean plate in the drying rack.

"When I first took the case, you told me he was clean. No boy scout, but clean. He liked to drink, stay out late, flash a little money around..."

"Yeah, he was a real character." She laughs. "But he couldn't hurt a fly and he wasn't involved with anything serious."

"What was his game?"

"He liked to gamble. Few years ago, he was into some guy for maybe a couple hundred, no more than that."

"Who?"

"A neighborhood bookie. No one connected."

"But this bookie sent muscle to knock on his door, send him a message?"

"Just a friendly warning. Pay up or else."

"Did he?"

"Yeah, about a week later. That's when he stopped gambling. Well, stopped betting more than he could lose, anyway. Still made a few nickel-and-dime bets."

"Scared straight."

"Like I said, he was just a kitten, a little boy. Not a real man like you."

He doesn't mind the flattery, or anything else so long as it comes from her lips. "I'm just like anyone else, Lana. I bleed when I get shot, and it hurts like hell."

"Yeah, but you don't curl up in a ball and cry."

"Not usually. So how do you know about Kovacs' little run-in with the bookie?"

"He told me, soon as we met. He told everyone."

"So they'd know he'd been around the block a few times?"

"Exactly."

"And the fake names. What was it, Kupchak and...Corrington?"

"Covington. He just thought it was fun, I guess. Like being a spy. Or maybe he gave different names to different women, to keep them off his trail. I don't know for sure. You'd have to ask him."

"I'd like to, but first I have to track him down."

"There's the rub."

The dishes are done. Lana's standing on the far side of the kitchen, by the icebox. Leaning against the counter. Horvath watches her lips and her eyes, thinking.

Everything she says makes a lot of sense, and she's got an answer for every single question I ask. It all adds up, but it adds up a little too neatly. Like she's reading off cue cards. The one thing he's learned is that life isn't neat, especially in his line of work. It's messy and the columns never quite add up.

He pushes his chair away from the table and crosses his legs. "So who's house is this?"

"A friend."

"Yeah, you said that. But who?"

She looks at Horvath, opens her mouth, turns away. She looks at him again, and pauses. "Look, I haven't been straight with you. Not completely."

"So I gathered."

She sits down next to him.

Horvath reaches across the table for the ashtray and pulls it closer. He lights up and stares

at Lana, trying to forget how he feels about her. It's not easy.

Her arms are on the table, hands folded tight. She's worrying her fingers and staring at the salt and pepper shakers.

He's had enough conversations like this to know it's not going to be a good one.

"I'll put all my cards on the table."

"I was sort of hoping you would."

She looks up at him with a closed mouth and rueful eyes. "I came to you because I wanted you to find him. He's missing and I'm worried about him." She crosses her arms. "We're not an item or anything. I don't even like him that much. But we're—"

"—friends."

"Yeah, friends. We run Frank's together. I've known him for three or four years. I trust him."

"So why'd he go missing, do you think?"

"Can't say for sure, but we were getting leaned on pretty hard. You know how it is when you open a bar. Liquor license, cabaret license, business license, food service certificate…"

"Yeah, the city really puts the squeeze on you. It's the same all over."

A couple of songbirds warble outside the kitchen window, and Horvath can just about hear them.

"It's not just the bureaucrats. Cops were asking for a cut, too."

"Let me guess, Gilroy wanted a piece."

"A few of his guys came by to talk with Kovacs."

"Just once?"

"Few times. I don't know who sent them, but they were trying to strongarm us."

"They did more than try."

"Looks that way."

"So where's all the money come from? You're not bringing in much at that bar of yours."

"Not anymore. The cops chased off all the decent customers. Now we've just got drunks, old-timers and two-bit crooks."

"What'll you do for money?"

"Sell my car, my apartment, join a convent, whatever it takes."

"They won't let you wear silk stockings in a nunnery. You know that, right?"

"Not even a fishnet wimple?"

"Fraid not," Horvath says. "Back to the money. Any other sources of income?"

She looks down at the floor, then back at Horvath. "Kovacs had a little operation on the side."

"Drugs?"

"He was a fence."

"I thought he was scared straight?"

"He only did it a few times, when we were short. Cars, jewelry, silverware…"

"I get it." He stamps out his cigarette. "You wouldn't cough up for the cops and the wise guys, so they grabbed Kovacs."

"That's about the size of it. Except we did cough up, just not enough. We couldn't afford it."

"They didn't believe you?"

Lana shakes her head. "You can't get blood from a stone."

No, he thinks, but you can get a hell of a lot from a cheap hood.

"Why'd you lie to me?" he asks.

"I didn't want you to know I'd worked with Kovacs for a couple years and knew him pretty well. I didn't want to be involved."

"You're involved, Lana. Whether you like it or not."

"I know."

He stands up, takes a glass out of the cupboard, gets a glass of water from the sink.

"I didn't know if I could trust you," she says. "That's another reason."

"So why me? You see me in a diner and suddenly I'm your guy?"

"I was just getting a bite to eat. Trying to sort out my next move. When I looked over at you, I liked what I saw. Here's a guy who can handle himself, I thought, and he's not too hard on the eyes. Then something occurred to me."

"What?"

"I didn't know you from Adam. Which means you didn't know me."

"So I was a sucker, someone you could lie to and get away with it."

"You were a fresh start. Someone who wouldn't make assumptions about me, or so I thought."

"When you start telling lies, people will assume the worst."

Lana leans back, folds her arms. "And you were obviously from out of town."

"How'd you know?"

"It was written all over your face. Anyway, a stranger was perfect. You might see things more clearly."

"And I wouldn't be afraid to poke my nose into the syndicate's business."

"Not only that, but I thought you might just be honest. Lord knows, you can't trust anyone around here."

He stares at the cutting board and knife, drying on the rack.

"I'm sorry," she says. "For what's it's worth."

It's not worth much.

"And I like you. You know that, right?"

He nods. She looks contrite.

Horvath thinks it over. Lana's very convincing.

But he's not convinced.

"One more thing," he says. "You never told me who owns this place."

"A friend."

"You already said that."

She shrugs. "Girl's got to have her secrets."

Lana smiles like a cat with a dead bird in its mouth. She stands up, walks across the room, and climbs the stairs.

Horvath wonders if it's any safer here than back in the city.

Upstairs, dresser drawers screech open and shut. Closet doors swing and click.

The neighbors scream at each other. He waits for the sound of dishes smashing against the kitchen floor.

Horvath tries to find his way through the problem, but every street's a dead end. He stands up, yawns, looks out the window. Nothing but gray sky and identical suburban houses.

He shakes the percolator, but it's empty.

Her footsteps creak on the wooden floor above his head.

He walks through to the living room, looks around.

A door closes. Running water. She's in the bathroom.

Her handbag is on the sofa. He thinks about it for a second, wonders just what she's capable of.

He picks up the bag, looks through it. Lipstick, compact, cigarette case, pillbox, keys, coin purse. All the usual gear. He sets each item on the sofa cushion.

A small wallet. He looks inside.

$23, ticket stub, driver's license.

Doris Schmidt. Brown hair, blue eyes, 5'6".

Doris? He wonders if this is her real name, and what the truth is. If you gave her half the chance, she'd probably lie about her height.

He hears the staircase groan and then feels her shadow creep over him. He doesn't hear a pistol cock, so that's something, and when he turns around he's not staring down cold metal.

"What are you looking at?"

"Your name is Doris?" He holds up the license.

"Going through my handbag?"

"When I walked by, it just sort of opened and the ID fell out."

"Not very likely."

"Well," he says, "I've heard a lot of things today that aren't too likely."

"Look, there's a good reason for the name." She approaches Horvath and takes the license from his hand. "I know you don't want to hear a sob story, so I'll keep it short. Bad marriage, worse husband. He liked to knock me around. Bottle of rum and a black eye–that was our Saturday night. So I got out of there, changed my name, and started over."

"Sounds pretty simple."

"It is. I'm telling the truth. I never got around to legally changing my name."

"Sure. Makes sense." He reaches down and picks up her keys from the sofa. "I'm going to borrow your car, but don't worry. It's in safe hands. I'll call Frank's later and let you know where I parked it."

Lana doesn't say anything.

He walks out the door.

A boy in a crewcut and striped shirt rides by on his bicycle. It's 9:46 on a Tuesday morning. Shouldn't he be in school? Horvath wonders if it's a holiday or if the kid's just playing hooky.

He gets in the car, turns over the engine, and pulls away from the curb.

It feels good to get behind the wheel. He drives slow and tries to make sense of what he knows. Or at least what he's heard. Horvath isn't sure if he knows anything.

Did she kill him?

Maybe that's why she hired me, to throw the cops off her scent. *Kill him? I hired someone to find him.*

I'm her alibi.

Could she do it? He tries not to think about the question.

Back in the city now. The wide streets and green lawns are behind him. The air is thin. He can feel the steel and concrete press forward and block his path, follow him wherever he goes. The city is a pair of filthy hands around his neck.

A garbage truck is blocking the street. A man hops off the back and walks toward the curb. He's in no hurry.

A woman hands over a crumpled dollar to the hot dog vendor.

Horvath can smell peanuts, smoke and gasoline. If the wind blows in the right direction, you get the bitter reek of hops from the brewery.

A cop stands on the street corner twirling his nightstick. He tips back the brim of his cap, wipes his forehead with a handkerchief.

Horvath parks downtown, swallows a few aspirin, and gets out of the car. He looks around, but there's not much to see. He hits the pavement and heads back to the hotel.

27

THE SECRET ROOM

His alarm clocks goes off—two men shouting in the alley outside his window.

He remembers that first night in the Executive. A fistfight woke him up. When he went outside, there was a dead body and a pool of blood on the jagged bricks.

That was his first clue, if it was one.

Who killed him? Who paid the guy to do it? Why did it happen right outside my hotel room?

And who wanted me to find the body?

Two sharp raps on the door.

Horvath slips into the pants he was wearing last night, hanging over the back of a chair, and walks softly toward the door. He squints through the peephole.

Gilbert.

He opens the door.

The hotel manager puts a finger to his lips, steps inside, closes the door behind him.

He looks older, Horvath notices. His skin's pale and doesn't shine the way it used to. Flecks of gray in his hair. How could he age so much in just a few weeks?. Maybe he always looked that way, and I just didn't notice.

"There was a man downstairs. Few minutes ago."

"Muscle?"

"Doubt it. He looked like a detective. Older than you, gray suit, dressed...discreetly."

"No red carnation in his buttonhole?"

"Not even a lavender pocket square."

"He still down there?"

"I don't think so. Guy walked in, sat in the lobby a few minutes, pretended to wave to someone, walked out a few minutes later."

"Ever seen him before?"

"He did the same thing yesterday afternoon."

"Did he ask about me?" Horvath asks.

"Didn't say a word to anyone. Like I said, discreet."

"Except you clocked him."

"It's a slow day. And the lobby's not exactly jumping."

"Plus, it's your job to see everything that goes on around this place."

"It is." Gilbert doesn't smirk. He's worried.

"Good man. Anything else?"

"No. Guy didn't say anything or do very much, but I have a feeling."

"Well, in my experience those things are usually pretty accurate. What kind of feeling?"

"He's looking for you, and he wants to put a few holes in your chest."

"Well, he'll have to wait in line. Lot of people have the same idea." Horvath pauses, looks at the hotel manager. "We'll get through this alright. Keep your head up."

"I'm fine."

Two simple words that are almost always a lie.

"One more question," Horvath says. "Where can I get a look at some public records? Who owns a particular building or business... something like that?"

"City Hall."

"Thanks. You got anything else for me?"

Gilbert shakes his head, turns, opens the door, and walks into the hallway. A few lightbulbs need to be replaced, but he doesn't seem to notice.

A HULKING GRAY building with stone lions guarding the front entrance.

A few people come and go, but no one speaks or smiles. They carry briefcases, folders and handbags. Almost everyone is alone.

He walks up the smooth stone steps, each corner as sharp as a knife blade.

Inside, the first door to his left has a brass plate at eye level. *Information.*

He walks in.

A tall broad-shouldered woman stands behind the counter, looking down at a sheaf of papers. Horvath stops a few inches from her desk, but she doesn't acknowledge him or make eye contact.

She's got cat glasses, pale gray skin, and gray hair tied back in a severe bun. Her white blouse has been starched and pressed until it's more of a shield than an article of clothing. He thinks of the nuns from elementary school, who carried wooden yardsticks like billy clubs and weren't afraid to slap them across your knuckles. They were so good at making your conscience burn that you felt guilty for crimes you hadn't committed and sins you'd never even heard of. If Jaworski's looking for new muscle, Horvath thinks, he should try the Sisters of Infinite Mercy.

He knows better than to speak or cough. This woman's a self-important functionary who'll hold it against anyone who tries to interrupt her or waste her precious time.

Eventually, she looks up. "Yes?"

"I'm looking for records. Business licenses and—"

"—Basement. Archives."

"Okay. Thanks."

The woman stares at him with a withered prune mouth, and he stares right back. She holds his gaze with a narrow squint as if daring him to ask another question.

He doesn't.

Horvath leaves the office.

Stairway is in the corner. He walks across the atrium. Men in suits and women in skirts cross the room without speaking, heads down, shoes clacking on the slick tiled floor. High ceilings, white fake-marble columns, and a wide stone staircase leading up to the mezzanine. The walls are lined with oil paintings of important scowling men. Crooks and liars, he thinks.

He walks down a flight of stairs and through the door on the landing.

A long dark corridor with worn carpeting on the floor. Most of the doors are unmarked. None are open. He can't see a light or hear sounds coming from any of the rooms.

At the end of the hall there's an exit sign and another door.

He opens it and walks into a cramped, dank stairwell. The floor is concrete, painted with thick coats of blueish gray. A light flickers near the ceiling and two steps lead down to another door.

He goes in.

Another hallway. It's hot and humid down here and he soon learns why. Third door on the left is the boiler room. Two men sit on upturned wooden crates drinking from chipped coffee mugs. When he walks by, they turn and stare but don't speak or even open their mouths.

Horvath can tell they're not drinking coffee. He nods, keeps walking.

It's a short hallway that ends in a white door made of cheap scarred wood. Someone has typed *Archives* on a sheet of white paper and thumbtacked it to the door.

He steps inside.

Short counter with a stool behind it. Beyond that, what looks like a small warehouse. Tidy rows of metal shelves run from floor to ceiling, packed with carboard boxes.

There's a bell on the counter but no one manning the desk. He smacks the bell.

No one answers, but a few seconds later he hears someone shuffling over from a side room behind the counter.

He's an old man, lean and bent with a sunken face and dry yellow skin. His hairline has receded into a horseshoe pattern, maybe for good luck. He wears a tattered cardigan, ripped at one elbow. His checked shirt is buttoned to the top but with no tie, and his eyeglasses are covered in a blanket of eyebrow dander.

The man adjusts his glasses. "Can I help you?" His back is curved into a capital C and his shoulders are hunched up by his ears, like a vulture.

"I'm looking for some documents."

"Aren't we all." The man laughs, softly and slowly, staring past Horvath at nothing in particular.

"Frank's Tavern, downtown. I want to know who owns the building, who holds the liquor license...whatever you got."

The man nods.

He waits a few moments before turning around and consulting a ledger. Afterward, he walks into the warehouse, heads to the right, then makes a left into one of the rows.

The man walks up and down the row, stops, squints at the white label on the side of a box.

He stops for a minute, scratching his chin, then breaks into a soft giggle.

Whistling a popular showtune from 12 years before, he turns right and disappears into the archives.

Horvath looks around but there's nothing much to see. A chair with ripped upholstery, a bit of stuffing poking out. Wall clock that's seven minutes slow. Wilting cardboard sign listing the office hours. Brown paper bag, folded over at the top. The clerk's lunch, probably.

The man shuffles back to the counter, smiling. "Forgot something."

He bends down, picks up a stepstool, heads back to the archives.

Horvath shakes his head, unamused. I'll be his age before I'm out of here.

18 minutes later the man comes back, holding a thin folder and two flat boxes the size of paperback novels.

He's disappointed that there isn't more, but also relieved. At least the old man didn't fall off his stool and die. Then he'd have one more body to explain.

"Here's what I've got, son." He lays the items on the counter.

"Thanks." Horvath points to the box. "What's in here?"

"Microfiche."

"What's that?"

"I'll tell you one thing, it's not a small fish. Ha-hu, ha-hu." The old man slaps the counter, stares at Horvath.

"Good one, pops, but really, what is it?"

"C'mere, I'll show you."

The man shambles along behind the counter and pops out a side door in the lobby. He jerks his head for Horvath to follow, walking toward a brown wooden door. He opens it and keeps going, without looking back.

Horvath follows him down a short hallway that empties into a small square room.

The old man flips on a light.

The walls were painted white, many years ago. Now they're grayish yellow with mildew in the corners and water stains on the foam ceiling tiles. The light works, but not well. There's no clock, nothing on the walls, no decoration. Unless you count a blood-splattered mosquito squashed onto the back wall.

The only objects in the room are two wooden carrels. He thinks back to the library in college, where people would would sit in carrels like this to study. It seems like another lifetime, or someone else's life. Each carrel has a bulky machine sitting on top with a heavy wooden chair tucked in.

"Newspaper and magazine articles, historical documents, administrative paperwork...it's all on the microfiche."

The man sits down, opens one of the boxes, threads the

microfiche film onto the spindles, and adjusts the tension. He presses a button and the machines comes alive, thrumming like an electrical transformer, lights blinking and sputtering.

"You make your way through the film like this." The man shows him how to use the knobs and levers. "Got it?"

"I think I can handle it."

"Hope so. You never used one of these?"

"Never even heard of them."

The man gets out of the chair, plants his hands on his hips. "Well, you learn something new every day, don't you?"

"At least once a month, anyway."

"You're right about that. Er, one thing I forgot to mention. No eating or drinking back here, keep pens and pencils away from the film, and absolutely no smoking. That stuff's highly flammable."

"Will do."

The man nods, stares at the carpet. "Alright then, I'll leave you to it. Good luck."

He starts walking away, but after a few steps he stops and turns around. "Say, you got a sweetheart?"

Horvath doesn't know where the old guy came up with a question like that. "I'm not sure."

"Not *sure*? Pff, what's wrong with you, son?"

"Good question, pops."

The man walks off, muttering in disgust.

He's not quite ready for the humming machine, which gives off heat like an animal. The modern world, he thinks, shaking his head. Machines aren't going to solve all our problems.

He opens the folder. It holds about 15 documents, maybe more.

Frank's Tavern. 634 22nd Street.

Property Deed. Title. Purchase Agreement. Tax Assessment.

Names, dates, signatures. Lawyers.

Papers of incorporation. Mortgage. Liquor license.

One thing's missing. His sweetheart. There's no Doris. Or Lana. No women at all.

He looks over the papers once more.

There's no Kovacs, no Kupchak, not even a Bill goddamn Covington.

The building is owned by Douglass Unseld.

His signature is on every paper, countersigned by a lawyer, Paul W. Tubbs.

He closes the folder and starts browsing through the microfiche. Nothing useful. Just a few photos of the building in local papers. A parade passing by on V.E. Day. A man stabbed to death on the sidewalk out front.

The second film is better. Photos of Unseld and Tubbs, standing together on the courthouse steps. Unseld shaking hands with a man named Turner. A shot of Tubbs with Earl Peters, Chief of Police. No surprise there, he thinks. Peters is dirty. Unseld and Tubbs must be dirty, too. And Doris.

She's been lying to me all along. I don't mind, not much anyway. I've suspected it for a while now. The whole time, maybe. But she's been using me. That, I don't like. Maybe she's doing more than using me. I don't know yet.

He stares at the photos and tries to remember their faces, for later. But the images are grainy and oblique. The film is old and the machine makes everything glow with an unearthly gray-yellow haze. Looking at the faces is like trying to find your way home in the dark when you're stumble-down drunk. Everything shifts and floats. There's nothing to hold onto.

He keeps scrolling but doesn't find anything new.

It's getting late, and he needs to eat. He needs a drink and a smoke. He needs to stand up and move around. Who knew there was so much research involved in this line of work. So much sitting and waiting.

Horvath scrolls a little more, listlessly. He's near the end of the film.

He stops at a half-page photo on the front page of the Metro section. The mayor and Chief Peters are standing in front of a new hospital holding a pair of giant scissors. The front doors are wrapped in yellow tape like a sash on a woman's robe, and they're about to cut their way in. Big fake smiles painted across their faces. Must be thinking about all the money they skimmed off the top to get the hospital built.

There are two men standing off to the side, next to a row of young girls in white dresses with ribbons in their hair. The one on the left is Tubbs. Looks like he's trying to hide from the camera. The other guy is smiling so wide it looks like he's about to swallow one of the girls.

Horvath bends down and reads the caption.

Robert Van Dyke.

Finally, I'm getting somewhere. He smiles and slaps the carrel hard with the butt of his hand. He wants to shout and jump for joy. But no, he's got work to do. This is just the start.

He goes back to the front desk and asks for whatever they've got on Van Dyke.

No papers. Another film.

He scrolls through the microfiche, but there's nothing helpful. Just a few murky photos with his name at the bottom. This tells him nothing about the man inside.

So everyone's dirty, everyone's involved. Lana can't be trusted.

Van Dyke is friends with these guys.

No one at the firm told me that.

Horvath packs up the film and brings it back to the counter.

"Find what you were looking for?" The old man pulls a wrinkled tissue out of his sweater and honks his nose.

"Just about."

LATER THAT DAY, he calls the office.

Lourette picks up. "Yeah?"

"It's Horvath."

"What do you got?"

"A lead, no thanks to you."

"Smart guy, huh?"

"Doesn't feel that way," he says.

"So, what's this big lead you got?"

"I'll tell you next time, after I look into it a bit more. First, I need to double-check a few things."

"Alright." Pause. "You almost got this guy or what?"

"Soon, I hope."

"Better be. Your time's running out."

"I just need another week or so."

No one speaks.

"Anything else?" Lourette asks.

"No, I'm good. Hold on, there is one thing."

"Yeah?"

"Van Dyke. Who does he know around here? Got any idea who could be hiding him?"

"We told you all that weeks ago."

You told me nothing.

"We gave you a couple address, right? A license plate? Whatever we had."

"Yeah, that's right." You didn't tell me about his connection to Peters and the mayor, or how they're connected to Jaworski and Gilroy. "Is McGrath there?"

Pause. "No."

"Where is he?"

"Out of town."

The operator tells him that, if he wants to keep talking, he'll have to stick another dime in the machine. He mumbles something to Lourette and hangs up.

28

TOUGH GUYS DON'T DANCE

For the fourth time, all roads lead to Mayor Childers.

His family runs Smith's Tavern, Horvath thinks. A shady bar. He had a big party and all the bad guys in town showed up. Even Gilroy, head of the syndicate. His basement's a dungeon and his goons tried to break my legs. And now this. He's connected to Tubbs, who owns Frank's. Which means he's connected to Lana. And he knows Van Dyke, the guy I've been sent to hunt down.

What does it all mean?

Someone at the firm knows more than he's letting on. Is it Wilson? Atwood? Who doesn't want me to find Van Dyke, and why?

Horvath finds himself on the front steps of City Hall, again.

Not that it was very pleasant the first time. That bitter shrew at the information desk was more intimidating than a whole army of heavies. And that old coot in the basement archives was slow and creepy.

But on the way out, after hours of combing through old film and dusty papers, something occurred to him. Something obvious.

This is where the mayor works, City Hall. He's right upstairs. It's a public building. They couldn't very well toss him out, or pull a gun on him, just for being nosy. At least not with everyone watching. City Hall was the safest place in town to look for answers.

He walks up the concrete staircase, pats one of the stone lions on the head for good luck, and passes through the front entrance.

He's wearing a fedora today, so he pulls it down low and heads for the elevator.

Women and men wait in silence before the shiny chrome doors.

The elevator dings but no one gets off. Seven people push in. No one makes eye contact.

He presses the glowing white button for the 6th floor, right next to a thin plaque—*Mayor's Office.*

For once, life is easy.

But he's not dumb enough to think the rest of it will be just as simple.

He's alone when he gets off at the top floor.

The hallway is large and open. Deep brown carpeting. Discreet lighting. A glass table with a blue vase and fresh-cut flowers. Modern art on the walls, like a kid spilled all his paints and he's waiting for his dad to get home to give him what for.

At the end of the hallway is a desk and a pretty secretary. The phone rings so she picks it up.

Four easy chairs and a coffee table are arranged in a waiting area to the side of her desk.

No bodyguards, no thugs. Just a tall lurching kid from the mailroom with a lazy eye rattling a cart down the hallway. This is a city government office. Nothing more. Anyone can walk in and make an appointment. They might not let you talk to the big man, but if you have a good reason they'll probably let you see one of his assistants.

There's another hallway intersecting this one at a t-juncture. He turns right and acts like he knows what he's doing. The secretary doesn't blink.

There are no paintings on the wall back here, and the lighting is more severe.

Break room. Toilets. Supply closet.

Conference room. Unmarked office space for the junior staff.

He walks deeper into the municipal turf. City Comptroller. Director of Public Works.

City Manager. Budget & Finance. Housing Director.

He gets to the end and walks back the way he came.

At the intersection he keeps going straight. This wing looks very much the same. Closet. Copier room. Office. Conference room.

But there's one difference. At the end of the hall there's another lobby, another secretary, another desk. The mayor has his own set of offices, a city within a city.

He doesn't have a plan.

"Can I help you?" the secretary asks, when he stops at her desk.

"Comptroller's office? I'm late for a meeting."

She smiles, just like she was taught in orientation, just like she does 1,000 times a day. "Turn around, go to the other end of the hall. Can't miss it."

"Thanks."

He'll come back another day, finish what he started.

Horvath walks back to the elevator, pushes another button, and takes it down.

THAT NIGHT, he walks for hours without any destination in mind, pounding the pavement until it starts to pound him back. His knees are getting old.

He thinks about the case by trying not to think about it. The walking and the city wear him down until his mind is empty and the puzzle pieces start to align.

But at the end of it all he still needs a drink.

He walks into a crowded bar without looking at the name above the door.

People come in here to feel good, or they toss back enough drinks to convince themselves that they do.

He sits at the bar and orders a double. Lights a cigarette, loosens his tie.

The first sip is magic, like always. His body softens and he sinks down into the chair, the floor, the room. Whiskey's like a hot bath and a Chinese massage all in one. Makes a tense, aching body turn into an amoeba.

He stamps out the butt and orders another whiskey.

He's getting close. He can feel it. His arms and legs are electric.

Someone else is getting close.

He clocked the blonde as soon as he walked in. Young, hopeful, stupid. Too much make-up, not enough dress. She grew out of hers three sizes ago. She thinks the world is about to open up and give her everything she wants, but in the end she'll only get what she deserves. Same as the rest of us. A few minutes before, she was sitting three stools away from Horvath. Now their elbows are touching.

"Sorry," she says.

Like a lot of words, this one's usually a lie.

"Don't worry about it."

"Buy me a drink?" She's nursing a sloe gin fizz.

"Sure." He nods to the bartender, who's mopping up the bar and pretending not to eavesdrop.

"I'm Cindy."

"Jay McDevitt." Never use your real name—a sacred rule. "Pleased to meet you, Cindy."

"You too."

The bartender brings her another highball.

They raise their glasses and drink.

She wonders if he's carrying a piece.

"So what do you do, Jay?"

"This and that."

"Mm, a man of mystery."

She throws him a seductive glance. Horvath is her type of man. Big, strong, rough around the edges. Maybe a little bad.

"You're a pretty big guy." She shifts in her seat, making sure that her dress rides up her leg a few more inches. "Play any ball?"

"Rugby."

"What's that?"

"It's like football, but without pads or a helmet."

"So you're a tough guy, huh?"

"Not really. I'd just feel like a fool wearing all that safety gear. Like I was a kid and my parents were afraid I'd get hurt."

"Never thought of it that way."

He lights a cigarette, takes a sip. Better than talking.

"Want to dance?" she asks.

"No thanks."

"Aw, come on, sport. Do it for me." Cindy hooks her arm into his.

"I'm no good."

She smiles with all her teeth, if not more. "Oh, I'll bet that's not true."

"You'd lose that bet."

"Please?"

"Look, I don't dance."

"What do you want to do, then?"

He starts to speak, but she cuts him off.

"Don't answer that. You probably want to play pinochle." She smiles at her own joke. "Or no, a few hands of bridge."

"I don't want to play any games."

"Me either."

She leans closer to Horvath. Their legs are touching. She looks away and sips her drink.

This is when he's supposed to settle up and take her home, but he doesn't feel like it.

And for some reason it seems wrong. He shouldn't feel any loyalty toward Lana, not now, but he he can't help it.

Cindy lays her hand next to his.

He stares at it and then takes out his billfold.

29

THE THIN MAN

HORVATH GOES BACK TO THE MAYOR'S OFFICE THE NEXT DAY, AND THE one after that, but nothing much happens. He rides the elevator, walks the halls, looks for clues, nods to city employees in the hallway. Secretaries smile at him as if they mean it.

He still doesn't have much of a plan.

The mayor's secretary rarely leaves her post and, when she does, one of the girls from the typing pool fills in for her. There's no way to slip by and sneak into Childers' office.

The other hallway would be easier. There's no secretary at the end. He could sneak into one of the offices and look around, maybe find something useful. But he's only interested in the mayor, not the city comptroller.

The only real possibility, from what he can see, is an empty office next to the conference room. Yesterday, he saw a custodian remove the nameplate from the door. *John Klein*. He wonders if the guy transferred, or if they put a knife in his back.

AFTER BREAKFAST, he buys a pair of reading glasses at the drugstore. Not much of a disguise, but it's better than nothing.

He picks up two more books and a new pair of shoelaces. Money's running low. Soon, he'll need a reup. Unless he can solve the case before then.

Before he walks into City Hall, he slips on the glasses. No hat today.

He remembers Cindy and the fake name he used. Jay McDevitt. Between that and the pair of glasses he doesn't really need, Horvath's starting to feel like Kovacs. Or whatever his name is.

He wonders if the guy really exists. If so, is he missing or just hiding out?

Can't believe anything Lana says.

She left a message at the front desk, but he hasn't called her back. Not yet.

The elevator's full. No one will notice one more man in a dark suit.

Sixth floor.

He gets off last and walks down the corridor, turns right at the intersection.

Something's off. The hallway is more crowded than normal, but also more quiet. There's a tense, uncertain feeling in the air. A few guys are surveying the area, glancing in his direction. They don't look like government drones. They're muscle.

Bathroom to his left. He turns quickly and starts to push the door open. Before he disappears inside, he recognizes someone. Gilroy. A small thin man surrounded by bodyguards, sycophants and public servants. The mayor's got to be around, too, but Horvath didn't see him.

He splashes cool water on his face and dries it with a coarse paper towel. He takes a few deep breaths to calm down.

He can't help but wonder why Mr. Big would show up today in the mayor's office. Something must be going down, or maybe it already did.

Mr. Big. More like Mr. Small. Skinny as a rail and only half the size of a regular man, like whoever made him got bored halfway through. Gilroy's got a little brush mustache, as if that would make him look taller, but it just makes him seem like a little boy playing dress up. He looks more like an actuary than a crime lord, which makes sense. He knows all about the dangers out there, and exactly how much a human being is worth.

Should have brought a briefcase or a folder, he thinks. So I'd look like I worked here. But no, I'd feel like a jerk walking around with a bunch of fake papers.

He pops a few aspirin, opens the bathroom door, and walks out.

The crowd is still there, congregating by the conference room. He doesn't see Gilroy.

A big man with a bulge under his jacket looks over, but only for a second.

Horvath can't just stand around with his thumb up his butt. He's got to do something.

He walks past the crowd and casts a sideways glance, but he can't see much.

No one notices Horvath. People come and go, scurrying like rats. He walks briskly and smiles like a fool, to fit in.

At the secretary's desk he turns right and walks down a short hallway.

Not much here.

He turns around and walks back to the lobby.

There he is, the mayor, talking to a man with bushy eyebrows and an oversized black suit. A developer or banker. Maybe someone from the concrete business. Whatever they're calling criminals these days.

Politicians. City fathers. Pillars of society.

A woman with short brown hair and dark red lipstick stands two feet behind the mayor, clutching a bundle of papers to her chest.

One of the goons looks at Horvath.

He grabs a ledger from an unoccupied desk, smiles, and waves at someone across the lobby.

The goon turns to the man next to him.

Horvath walks back toward the crowd, lowers his head, pivots quickly to the left, and walks past the conference room.

He opens the door of the empty office and slips in.

Lights off, no one here.

Footsteps outside the door. He hides under a desk.

Silence.

In his mind, he sees a large man listening at the door, reaching under his jacket.

Horvath closes his eyes, slows down his breathing.

The door opens. A click, and then light floods the room.

The man doesn't move or step inside. He just holds the doorknob and looks around.

An urgent voice in the hallway.

Lights off, door slams shut. The man walks off.

He waits two minutes before standing up.

People are starting to enter the conference room. He puts his ear to the wall. Three voices, maybe four.

The hallway is clearing out. Everyone's going back to work.

His eyes are adjusting to the darkness. A vase squats on a small table next to the desk. He dumps the water and flowers into a trashcan and uses the glass vessel to listen at the wall.

A few more people enter the room and sit down.

He can hear the voices more clearly now.

Silence. The pleasantries are over. The men sit and think about what comes next.

The little big man starts speaking. Gilroy's voice is soft but distinct.

They're settling an issue about city contracts. Gilroy's nephew owns a waste disposal company, and his offer to clean the streets and collect garbage was accepted by the Department of Public Works. Horvath guesses it wasn't the lowest bid. The problem, it turns out, is that he wants more money, and Gilroy can't understand why he's not getting it.

The mayor is uncomfortable. His chair squeaks and he clears his throat twice before speaking.

In the end, they come to an agreement. The mayor coughs up more money, and Gilroy doesn't have to shoot anyone.

The lawyers are talking now, so things get even more nasty. They keep interrupting each other, which means Horvath can't hear them very well.

Another silence, longer this time.

Van Dyke. He hears the name spoken as if it was shouted. He's been thinking about the guy for so long that Van Dyke's name is as familiar as his own.

The Dorsett. Tomorrow night.

The next few sentences are garbled.

Van Dyke again. But no, that's not it. *My man Ike.* Or something like that. Horvath is hearing things. He wants to find Van Dyke so badly that his ears are playing tricks on him.

Schwartz. Jaworski.

The door opens and, before Horvath can react, the lights go on.

A tall thin woman in a yellow blouse stares at him, mouth open. She bleaches her own hair, and it looks that way.

Horvath doesn't say anything, but he puts down the vase and struggles to raise a smile.

The woman's eyes change color. "You're Fred Dawson, right? From Accounting?"

"Yeah, hi."

"Delores told me about you."

"She did?"

"Yeah." She gives him the once-over. "She's right, you look just like that guy from *Spartacus.*"

"Kirk Douglas?"

"No, the other one."

He's fresh out of names.

"I'm Vicky."

"Nice to meet you, Vicky."

"You too." She clasps her hands behind her back. "Say, what are you doing later? Some of us are going to Reggie's over on Claremont."

"Oh, yeah? Sounds like fun."

"Why don't you stop by?"

"Sure, why not."

"We're meeting at 5:30."

"Okay," he says, "but I may be late. They run us pretty hard up in Accounting."

"That's what I heard." She laughs. "Hey, have you seen Connie Lewis? That's what I'm doing in here, looking for her."

Horvath shakes his head.

"Alright, see you later." She starts walking out, then stops. "What are you doing in here, anyway?"

"Playing a joke on Philips."

Her face is a blank.

"Works for the Housing Director. It's his birthday. I'll tell you all about it later."

"Oh, okay."

"Can I bring him along tonight?" Horvath asks.

"Sure."

"See you then." He puts a finger to his lips. "Don't tell anyone you saw me, okay."

She nods, smiles, and tiptoes out the door.

He picks up the vase and starts listening again, but the meeting is breaking up.

That's alright, he thinks. I've heard enough.

30

HIGH AND LOW

HE WAKES UP EARLY. IT'S STILL DARK OUTSIDE AND THE STREETS ARE quiet.

There are no footsteps in the hallway, no elevator dings, no doors clicking shut.

He reaches for his book, *Six Chambers of Justice*, and reads the first chapter.

A man whistles outside the window as he starts Chapter 2. He puts the book down.

Shower, shave, clothes. Billfold, cigarettes, lighter, key.

He leaves the room and walks down to the cargo elevator.

Inside, a man and a woman are shoved up against the wall, going at it pretty hard. The guy is one of the bellhops, Skip. He's never seen the woman. Their lips are all over each others' faces and necks, and their hands can't sit still. He wonders if they're early risers or if they still haven't called it a night. Horvath presses the glowing *L* and looks away.

He walks around the corner and into the back of the lobby. There's not much light here, no chairs, and no hotel guests. He can see the front desk to his left and, beyond that, the front entrance. He stands against the wall by a potted fichus.

Gilbert gives him the signal, so he approaches the desk.

"Bit early for you, isn't it?" the clerk asks.

"Wanted to see what you look like before sunrise."

"I look just as great first thing in the morning as I do at night." Gilbert adjusts the faultless knot in his yellow tie.

"Question: what's the Dorsett?"

"Cheap hotel in Koreatown. You checking out?"

"No, this place is cheap enough."

Gilbert maintains his composure. No laugh, not even a smirk.

"So where's Koreatown?" Horvath asks.

"Due east of Chinatown, where do you think?"

"You're a funny guy, you know that."

"I do, sir. Thank you very much."

"How do I get there?"

"Few blocks east of Pulaski Plaza, corner of Lindell and Pine." Gilbert has been signing a form. Now he looks up at Horvath. "Why you going there?"

"I need to look into something."

"It's a bad part of town."

"Just the way I like it."

"Well, just be careful."

"I always am."

Gilbert raises an eyebrow, just a fraction of an inch.

"Okay, maybe not always."

"The Dorsett...I thought they tore it down. Seedy place." The desk clerk pulls a face.

"Too vulgar for your taste, Gilbert?"

"Oh, there's no taste at all, not at the Dorsett. You'll see."

"I'll be sure to wear my second-best suit. One more question. Any idea who Schwartz is? Friend of Jaworski maybe?"

"Probably. He's connected."

"Go figure." Horvath lights up. "What's his game?"

"Owns a few bars and nightclubs. Legitimate businesses."

"I'm sure they are."

"But he's also a middleman. At least from what I hear."

"I'm sure you're hearing's just fine. Go ahead and spill."

"He sets up meetings between sellers and potential buyers. Stolen goods, narcotics, guns."

"People?"

Gilbert shrugs. "I don't see why not."

He thinks of the warehouse, the women and children Jaworski peddles.

"He also mediates when there's a turf war, labor dispute, any kind of disagreement on the street."

"*Mediate*? *Labor dispute*? You work for the mayor's office now?"

"I work at the Executive, sir."

"Good answer." If you want the straight skinny, ask a hotel employee. Everyone knows that. "Any idea where I can find this Schwartz?"

"Hard to say. I hear he likes to hang out in one of his uptown joints. Jazz club called the Green Note."

Sounds about right. "Thanks."

"It's close to the Dorsett. Seven blocks up and one over. You can't miss it. Big bright orange sign, always blinking. Good luck."

"I'll need it."

Gilbert starts to say something else, but Horvath is already halfway to the back door. Breakfast is calling.

HE LIES IN BED. Eyes closed, not sleeping.

The plan is to get to the Green Note by 7:00, before the smoke is so thick he can't taste his own cigarettes.

Raindrops pelt a metal awning in the alley outside his window. It reminds Horvath of that syncopated jazz he can't stand.

He puts on a hat and a raincoat before heading downstairs.

The first two cabs zip by without stopping, even though their flags are up.

The third one stops and he gets in.

"Uptown, the Green Note."

The driver nods, puts the car in gear, and jumps into traffic.

He stares out the window at the black of night and the electric lights that cut through it all. A red neon sun gives off no warmth and no comfort. Horvath tries to read the signs hanging over shop windows but the rain comes down hard so everything is blurry and distorted. He looks at the people walking by and their faces look like they're melting off. The whole city is a funhouse mirror and he feels sick to his stomach.

Gilbert knew what he was talking about, he thinks. Right down to the directions from the Green Note to the Dorsett. Guy sure knows his way around town. It's almost as if he knew what questions I was going to ask before I ever opened my mouth.

The cabbie pulls over to the curb.

Horvath reaches across the front seat and hands him three folded bills. "Keep the change."

The rain is letting up. He steps from the taxi and looks at the jazz club. A green treble clef blinks on and off.

Inside, he stands in a small square vestibule with no overhead light. It takes a few moments for his eyes to catch up. On a dark table to his right, a lamp is draped in a red scarf.

The hostess smiles like he's an open wallet and her hands are about to reach in. She'd almost be wearing more clothes if she was naked.

Up and to the left is a small bar. Five empty stools and a tired bartender. Straight ahead is a low wall of dark wood. To the right, down one step, a dark room scattered with little round tables. Candles burn inside cut-glass fixtures. Most of the tables are empty, and a jazz combo is setting up their gear onstage.

"Can I get you a table, sir?"

"I'll sit at the bar."

Horvath walks away and the hostess follows him with a frown.

There are no other customers at the bar. He takes the first stool. "Bourbon, neat."

The bartender, standing two feet away, doesn't stir. He leans against the register, arms folded. White cloth draped over his shoulder. After a few seconds, his eyes shift toward Horvath.

"Make it a double."

The bartender waits a moment before pouring the drink. He sets it down, wordlessly, in front of Horvath.

A portly man walks in with a younger woman, fur stole wrapped around her shoulders. Her low-cut dress sparkles. She's definitely not his wife.

"What time does the crowd roll in?" he asks.

The bartender grabs his cloth, wipes a pint glass, sets it down next to the others. "Soon."

"What about the band? What time to they start?"

The bartender holds up a bottle of gin, to see how much is left. "Depends."

"Say, I was wondering. Is there another room here? More private?"

"No."

"Not even for big spenders."

The bartender glances at him for a few seconds. "No."

"You're not going to let me get a word in edgewise, are you?" He laughs, thinly.

A stone wall stares back at him. The bartender walks down to the far side of the bar and starts leaning again.

Horvath takes a big sip of whiskey, lights a cigarette, reaches for an ashtray.

A young man with a briefcase sits two stools away. The club is slowly filling with voices now, heels tapping the wooden floor, chair legs skidding, waitresses hustling for tips.

He raises his hand for another drink.

After the bartender brings it, he turns around and looks over at the main room. The band is playing. It's modern jazz, simplified and fast. Almost like rock 'n roll. Horvath doesn't realize it, but he's frowning. He doesn't like teenage music. Too primitive. The musicians aren't really musicians. He takes a deep breath. Not to worry, he thinks. It's just a stupid fad. Soon, it'll die out. He looks over at the band. At least it's not folk music. Christ almighty. I'd have to walk out.

The bartender's taking an order from the young man. When he's through, Horvath leans over. "Where's the can?"

Instead of speaking, the bartender points to the left with his head.

People are dancing now. Horvath glances over on his way to the toilet. They look like apes, he thinks. Shaking their bodies without any rhyme or reason. Stupid grins on their faces. It's like they're having nervous fits. What's the world coming to?

He walks through a velvet curtain, down a hallway. To his right a curvy woman in a short skirt is screaming at the telephone. The guy she's talking to is shouting right back. He can hear every other word. Seems as if she's a loudmouth shrew and he's a no-good cheater. Seems about right.

He goes into the bathroom, has a slash, washes his hands and face.

No paper towels.

While he's dripping dry into the sink, a drunk stumbles in, mumbling incoherently. He crashes into a stall door and then bounces back against Horvath.

"Easy there."

He rights the man, who turns around and sneezes. Then he adjusts his lapels and stares at Horvath with red unfocused eyes.

"Thanks, pal."

"Don't mention it."

The drunk stares at Horvath, takes a step closer, points a finger at his chest. "You really think you're something, don't you?"

"Easy there, friend."

"Oh yeah, sorry. It's fine." He pats Horvath on the shoulder. "It's okay. It's fine."

He figures it's safe to ask this guy a question. He won't go blabbing to anybody. And even if he did, no one would know what the hell he was talking about. "Hey, you ever heard of a guy called Schwartz? I think he owns this place."

The drunk was rubbing his arm like it's sore, but now he stops and clears his throat. He looks at Horvath and then over at the sink before speaking. "No, never heard of him. Why?"

He sounds almost completely sober now.

"No reason."

"No reason? You gotta have a reason, pal."

"Just wanted to thank him. You know, tell him I appreciate what a nice place he's got here."

"Uh-huh." The drunk turns and walks back out.

Horvath takes out a handkerchief, dries his hands and face.

He starts walking back to his seat, but as soon as he parts the velvet curtain he feels the bartender eyeballing him.

A tall dark man stands behind the wall, facing the bar. He's Armenian, or maybe a Turk. Whatever he is, the guy's not in customer service.

Time to leave. He glances at the bar, where his lighter and cigarettes are mingling with half a whiskey. Too bad, he thinks. I really liked that lighter.

He walks past the bar, quick as a waitress, and doesn't quite catch whatever the hostess is saying.

Outside, he heads uptown just like Gilbert said.

Can I trust the desk clerk? Felt like the bartender knew who I was. He was waiting for me. The drunk couldn't have told him I asked about Schwartz, not that fast. And it wouldn't have meant much, anyway. Some guy asked about the owner. So what? That's not enough to unleash the Armenian muscle. Maybe old Gilbert called ahead and told them to expect me.

The storm is over, but the streets are still wet and filthy. The rain didn't clean up this town, he thinks. It just stirred up all the dirt.

He's walking uptown but the streets lead downhill.

Up ahead, a woman locks her car and steps onto the sidewalk. As Horvath passes by, she slips on the wet cement. He catches her elbow and keeps her from falling down, but she scowls and yanks her arm away.

I didn't need a *thank you*, but a smile would've been nice, or even a small nod.

It's a short walk to the Dorsett, but not a quick one. The sidewalks are congested, cars double-parked on the street, small groups of men gather in front of shops and restaurants, stumble out of nightclubs. Car horns, squealing tires, music, voices, laughter, angry shouts. A car backfires but he knows better than to think it sounds like a gunshot.

On the next block, the sidewalk and half the road are closed for construction so he takes an alley that runs nine blocks before ending at the brick wall of the old city armory.

A man sits in a folding chair on the tarpaper roof of a three-story building. Horvath looks over at his quiet shadow.

Apartments, small grassy yards, and a detached house back onto the alley.

Dirt and gravel lie at his feet. Stray cats slink and sniff along a row of garbage cans.

A car drives slowly down the alley so he stands sideways, against a rusting chain-link fence.

Across the alley, two men warm their hands in a fire they've made in an empty oil drum. Summer is over, and the nights are getting colder. One of the men grabs a can of beans cooking in the fire. The other one feeds a busted two-by-four into the flames. Newspaper pokes out from the tops of their shoes.

The alley becomes more narrow with brick and concrete walls on either side. Dirt lots and ash heaps sit between the buildings. No room for a car to pass by. Industrial trash bins. Old mattresses. Broken bottles. A fat man and a working girl go at it in a doorway set back from the alley. Four bums stand around smoking and drinking out of paper bags. A man sits on the ground with his back to the wall, asleep. Someone sings an old Scottish song.

After the next block, there's a plywood shack built in a recess of the alley. Alongside the brick walls, men and women sleep under cardboard and newspaper. Hooverville.

A squirrel jumps off a fire escape and the metal clangs.

More fires burn. A man in an undershirt opens a third floor window and throws a bucket of slop onto the ground. A dog yelps and runs off into the night, but the bums don't bother moving. A woman with drooping knee socks and a grocery bag heads south onto the main street.

Horvath turns right and stops for a moment on the sidewalk to orient himself. Two more blocks. He keeps going.

The elevated platform is straight ahead. When he gets close, a train rumbles into the station and stops. The faces in the windows don't look too excited to get wherever it is they're going. He walks under the platform and past the station.

Almost there. The signs turn from English to whatever it is that Koreans use. The faces are different here, and the shops are smaller. The streets are less rowdy but even more steep and constricted, no wider than the alleyway he just left. The people walk or ride bicycles. He leans forward and plunges downhill past red lanterns and glowing yellow signs. It feels as if he's walking into the fiery bowels of the earth, and maybe he is.

Grocery store, butcher, deli. Bar, restaurant, corner store. Men, women, children, grandparents. Everything's the same here, only different.

He sees the hotel, on the other side of the street.

The sign is orange but it's not bright and it doesn't blink. It's not even on. Gilbert was wrong about that, if nothing else.

They didn't tear the place down, but it sure looks like they tried.

The windows are missing, or boarded up. Trash is piled up in front of the building, and on both sides, like some kind of sick landscaping. The front stoop is covered in graffiti and the front door is missing. This place looks worse than 436 Cantrell, where he got shot. The wound in his arm stings as if it has its own memory.

Koreans walk on the other side of the street. They don't even look over at the Dorsett. Maybe they're pretending it's not there.

He doesn't see anyone who's not Korean.

There's a bookstore 30 yards ahead, across from the hotel. *Giebenrath's Books*. It's the only shop around with a sign he can read.

He'll go inside and keep an eye on the Dorsett from there. See who goes in and who comes out. Get his bearings before taking the next step.

He walks in and looks around. It's just like a regular bookstore, but with a whole wall of foreign titles. Korean, Chinese, maybe Japanese. French, German, Russian, Spanish. Other languages that he can't even guess.

A clerk makes eye contact with him from behind a counter. Horvath nods and the man bows, unsmilingly.

He picks up a book at random, reads the spine. *Franny & Zooey*. What the hell kind of title is that?

After browsing in the stacks for a few minutes, he walks toward the front of the store and stares out the window. There are no lights in the building. No one outside on the front stoop. No one walks in or out.

The Dorsett is more rubble than hotel. There's a hole in the wall on the ground floor. You could stick your arm through it. It reminds him of photographs from the war. London burning after a German air strike.

Horvath was too young for World War II, and he never got called up for Korea. He thinks of his father.

He pretends to read the first page of the novel, or whatever it is.

No one uses the crumbling sidewalk in front of the hotel, except for an elderly couple. They walk past the Dorsett arm in arm, heads down. Every step is slow and carefully planned. Pretty soon, Horvath knows, they won't be able to live on their own. What then?

The clerk comes up behind him, quietly. He coughs. "May I help you, sir?"

"No thanks. I'm just looking."

The clerk backs off, returns to the counter.

Time to earn my pay. Horvath puts down the book and walks outside.

Outside, two street toughs are hassling a middle-aged woman. They can't be more than 11 or 12 years old. They're trying to steal her purse, but she's putting up a fight. One of them punches her in the back. A man watches from a nearby window, smoking a cigar, and a young couple walks past, but no one stops to help the woman.

Horvath walks over, grabs one of the kids by the scruff of the neck, and pulls him off the woman. "Get out of here, you two."

"Mind your own business, old man."

"Yeah, get lost."

He's not sure what's worse, theft and assault or the way they're talking to him. They're still kids, and this is what they're up to? What happened to pinball and chasing girls? And look at their hair. It's down past their shirt collars.

The kids leave the woman alone and turn to Horvath.

One pulls a switchblade out of his back pocket, flicks the blade, takes a step closer.

The woman runs off.

The two boys walk toward him, crouched like wrestlers.

Horvath stands still, as if he's not going to do anything.

The boys look at each other.

In the time it takes the boys to look back at Horvath, he's lunged forward and popped one of them in the face. The other kid steps forward and holds up the knife. Horvath grabs his wrist, twisting it around until the boy screams out in pain and drops the blade. He picks him up by his lapels and throws him against the wall of a corner grocery.

A few seconds later, the kids run off. They don't feel so tough anymore, but soon they'll graduate to guns and armed robbery, grievous bodily harm and manslaughter.

The last thing he wanted was to draw attention to himself.

He pulls his hat down, walks quickly across the street, and passes through the doorless remains of the hotel.

His shoes clatter on broken floor tiles.

Straight ahead, there's an empty space where the front desk used to be. The wooden counter and pigeonholes have been pulled off the wall, probably for firewood. Horvath can see iron-gray shadows on the white wall, where the objects used to hang.

To his right is a staircase. A dead rat is sprawled on the first step, like a sleeping bellboy.

He can hear footsteps overhead so he steps over the dead vermin and walks up the staircase.

I feel like a rat, he thinks. Running around in circles. Never getting anywhere. Feeding off scraps.

Always finding myself in filthy hovels like this.

Horvath walks slowly, back against the wall, cigarette butts and bottle caps under his feet.

He waits on the landing. The voices and moving bodies have stopped.

Slowly, he turns to the right and walks down the hallway.

Another day, another cheap hotel. Maybe I'll get shot again, he thinks. Maybe I'll bleed some more.

Second room on the left. Door is halfway open.

He stands and waits. Nothing.

With his left foot, he shoves the door open and stands back. If there's a pistol waiting for him, he wants time to run.

Nothing.

He leans forward, peers around the doorframe.

It's dark, but he can see shadows spread throughout the room.

He walks inside.

A dark form turns its head sluggishly, then turns back. No one else moves. No one speaks.

The stink is overwhelming. He's met three-day-old stiffs that smell better than this.

Horvath lights a cigarette, so he can see what's going on here.

When the lighter sparks, he can see faces, five or six of them. One woman. Pale, gaunt, Asian.

A chair, two threadbare sofas. A few overnight bags, trash can overflowing with debris.

Dope fiends, neither dead nor alive. Ghosts haunting the city of their old lives.

The Dorsett is a drug den. Why doesn't the city do something about it? Close this place down. The mayor's probably in the dope racket, that's why.

"Heya..."

He turns to see a skinny young man, a boy really, lying on a thin mat in the corner of the room.

"Eye, whu..."

Horvath isn't sure if the kid's speaking Korean, Japanese or just mumbling in English. Maybe he's dreaming.

He steps over a mound of clothes and trash, bends over, looks down at the guy. He's wearing ripped pants and a stained undershirt. His belt is wrapped tight around his right arm, which is dotted with dry blood. A syringe lies next to him on the mattress, as if it was his girl.

The kid raises his head, smiles and starts to open his mouth, but then he drops down and closes his eyes.

Horvath turns and looks around the room. This isn't what he came here for.

He walks out, keeps going down the hallway.

There's a man-sized lump on the floor against the far wall. He walks over and nudges it gently with his left foot. The lump doesn't flinch. He's either dead or nodding off. Horvath can't tell, and he's not even sure there's a difference.

He wonders if life really was better before the war, like the old men say.

Maybe so.

But then he remembers the Great Depression, and the first world war.

Back to the stairwell.

He looks up to the third floor, puts a foot on the first step.

No, whatever's going on, it'll be in the basement. Always the basement. It's darker, fewer people around, and there's always a back exit.

He walks down one flight and then stops to listen. Nothing. He drops the cigarette and grinds it into the floor.

Even more cautiously down to the basement, hand on the railing. Light footsteps.

No door at the landing. He stops and waits, but he can't hear anything over the pounding of his heart.

He edges forward, hugging the wall. One long slow step every three or four seconds, like a dream where you're getting chased but your legs just won't move fast enough.

It's cold and dark. Square objects line the walls. Laundry room. The brass and copper pipes have been stripped off and sold for scrap.

He walks through to a smaller room. Storage. Shelves and cabinets. A pantry.

The basement is long and narrow, a series of rooms connecting like boxcars.

A noise. He stops, goes flat against the wall.

Shuffling feet, voices, a yawn. The sounds are coming from behind him.

He slips into the next room.

The kitchen is larger than the other rooms. Some of the workstations have been removed, but the stoves remain. A few pots and pans are lying around. There's a back door up ahead, to the right.

The footsteps are getting closer.

He steps into the walk-in icebox. The power's out, so he won't freeze. Anyway, the round window in the door is cracked; a large piece of glass is missing and smaller pieces hang by spidery threads.

He takes off his hat, stands in the shadows, and watches through the busted window.

Three men enter the kitchen. They gather around a metal table four feet away from the icebox.

Another man, smaller, walks in behind them. Gilroy?

The back door lets in a little light, but not much. He squints into the gray room.

He doesn't see Jaworski. Maybe he sent one of his henchmen. One man wears a long dark coat with a fur collar, acting like he's in charge. That's probably him.

There's a short round guy wearing a three-piece suit. Must be Schwartz.

He can't see the smaller man.

The last guy is big and square, muscle. It might be Marco. He's not sure.

The big man is holding a large satchel. He sets it on the table, opens it up.

Jaworski's henchman reaches in and takes out a square bundle, the size of a brick. He weighs it in his hand. The men speak. Voices get louder. They're arguing. Shoulders, biceps and jaws tense up. The veins in the goon's neck begin to twitch.

A drug deal.

Jaworski's man lights a cigar, takes a few puffs, blows a thick rope of smoke into the air above his head. He rocks on his heels, gently, and then points at the short man with the end of his cigar.

The short man shrugs, says something too quiet to hear from inside the icebox.

Horvath looks at Jaworski's man. The skin on his craggy face looks thin and yellow. The ridges of his cheekbones are sharp as a machete, and he seems eager to cut someone.

Fear, excitement, anxiety. With all the adrenalin rushing through his veins, he feels as doped up as the people nodding off on the top floor. He might die tonight, but he feels more alive than ever. McGrath didn't teach him this, but he gave him the chance to learn for himself.

There's something long and heavy on the floor. Horvath bends down and picks it up. A lead pipe, jagged on one end and starting to rust. He feels the heft in his hand. It'll do the job.

He hears the flint and cogs of a lighter, sees the blue spark and orange flame.

The small man steps forward and looks into the bag of drugs, moves the bundles around and counts them. He takes a roll of cash from his coat pocket and hands it to the muscle.

But it's not a man's face. It's a woman. Lana.

The truth, at last.

31

HARD-BOILED WONDERLAND

HE CAN ONLY HEAR A FEW WORDS HERE AND THERE, LEFTOVER SCRAPS of conversation. But the main idea is pretty clear. Sell the drugs, burn down the building. Kick back a percentage to the mayor and the police.

Jaworski and his men are really earning their keep, he thinks. Guns, arson, drugs, women, children, beat-downs and murder. Fixing the fights. They've got anything you want all in one place, like a department store.

And Lana. She's been playing me the whole time. Feeding me lies, keeping tabs on me, reporting back...to who? Jaworski? The firm?

I fell for the oldest trick in the book. A good-looking woman turned my head. I lost focus. I lost control of the case. They knew every move I was about to make, because she told them.

How does Van Dyke figure into all this?

He can't answer any of these questions, not yet, but he's getting closer.

The meeting is breaking up.

"We'll leave first," says the man in the fur-lined coat. "Wait a few minutes before you follow us out."

Schwartz and Lana nod.

The men walk over to the door. The big man unlocks it and, with some effort, pulls it open.

He can hear the heavy door scrape against the jambs.

They walk out into the night. The goon slams the door.

Lana says something to Schwartz, who laughs without joy.

Horvath grips the pipe and stands tall. He's ready to do what he has to do. The back door is only a few feet away, so he doesn't have the time or space to creep up on them.

Lana picks up the bag. Her shoulder drops from the weight.

His tightens his grip on the pipe. The muscles in his arm twitch and sweat runs down the side of his face.

Schwartz lets her go first because he's such a swell guy.

He leaps out of the icebox and swings wildly. He connects with the side of Schwartz's head, but it's only a glancing shot. The man buckles and his knees drop to the concrete, but his body doesn't collapse.

Lana doesn't bolt out the door, which would be a more useful instinct. Instead, she turns to see who's there and what he's doing. Horvath can't see her face through the darkness.

Schwartz gets up and reaches into his pocket for a knife.

Horvath takes another swing and this time he hits a triple. The jagged tip of the pipe slices through Schwartz's ear. He can feel the metal cut through skin. The man screams and Horvath hears the pink flap of skin fall to the floor and land on a bed of its own juices.

Schwartz stares at him for a second with milky eyes before lunging forward. He raises the knife and swings wildly, but Horvath smacks his arm away and hits him across the back with the pipe.

Lana hasn't moved. He keeps an eye on her so she doesn't escape through the back door.

Schwartz has dropped the knife. He reels, takes a step forward, puts up his fists.

Horvath tosses the pipe away. He can tell that Schwartz doesn't have much left in him. He didn't have a lot to start with.

Schwartz fakes a left hook then tries to land a right, but his arms are short and his reflexes are slow. Horvath swats away the punch, jabs him in the gut twice, then uses his weaker left hand to flatten the guy's nose.

The fat man is out cold on the floor.

Horvath doesn't feel good about it. It's only a real fight if both men have a chance.

For a second or two, he's lost sight of Lana, but then he hears her breathing hard, trying to get the door open. She can't do it, especially with the heavy satchel in her hand.

Horvath steps closer. "Don't try to run. I'll hit you if I have to."

"And here I thought you were a real gentleman."

It takes her a few seconds, but Lana turns around.

She's holding a snub-nose .38 and it looks like she's prepared to use it.

"So now you know, huh?"

"I've probably always known, if I'm being honest. But who wants to do that, right?"

She doesn't say anything.

Horvath lights a cigarette, stares at her arms for a trembling that never comes. This isn't the first time she's held a gun in her hands. "I guess it was always coming to this."

"Only if you wanted it to."

"I never wanted this."

"Me either," Lana says, "but here we are."

"Life's a terrible business, isn't it?"

"It can be."

They don't speak for almost a full minute. He notices small windows high up on the wall, covered with tattered blinds.

She waves the gun. "Move over there, two big steps."

He holds up his hands, walks backward. "Were you working me from the start, or did they turn you?"

"From the start."

"I'll say this much, you're a hard worker. Drugs, whores, kids—"

"—I got nothing to do with those kids."

"But you weren't doing anything to stop it, either."

"What could I do? The syndicate's going to do whatever it needs to do."

"Sure, sure. You're a real saint."

"Maybe not, but I draw the line somewhere."

He pauses. "You're a pretty good actress, too."

"I did like you, Horvath. I still do. That's the truth."

"Yeah, right. You wouldn't know the truth if it got up and bit you on the ass."

But he can see it in her eyes. The feelings were real. Maybe they still are.

None of that matters, not anymore.

"And Kovacs?" he asks.

"There is no Kovacs, but you've probably figured that out by now."

He nods.

Schwartz groans.

Horvath looks over at the poor bastard. His clean white shirt is covered in blood. Half his ear's gone, and a chunk of skin from his neck.

"I did help you, you know? There may not have been any Kovacs, but I really did try to help you find Van Dyke."

"Uh-huh."

"I'm telling the truth, Horvath. I was on your side."

"Sure you were."

"I didn't tell them everything."

"So what, it was a double-cross? Triple? Quadruple? You were playing all the angles. The whole thing's as messy as this guy's ear."

"Don't tease him, Horvath. Shouldn't kick a man when he's down."

"No harm. He can't hear a word I'm saying."

"Good point."

"So who's side are you on?" he asks. "Or can't you tell anymore?"

"No one's side. I'm in it for myself." She looks down for a second. "Look, I'm sorry. I really am. The truth is, there was a Kovacs in my life. Hell, there was more than one. The rat took all my money and skipped town."

"And that's when you got into a life of crime?"

She shrugs. "Didn't have a choice. Not that I could see, anyway."

Her story's not so different than mine, he thinks. But I'm not going to tell her that.

He hears the roar of a V-8 engine. There's a tear in the blinds so he can see a pair of headlights sweeping by. He gets a better look at her face, too. Lana seems tired now, and older. The lines around her eyes are thicker and there are more of them. Or maybe it's just the lighting.

"I was hoping we could run off together," she says. "Leave all this behind and start fresh, just you and me. Go somewhere far away from this crummy place."

"Why would I trust you?"

"I don't know."

He drops the cigarette, crushes it under the heel of his shoe. "So who hired you?"

"You know I can't tell you that."

He nods.

"Sure you don't want to come along with me? I'm getting out of here, with or without you."

"No."

She moves a step closer.

"Come on," he says, "tell me who you're working for. That's the least you can do."

"Can't do it."

"If you really like me so much, prove it."

She aims the gun at his chest.

"What's the harm? It's not like anyone will ever find out. Dead men don't make small talk."

"Jaworski."

"Anyone else?"

"No. Just him."

"So what's next?" he asks.

"You know what's next. Time for a nap."

"What about a last wish? Don't you have to give me that?"

"I don't have to do anything."

He's quiet now.

"What is it?" she asks.

"A kiss."

"Not on your life."

"Okay, how about I just close my eyes and pretend. Then you can shoot me."

"Alright, if that's what you want."

He closes his eyes and a goofy smile floats across his face. He holds out his arms like a scarecrow and stands that way for 20 seconds.

"You almost through with this?" she asks.

"Just about."

He smiles even more widely, like a lunatic. She laughs.

After a few more moments, she starts to yawn.

When Horvath hears this, he imagines one hand going up to her mouth, and the other one slipping down a few inches. That's enough.

He lurches forward and kicks the gun out of her hand.

She rushes him, but he pushes back and she falls to the concrete, slamming against the side of a metal counter.

Horvath's not going to die after all, at least not tonight.

He kicked the gun out of her hand, and now he thinks about kicking her teeth in.

She can read the anger and bitterness on his face. "Go ahead, do it. Will that make you feel like a real man?"

"No."

"Well, do it anyway."

"I wouldn't want to ruin that pretty face of yours, no matter how many sides it has."

He takes out his handkerchief and picks up the gun. He kicks Schwartz's knife into the corner.

She stands up, brushes the dirt off her coat. Schwartz moans and twitches.

Horvath watches Lana, Doris, whatever her name is. He turns around, opens the door, and walks out.

The streets are empty, but a scrofulous dog follows him downtown for several blocks. The animal's losing his hair and there are red splotches all over his skin. Looks like he hasn't eaten in a while. Horvath waits for a car to pass before crossing the street. The dog looks up at him and coughs like an old man with emphysema. It's a long walk back home.

32

THE HIGH WINDOW

IN THE MORNING, STILL IN BED, HORVATH REACHES FOR A LIGHTER that's not there. He left it on the bar at the Green Note. That's no way to start a morning.

He gets dressed quickly and heads down to a corner store for cigarettes and a lighter. He grabs a couple of candy bars, too, because he doesn't feel like sitting by himself in the booth of a greasy diner, not today.

He remembers a Sunday morning when his wife made bacon and eggs with a side of crispy toast and as much hot coffee as he could handle. Seems like a million years ago, and someone else's memory.

He scarfs down the first chocolate bar on the way to the Italian deli.

Inside, the store is quiet. It's still early. He can hear the voices of children on the sidewalk, walking to school.

He orders a double espresso and brings it outside. With his back to the stone building, he sits at one of the two iron tables.

The owner follows him out, with a broom and dustpan.

He undresses the pack of Lucky's, taps out the first cigarette, and lights up.

Sip of espresso, lean back, relax.

He's in this alone, against the whole town and everyone he knows. They've got guns and knives and he's got nothing but his fists and, if not brains exactly, a bit of common sense. The odds are stacked against him, but at the moment he wouldn't trade his life for anyone's. He takes another sip to confirm the idea.

The owner has been sweeping the sidewalk in front of his store. Now he's getting the debris alongside the building and by the front entrance. He sweeps under Horvath's table, and right over the tops of his shoes.

He downs the rest of the coffee and his brain lights up like a pinball machine.

So Lana's part of it, he thinks. Figured as much, so that doesn't tell me anything new.

Jaworski knew my every move, at least the ones I told her about. And they probably had a guy on me from the start. They could have killed me a long time ago, but they didn't. Why?

Because I'm worth more to them alive than dead. What for, exactly?

That's what I still need to figure out.

I met Lana that first morning. The syndicate's been on to me from the word go. I haven't made any real progress. I've learned nothing, found nothing. He closes his eyes and thinks back to that first morning in town.

A fight outside the window. A dead body in the alleyway. A scrap of paper with a name on it. A chalk mark on the windowpane so the firm would know exactly where I was.

It all began from here.

The noise from the fight led me to the alley where I found the paper. That took me to Paradise City, where I got chased by two goons. Everything else can be traced back to that.

Who made sure a dead body turned up outside my window?

Who left the scrap of paper?

So many questions.

Who told me to leave the mark on the window? McGrath.

That's the only question with an answer. It can't be him. It can't be.

But it has to be.

Horvath's been circling the thought for a few days now, but it was too disturbing to look at. Now he has to pick it up and see exactly what it is. Getting double-crossed by Lana was bad enough, and now this? McGrath is his oldest friend, the only man he really trusts.

Maybe that was the problem. What did McGrath always say? *Keep your eyes open and your mouth shut. And don't trust anybody, especially your friends.*

The whole thing was a set-up. There is no Van Dyke. There is no stolen money. They didn't need to send me out on the road. I've been searching for a ghost.

Van Dyke, Jaworski, dead bodies. They were all diversions. McGrath's hiding something and he needs to keep me busy so I won't find it.

What's he hiding? And why me? Couldn't he find someone else to be the patsy?

McGrath sent me on a mission to find someone, but all along he was the person I was looking for. Who else is in on it, how much do they know, and what's the plan?

More importantly, how's it supposed it end?

His brain can't untangle all the knots. Each question leads to three more, and none of them gets resolved. His head is throbbing so he pops a few aspirin.

Lana, McGrath, his ex-wife. They all let him down, but Horvath is even more disappointed in himself. He got played for a sucker. He let his guard down and now he's paying the price.

McGrath taught him how to escape from tight spaces, but he can't seem to wriggle out of this one.

He stands up and walks back inside for another espresso.

IT'S A HOT NIGHT. Just when you think summer's over, it comes back stronger than ever.

The ceiling fan is broken. The curtains are drawn, but the door to the fire escape is wide open.

Horvath went to sleep three hours ago, but now he's wide awake.

He sits up in bed, lights a cigarette.

The bus ticket sits on the table several feet away. Tomorrow at 11:35 am, he's leaving town.

There's nothing more he can do here, and no one to do it for.

But what then? he asks himself. I could start collecting evidence about whatever McGrath's been up to, and bring it back to the firm. Make sure he gets what's coming to him, that none of it's pinned on me. Set up a meeting with Wilson or maybe the big man himself, Atwood.

No, none of it feels right.

He'll go somewhere new and start over, again.

Horvath shakes his head, angry at himself. He had the same feeling years ago, when he missed an important tackle on the rugby pitch and let his team down.

McGrath taught me everything I know. He's the only one who'd know where I was, what I was doing, and how I'd do it. It was so obvious, but I couldn't see it. The mark on the window was supposed to be for me. So I could spot my room from the outside. If I saw shadows moving around behind the curtains, I'd know something was up. And it would help them find me in case I needed help. But that was all a smokescreen. The mark was there so he could keep tabs on me.

McGrath's so good that he's teaching me even when he's not around. And he just taught me the final lesson—don't trust your teacher.

He thinks back to all the rules he learned over the years. How many are true, he wonders, and which ones are bullshit? He stamps out his cigarette and walks over to the window. He pulls back the curtain with one finger and looks down into the alley.

Horvath can see a bit of the sidewalk. A man in a dark coat and wide-brimmed hat stands by the side of a building. He doesn't move.

He lets the curtain close. Am I safe here? Should I spend the night somewhere else?

They're probably waiting for me in the lobby, or outside the front entrance. I could slip out the back door. Or if the man outside leaves, I could climb down the fire escape.

He moves toward the fire escape door to get a better angle.

Now he sees the leash and the gray terrier. Man's just walking his dog.

The clock says 3:17.

Horvath puts on his pants. It's too late to go back to sleep.

A soft noise, like a mouse scurrying inside the walls.

Someone's trying to pick the lock.

A weapon. He runs to the bathroom to see if there's a loose pipe under the sink. No. Curtain rod? Not heavy enough. Razor? I'm probably better off with my hands.

When Horvath comes out of the bathroom, he's not alone.

McGrath's in the center of the room holding a Luger from the second world war. He was at Ardennes, if you could believe the stories.

Now I know why he doesn't want me to carry a gun, Horvath thinks. That way, he'll always have the drop on me.

"I can read your face like one of those cheap novels you're always reading," McGrath says. "But don't feel too bad about getting conned. Happens to the best of us."

"The best of us, huh?"

"Just a figure of speech."

"Right." His hands are balled up into fists and his biceps are throbbing.

McGrath smirks. "You're not going to do anything stupid, are you?"

"Too late. I already did."

"Glad to see you haven't lost your sense of humor."

McGrath has gray hair, veiny hands, and his back is beginning to stoop.

"Aren't you a little old for this?" Horvath asks.

"Yeah."

"Then why are you doing it?"

"Because I have no choice."

"There's always a choice."

"At first, maybe, but not later on. After a while, you're at the mercy of all the choices you already made."

Horvath looks back through his life, which seems like nothing more than a long series of stupid mistakes.

"I'm staring at retirement now. Another year or two, they'll push me out. Thing is, I haven't saved enough."

"That wasn't very smart."

"It's not me, it's my wife. Always wants a new car, new clothes, an electric dishwasher, the whole bit. She spends money like it's going out of style."

"Money never goes out of style."

"You got that right. Anyway, I've been skimming for years, to keep up with her spending. I've got a bank account she doesn't know about, few towns over."

"Good idea."

"Trouble is, Wilson's been asking some unpleasant questions lately. He's getting close."

"So you got scared and cooked up this Van Dyke scheme?"

"Not exactly. I've had it planned out for years. It's a long con."

"How long?"

"Since the day I met you in that poolhall."

"You remember that?"

"Of course."

Horvath feels like a fool. It was all a lie, from the very beginning. He knew he was stupid, but he didn't realize he was a total idiot.

"So when Wilson and his lackeys came sniffing around, and they figured out that some money'd gone missing, I told them it was anyone but you. That I trusted you more than my own mother."

"They bought it?"

"Well, it's the truth. But at the same time, I planted evidence that suggested maybe you weren't so honest after all."

"Like what?"

"See, you haven't been at your desk in a while. They may have found a few incriminating receipts, a slip of paper with the firm's account numbers in your handwriting..."

"So now Wilson suspects me?"

"Everyone does. In fact, they'll be searching your apartment later today. They'll find money under the floorboards and a second set of books. An hour or so later, they'll send two guys down here to kill you."

"So why don't you let them?" he asks.

"From what Doris told me, you were starting to figure it out. If the firm's...Human Resources team came down here to manage your early retirement, you might start talking."

"Wouldn't want me to reveal any of your trade secrets."

"Exactly."

"Taking care of it yourself is Plan B."

"You know me, Horvath. I've got a whole alphabet of schemes up my sleeve."

"I'm sure you do. Maybe you even have one of those French e's with a tilted line over its head."

"I think that's a beret."

Horvath is too wound-up to laugh. "So what about Van Dyke?"

"You disappoint me, Horvath. There is no Van Dyke."

"I know he didn't take the money and that I'm not really here to find him, but he exists. I saw his picture in the paper, standing behind the mayor and the chief of police."

McGrath laughs. "Look, kid. You've been searching through libraries and archives for weeks now. Following people, snooping around condemned buildings, asking questions. You were bound to trip over someone named Van Dyke. It's just a coincidence.

"I don't believe in coincidences."

"Some things exist whether you believe in them or not."

"Okay, but why me?"

"No reason." He shrugs. "We needed a fall guy and you were him."

"Lucky me."

"I'd say sorry, but I'm not. You knew the rules, and the dangers. You know how the game works."

"Thought I did."

Horvath is shaking, inside and out. He knew McGrath was a rat, but it's different seeing him here in person, listening to him talk. He's a completely new man now that the con is over. Even his voice sounds different.

"You never knew?" McGrath asks. "You didn't suspect anything?"

"Not for a second."

"No offence, Horvath, but you're a chump."

"Guilty as charged." He pauses, looking everywhere but at McGrath. "I thought we were friends."

"Not by a long shot. You know what your problem is?"

"I'm guessing you're about to tell me."

"You look too hard for evidence of a crime. Blood, violence, murder, mayhem. Mobsters, corruption, kids in trouble...all the obvious signs. But sometimes all that stuff is nothing but a distraction from what's really going on. I left a bunch of breadcrumbs for you, and you followed them like a good little detective. But they were all meaningless, just red herrings."

"Don't forget Lana."

"She was biggest distraction of all," McGrath says. "See, you're a smart guy, but not quite smart enough. You were looking too hard, and in all the wrong places. A couple dead bodies fall in your lap, and you think they're important."

"Wouldn't anybody?"

"Maybe, but sometimes a body is just a body, 180 pounds of useless flesh. You have to pay attention to the little things, not just the blood splatters and busted jaws. A book left in the wrong position on a table. The unlocked door. The flower bed with a single footprint. A crime doesn't always look like a crime, and the evidence won't always slap you across the face. You have to slow down and see the little things, Horvath. You have to walk along the edges and stare at all the dark corners. I taught you this."

"No you didn't."

"Huh, thought I did." He smirks. "Guess I left out one of the rules."

Shock, regret and bitterness have walked out the door. Now he's filled with anger and vengeance. His blood is a thick rope twisting through his veins.

"You're a good man, Horvath."

"Oh yeah?"

"Yeah, and that's another problem right there." McGrath cocks the Luger.

"Breaking your own rules, I see."

McGrath looks down at the gun. "That's right. No hardware." He laughs. "I was just making it all up as I went along. You know that, right? There *were* no rules."

"I followed every one of them."

McGrath frowns and shakes his head at the gullible young man who's not so young anymore.

It's a good code, whether McGrath believes in it or not.

"Know why you made such a perfect mark?" McGrath asks. "Cause you were the last person on earth who'd ever think he was one. You trusted me too much."

"Looks like I'm chock full of weaknesses."

"I taught you to hide them, didn't I? So your enemies couldn't use them against you."

"Yeah, you taught me that. I just didn't know trusting you was a weakness."

"Well, now you do." He takes a step closer to Horvath, aims the pistol at his chest. "Last request?"

"You got time to fry up a steak for me? Maybe some mash potatoes on the side?"

"Sorry, left the hibachi in my other suit."

"How about a cigarette?"

McGrath nods.

Horvath reaches slowly for the end table, picks up the smokes and lighter. He tips one out of the pack, puts it in his mouth. He covers the ashtray with a paperback novel.

"Hurry up."

He fires up the lighter and takes a deep drag.

McGrath glances at his watch. He's thinking about the long drive back home, and where to stop for breakfast.

Horvath smokes down the cigarette quickly, which makes his heart thump and arms tingle.

"It's time," McGrath says.

He holds up the butt. "What do I do with this?"

As soon as McGrath turns his head to look for an ashtray, Horvath leaps forward, grabs the pistol, and tries to wrestle it out of his hand.

McGrath is strong for an old man, with broad shoulders, lean muscles, and large meaty hands. He screams like a savage and opens his mouth wide, baring his teeth. Before McGrath can bite him in the neck, Horvath headbutts him.

He's more surprised than hurt, but Horvath has a second to rip the gun out of his hand and clock him in the face.

McGrath doesn't waste any time. He rushes Horvath and tackles him before he can get a shot off.

The gun falls out his hand and rolls toward the window.

He jumps up first, but waits for McGrath to get to his feet.

The old man is winded, his face pale and clammy.

Horvath lets McGrath take the first shot. He blocks it with his left forearm, then jabs him in the nose and follows it with an uppercut to the jaw.

McGrath reels. Before he can compose himself, Horvath lands two rabbit punches, grabs him by the tie, and throws him to the floor.

Now it's Horvath who's breathing hard while his mentor is doubled up on the floor. He's not sure what the next step is.

McGrath pulls himself up to a kneeling position, one foot on the floor for balance. He looks close to a heart attack. Purple lips, tornado hair, blurry eyes. "Okay. I give up. You got me." He loosens his tie, tries to catch his breath.

Horvath stands three feet away, hands on his hips.

McGrath begins to stand, arms drooping to the side. In one swift motion, he reaches for his sock and pulls out a blade.

Horvath is ready for it. He kicks the knife out of his hand and it clangs against the wall.

"That's an old trick, McGrath. You taught me that one years ago."

"Did I?"

"Should've held that one back. Now I know all your tricks."

"Not this one."

McGrath sprints toward the open door, through the curtain, and jumps off the fire escape. He's taken the curtain with him. It's three stories down, but he must have gambled that the odds of surviving the fall are better than a gunshot at close range.

Horvath walks out to the fire escape, looks down. The body is unmoving, shrouded by the curtain like a stiff down at the morgue. The blood has already formed a wide shallow pool because he didn't jump quite far enough. McGrath's torso is impaled on the pointed iron spike of a small fence that surrounds three garbage cans. He didn't factor this in when he placed his bet.

He's retired now, Horvath thinks. And he didn't need Human Resources to file the paperwork.

33

LEAVING TOWN

H ORVATH CHECKS OUT OF THE HOTEL AND WALKS TOWARD THE BUS station on the southeastern edge of the city. It's a cold morning and the fog is a thick blanket.

His head is throbbing.

He stops at a phone booth and calls the firm.

Lourette picks up. "Yeah?"

"Horvath here."

"What's new?"

"There is no Van Dyke. McGrath stole the money, but he set me up. Not sure if you knew this or not."

"We suspected as much, and now we know."

"Did you search my apartment?"

"Yeah, we found the dough."

"I've got nothing to do with it."

"We know. Where's McGrath?"

"I cleaned up the mess."

"Good. You on your way home?"

"Yeah, I'm catching a bus now."

"Alright. Stop by the office tomorrow. Wilson will want to see you, get the lowdown."

"Sure. I'll be there."

The phone goes dead.

There's no way he's going back. The firm likes to tie up all the loose ends, even the ones that aren't so loose. They'll stick a knife in his back or a hunk of cold metal in his face.

He keeps walking.

At the depot, he goes up to the window and waits for the clerk to look up.

"How far will this take me?" He lays a couple of bills on the counter.

"About halfway to Denver."

"Then that's where I'm going."

The clerk slides a ticket and some change across the counter.

Horvath picks up the money and his ticket, turns, walks over to a row of wooden benches in the waiting area.

His bag is as weightless as the day he pulled into town.

Travel light.

That was one of his rules. Horvath decides to keep following them all, even though the code wasn't real and neither was McGrath. He's lost everything else, so he might as well hang onto this one thing. In any case, the rules work.

The bench is hard and unforgiving. He thinks of the pews at church when he was a little boy. He couldn't sit still for more than a few minutes at a time. His good shoes hurt and the necktie strangled his throat. He looks up at the high vaulted ceiling, the clerk and counter like a priest and altar. The arrivals and departures table hangs like a crucifix overhead.

This isn't god's house, though. It's a filthy bus station in a bad town. He'll be happy to leave it all behind.

It feels like the end of an era. Something's dying, but that's mostly a good thing.

Horvath checks his watch. The bus leaves in 20 minutes.

A bum looks through a trashcan for scraps of food.

A businessman walks across the lobby carrying a leather brief-case like some sort of medieval weapon.

A family of four walks up to the counter, smiling as though they've never been on a trip before.

He takes a book out of his pocket. *Kisses Kill.* It's a crime novel, but it might as well be Lana's autobiography. He laughs to himself. The lady to his left, in a scratchy fake-Chanel suit, scrunches up her face and slides a few inches down the bench.

THE BUS PULLS IN JUST when the story's getting good.

Horvath stuffs the book in his pocket, gets up and walks outside. He wants a seat in back.

Outside, the sky is gray. He has to wait for the driver to let him on.

He sits down. People are boarding, choosing seats, stowing bags. A few minutes later, the bus pulls away from the station.

He stares out the window and watches the city disappear in a cloud of dust and gravel.

He's all out of aspirin, but his head is feeling a little better now.

They pass a junkyard, a motor pool for the city cops, a plumber's union, the Oddfellow's Hall, a dog biscuit factory spitting black smoke into the sky.

He tries to imagine where he'll settle down, but he can't.

The city ends and they pass over a river, through farmland and forests.

Lake, silo, cows stoically grazing. Houses, fields of wheat and corn. Schoolhouse, church, diner, and all the rest of it. He watches everything and nothing.

No wife, no house, no car. No friend, no job, nowhere to go. No Doris. Not even a Lana.

Horvath closes his eyes. He sees a green field and, in the distance, a still pond. A deer stops, looks over, darts away. He sees a quiet town five states away. No one could ever connect it to him, not in a million years. No will would ever look for him there. He's kept it a secret for years. His ex-wife doesn't know about it. Even McGrath doesn't know.

He sees an oak tree and, three paces to the northwest, a patch of fresh soil.

Four feet down, there's a locked metal box filled with cash.

The trick was to take a little at a time, at random intervals, and to take it from a variety of accounts. No pattern, nothing to make anyone to notice.

They never knew. McGrath's problem was that he grabbed too much, too quickly, and always from the same till. He thought he was being smart. He thought it was a long con, but it was just a series of short and obvious ones.

I hid my tracks well. They'll never find out. But even if they do, Wilson won't trace it back to me. Neither will Atwood or any of the others. When they realize I'm not coming back, they'll assume it's because I'm afraid of being killed. And they won't send anyone to track me down. After all, that's my job.

He'll spend a few nights halfway to Denver. Maybe he'll grow a mustache. Then he'll work out a disguise and get back on the bus. The next day, he'll pay a visit to the field and the oak tree. He'll dig up his money and buy another bus ticket. He'll go somewhere far away and never come back.

He smiles and stretches out his legs. Time for a nap.

The bus picks up speed on the open road. The driver has things to do and he wants to make good time.

The hum of the tires on blacktop lulls him to sleep.

And the fog begins to lift.

Dear reader,

We hope you enjoyed reading *Dark End Of The Street*. Please take a moment to leave a review, even if it's a short one. Your opinion is important to us.

Discover more books by Andrew Madigan at https://www.nextchapter.pub/authors/andrew-madigan

Want to know when one of our books is free or discounted for Kindle? Join the newsletter at http://eepurl.com/bqqB3H

Best regards,
Andrew Madigan and the Next Chapter Team

ABOUT THE AUTHOR

Andrew Madigan is a freelance writer and novelist from Washington, DC. He's lived in Dubai, Okinawa, South Korea, Tokyo, New York, the UK, St. Louis and Abu Dhabi. In the past, he's worked as a professor, janitor, university administrator, columnist, editor, rugby coach, fraud investigator and Bill Murray's stand-in. His writing has appeared in *The Guardian, The Observer, The Washington Post, The Iowa Review, The Christian Science Monitor, The Believer, The New Haven Review, The London Magazine, Lucky Peach* and other periodicals. His first novel, *Khawla's Wall*, was published by Second Wind. He lives with his wife, three daughters, and a beloved record collection.

CPSIA information can be obtained
at www.ICGtesting.com
Printed in the USA
BVHW030059230221
600771BV00023BA/841/J

9 781034 445821